I0769599

RAINIER
PUBLISHING

THE

FIRST

HUNT

THE FIRST HUNT

AUDREY J. COLE

USA TODAY BESTSELLING AUTHOR

PROLOGUE

Seattle, 1984

THE BOY EYED his father from the backseat of the Ford Fairmont as it turned off the Pacific Highway and pulled up to the curb of a dingy side street. He turned down the volume on his AC/DC cassette that played through the Walkman his dad had given him earlier this year for his ninth birthday. When a young woman with dark undereye circles and heavy makeup approached the passenger side of the car, he didn't have to ask what they were doing here. Her fishnet tights and cut-off shorts were way too cold for the middle of winter in Seattle.

His dad rolled down the window. The woman leaned inside. She eyed the boy curiously in the back before speaking to the driver.

"Are you lookin' to have some fun this afternoon?"

His father leaned across the seat and opened the passenger door. "Get in."

She climbed inside without another word, and the Ford Fairmont pulled back onto the Pacific Highway.

She rubbed her hands together and held them in front of the heater. Her knuckles were red and cracked.

"I'm not used to being picked up with someone's kid in the back," she said. "And I've seen a lot of weird shi—" She looked back at the boy. "Stuff."

The boy's father didn't respond.

She smiled at the boy through her bright red lipstick. "Hi," she said. "I'm Sally."

"Don't talk to him," his dad said from the driver's seat.

Sally obeyed and turned back around. As they sped along the highway, the boy looked out the window at the cars in the adjacent lane. Families. Commuters. None of which, he guessed, had a hooker in the front seat.

The boy knew his dad had picked up women before. Before his mother died, he'd heard his parents arguing about it, although at the time, he'd been too young to understand what it meant.

Last year, his dad had picked up another hooker by the airport. They'd driven to a rundown motel, and his dad told the boy to wait in the car while he and the woman went into one of the rooms. The boy had fallen asleep, and when he'd woken, his dad had driven the woman back to the street where he'd picked her up.

Afterward, his dad had never spoken of it, and the boy had never asked.

They turned off the Pacific Highway onto a winding road lined with towering evergreens. By the time his dad finally pulled into an empty gravel parking area surrounded by green woods, they hadn't passed a single car.

The boy pulled off his headphones, hearing the gravel crunch beneath the tires before the car came to a stop.

"Get out," his dad said to Sally.

Sally glanced at the boy before opening her door. "What about your kid?"

"He's fine," his dad said, his expression stern. "Stay in the car. Me and her are gonna take a walk."

He slammed the door and motioned for Sally to follow him. She gave the boy a sheepish look before following his dad into the woods.

The boy waited in the car for as long as he could until his curiosity got the better of him. With his Walkman in hand, he climbed over the front seat and slipped out, leaving the door ajar so that the *wump* of it closing wouldn't alert his father of his disobedience.

When he reached the edge of the forest, he stopped, straining to hear what his father and the woman were doing. He took a few steps into the woods, wincing when a branch snapped under his foot. He paused before moving forward, heading in the direction he'd seen them go.

A woman's scream pierced the silent wilderness. The boy stopped in his tracks. It was a different kind of scream than he'd ever heard before, high-pitched and keening, almost like an animal.

Sally appeared in the woods ahead of him, running. She was naked, her eyes wide with sheer terror. Branches cracked under her feet, and she sprinted toward him. The boy took a step back and stumbled onto the damp ferns.

When Sally met his gaze, the fear he saw there rooted him to the spot. Then out of the trees came his dad, too focused on Sally to notice his son in the distance. He gripped her arm and yanked with such force that she flew backward onto the ground. The boy gaped at the dirty, bloodied soles of her feet.

Frozen, he watched his father grab her by the hair. Sally shrieked and whimpered as he dragged her deeper into the underbrush, branches breaking under her naked body, until they were out of the boy's sight.

The boy sat still, paralyzed with fear as he listened to Sally's screams and pleading cries grow farther away. He heard his father grunt. Then there was nothing other than the rapid beating of his own heart. The silence was worse than Sally's screams for mercy, even though he hoped it meant she was okay. But his gut told him there was only one reason Sally was no longer begging for her life.

The ground seemed to move beneath him. His father's face, when he'd come out of the woods and pulled Sally off her feet, with his gritted teeth and distant fury in his eyes, was that of a stranger. Pure rage. Evil. He'd known his father to be a stern man, but nothing like that.

The boy covered his face with his hands. He should've helped her. But he'd been so afraid. And after seeing the look in his dad's eyes, he knew there was no way he could've overpowered him. But it didn't lessen his shame.

The sound of twigs snapping caused the boy to leap to his feet. He turned and ran for the car, tripping as the forest turned to gravel but catching himself before he fell. He didn't dare turn back as he scrambled toward the faded blue car. He got in and closed the passenger door harder than he intended.

The boy slumped into the backseat and tried to catch his breath as his dad emerged from the trees—alone. He crossed the gravel parking area toward the car, his expression stoic, the insane look gone.

His dad reached the car and opened the driver's door. He held something square and blue in his hand, and the boy's heart sank when he recognized it. His father held it out for him.

With a shaking hand, the boy took his Walkman.

"I told you to stay in the car, John," his dad said, his voice strangely calm.

John swallowed. "Sorry." The word came out in a croak.

His dad took a deep breath and put both hands on the steering wheel. John was desperate to ask about Sally. What happened to her? But, after what he'd seen, he didn't dare.

His father turned and put his hand on John's leg. John looked beyond the wet spot around the crotch of his pants to his father's hand. He was sure his father could feel his knee trembling.

"How about pancakes for dinner?" His father's expression had softened, his demeanor restored to the man he'd known all his life. "It is Christmas, after all."

John nodded, afraid if he spoke, he would break out in sobs. His father patted his leg and turned forward in his seat. With trembling hands, John connected his Walkman to the headphones that still hung around his neck and pulled them over his ears.

As he stared out the window and turned up the volume, tears blurred his vision. Almost certainly, Sally was dead. His father threw the gearshift into drive and sped out of the empty gravel parking area onto the winding, paved road—leaving Sally alone in the woods.

PART 1

CHAPTER ONE

HOLLY

January 1985

IN HER EMPTY apartment, Holly blew out the six dotted-blue birthday candles in one breath. "Happy birthday," she said.

She looked out her second-story window at Mount Rainier's snow-capped peak, barely visible in the waning daylight, wondering if the parents who'd adopted her sister's child loved him as much as she did. She'd never laid eyes on her nephew, and probably never would.

Holly tore her gaze from the window before slicing herself a piece of chocolate-frosted yellow cake, licking the frosting off her finger before taking a bite. The lock on her apartment door released with a *click* before swinging open. Holly turned, mouth full of cake, to see her fiancé step into her apartment.

Holly placed a hand over her heart. "You scared me. I didn't think you'd be off work for another few hours."

Jared peeled off his coat and flung it over the back of her couch. "Yeah, neither did I. I got sent home early. My asshole sergeant told me to take the rest of the night off." He put his hands on his hips and began to pace back and forth in her small living room.

Holly set down her fork. "What? Why?"

Jared paused. "I gave him a piece of my mind about what's wrong with the Green River Killer investigation." Jared shook his head and resumed his pacing. "I spent *all week* chasing a lead only to find out a detective from SPD had already ruled it out. We've got to have better communication on the task force. It's no wonder they haven't caught this asshole by now." He spun toward her, jabbing a finger at the middle of his chest. "*I* should be the one running the task force."

Holly's eyebrows knitted together in confusion. "So, why aren't you still at work?"

"Because I ran my mouth off," he shouted. "I was pissed." His chest heaved with a sigh as he tilted his head toward the ceiling.

Now, Holly understood. Jared could be a loose cannon when his temper flared. She pictured Jared in his superior's office, voice raised and profanities flying, laying out every flaw in the investigation with the confidence of someone who'd been on the case for years—never mind that he'd been on the task force for less than a month.

"It's so damn frustrating. This is what I get for doing my job?" His fist impacted with her wall, making Holly jump in her seat.

Her mouth fell open at the sight of the hole in her drywall as her fiancé shook out his fist. "Jared!"

She stood as he spun toward her. The anger on his face faded, replaced with a softer, apologetic expression.

"I'm sorry." He gestured to the hole. "I'll fix that tomorrow."

In stunned silence, Holly watched him move toward her. She'd seen him angry before, but not like this. The thought surfaced unexpectedly—*Maybe giving him a key was a mistake.* But almost as quickly, she pushed it aside. He was frustrated, that was all. Anyone would be, given the circumstances.

When he got closer, she noticed the glassy sheen on his eyes. "Have you been drinking?"

He shrugged. "I had a few beers on my way home." His gaze landed on the cake, noticing it for the first time. "What's this? Did I miss something?"

Holly stared at the blown-out candles. She'd planned to have it all cleaned up before Jared came over, but it was too late for that. Plus, they'd be married soon, so she might as well tell him.

"I celebrate Meg's son's birthday every year." She lifted her gaze to meet Jared's glazed eyes. "This year he's six."

Five years ago, when Holly had gone to the group home to retrieve the few belongings Meg had left behind, she found the adoption paperwork. She hadn't even known about her sister's pregnancy. Because it had been a closed adoption, Holly had no way of finding out who'd adopted Meg's baby boy, even though she'd tried.

His mouth twisted into a frown. "And you think that's healthy?"

She felt a jab in her chest at his insensitive response. *He's just had a bad day and too much to drink.* "If eaten in moderation," she replied, trying to lighten his mood.

He didn't laugh—or smile—at her quip. Instead, his brown eyes narrowed. "You don't even know his name. Hell, you don't even know if he's alive."

Holly's shoulders stiffened. That was enough. "Go home. And when you're sober, I expect an apology."

"Holly." Jared cocked his head to the side. "Come on. Seriously? I've had a shit day."

"Go home, Jared. If you need me to drive you, I will."

He scoffed. "Don't be so dramatic." He turned, but instead of moving toward the door, he strode toward her spare bedroom that she'd converted into an office. He paused beside the open doorway and looked inside. "Fine. I'll go." He spun around. "But when we move in together, this room has to go. I'm not having a shrine to the Green River Killer in my house. You're not a detective. If Major Crimes couldn't solve your sister's murder, you sure as hell can't."

Holly's face burned hot. When she first told Jared about Meg, he'd seemed so supportive. Did she even know him at all? She swallowed over the lump in her throat.

Her fiancé stood at the end of the short hallway, his face softening as he saw her bristle from his remarks.

"Get out."

"Look," Jared said. "I care about you, and I'm sorry about what happened to your sister. But you need to move on. The Green River Killer didn't start killing until two years after Meg was murdered."

Holly disagreed. She just couldn't prove it yet. But she wasn't going to argue with Jared about it tonight. "Please, go home."

Jared flashed her a look of disappointment before cocking his head. "I'm only telling you this because I'm worried about you." He pointed inside the room at the wall covered by a large map of King County where she'd marked every location of unsolved cases involving young women found strangled in the last five years. "This is crazy, Holly. It's obsessive."

A heavy silence filled her small apartment as he swiped his coat off her couch and left without saying goodbye. After he left, Holly exhaled and turned the deadbolt.

Maybe it is, she thought, sitting back down at her kitchen table. *But so what? Wouldn't anyone be obsessive if their sister's murder remained unsolved five years later?*

Yes, making a cake and blowing out candles for a nephew she'd never met was strange. But he was all she had left of her dead sister, aside from a shoebox filled with Meg's things. And aside from her mother, who didn't really count. For as long as Holly could remember, Meg and her mother had always been at odds. While Holly was obsessed with finding out who killed Meg, her mother had chosen to forget Meg had ever existed. It's why her mom had moved to Spokane with her new husband—Seattle was full of too many reminders of Meg's short, troubled life.

After taking another bite of cake, Holly ran her thumb along the thin gold band on her left ring finger. She knew Jared had an edge—a temper—but tonight had been the first time he'd ever lost it like that, punching a hole in her wall. The first time he'd ever reminded her of her father.

Maybe she and Jared were taking things too fast.

She shot a look over her shoulder at the fist-sized hole Jared had left in her living room drywall, then shook the thought away. *He's stressed out from work, and he's worried about me. That's all. He's nothing like my father.*

Jared got drunk only occasionally. He had a stable job, wanted to have a family, and promised to be a good father to their future kids. Jared would stick around and be a part of their kids' lives in a way that neither of their own fathers had been. *Although*, she thought as she swallowed her cake, *picking bad men does run in my family.*

She scraped the last of the frosting off the plate with her fork. Every year, she made a different kind, hoping to at least once make her nephew's favorite. With her other hand, she grabbed the framed photo she'd brought to the table with the birthday cake.

She smiled at the photo of her and Meg in front of their parents' Ford Pinto. Her thirteen-year-old sister wore overalls, and Holly's arm was slung around her younger sister's shoulder as she laughed at something Meg had said. Even though Meg was three years younger, she towered over Holly's petite frame. Holly's long dark waves were a stark contrast to Meg's pale blond hair. Those were happy times for the most part, dampened only on the occasional night when her father went into a drunken rage, which grew increasingly frequent in the year after this photo had been taken. Looking back, she'd realized that her mother and Meg had taken the brunt of her father's anger, while Holly had hidden away in her room writing love stories with fairy tale endings and articles for made-up travel magazines, imagining she was anywhere else.

The following summer her father had drunkenly slapped Meg one night, and Holly's mother ordered him out of the house—the last time any of them saw him. A few months later Holly left for college in eastern Washington, and not long after that, Meg got into so much trouble in high school that their mom sent Meg to live with their overly strict aunt and uncle in a neighboring suburb. Before Meg ran away and was placed in a group home. Before she got pregnant and put the baby up for adoption. Before she started working at a seedy strip club. Before Meg was murdered.

With a heavy heart, Holly set the photograph beside the cake. In another life, she, Meg, and Meg's son could've celebrated their birthdays together. She got up from the table, leaving her empty plate, and moved down the narrow hallway to her "obsessive" home office.

She sat at the desk and sifted through the mess of handwritten notes beside her typewriter, along with a stack of write-ins she had yet to open. Ever since she'd covered the infamous murder of popular radio host Cassidy Ray two years ago, her write-ins had been hard to keep up with. When she'd taken the job as a crime reporter for the *Tribune* to find out who killed Meg, she hadn't expected to gain such a following of readers.

Two pieces were due tomorrow at the *Tribune*: one was her ongoing coverage of a string of burglaries that had been happening at Seattle convenience stores, and the other was an update and a request for information from the public on the disappearance of Jennifer Duran, the twenty-year-old waitress last seen waiting for a bus after leaving a friend's house on the evening of January 10. Duran's disappearance had garnered so much public interest that Holly's boss wanted her to publish an update every week and ask for the public's help in finding her, regardless of new information.

Holly lifted her gaze to the opposite wall, where the only article ever written about Meg's murder was tacked, headlined *STRIPPER FOUND DEAD. Stripper.* Not her sister's name or her age. *Stripper* had been all the public needed to know. Holly wondered how many people who'd read the short article thought Meg had actually deserved to die.

Like Jennifer Duran, Meg had also been last seen at a bus stop before accepting a ride from someone driving a blue car. On Holly's handwritten draft of Duran's disappearance, Holly scribbled *GRK?* before sliding the pen over the top of her ear, using her thick dark curls to help hold it in place while she typed.

It was largely believed that the Green River Killer's victims were mostly sex workers or runaways, like Holly's sister, even though police refused to believe Holly's theory that the Green River Killer murdered Meg. But when women like Jennifer Duran went missing, it fostered a growing panic in the public: not only was a serial killer on the loose in King County, but no young woman was safe.

Holly pulled the half-typed page from the typewriter, then leaned back in her chair and rubbed her eyes. Outside, an ambulance siren wailed. She had ten pages of notes to weed through before drafting her piece on the convenience store burglaries.

Becoming the *Tribune's* youngest primary crime reporter had come with its drawbacks, but she was at least now getting called to the scene when a Green River Killer victim was found, getting a first-hand look at the work of the man who'd killed her sister.

Holly mindlessly unwrapped a stick of gum from the half-empty pack on the desk before getting up. She folded the gum into her mouth as she stood facing the map on the wall behind her. Crossing her arms, she studied the spot where Jennifer Duran had gone missing in relation to where over fifty women—including Meg—had been found strangled in King County in the last five years. All those murders remained unsolved. *What if Jared was right? I'm not a detective. Am I going to spend my life obsessing over the Green River Killer in the hope of finding a lead in Meg's murder?*

She looked up at the red *X* on the map that marked where Meg's body had been found in the yard of an abandoned house in White Center. Holly swallowed the lump that formed in her throat. That was a week after she'd been last seen. No one had even reported Meg missing.

Her phone rang in the kitchen, making her jump. She turned from the map and took a deep breath as she stepped into the hall. It was probably Jared calling to apologize.

She pulled the transparent phone off the hook of the kitchen wall.

"Hello?"

"Holly?"

The gruff voice wasn't Jared's. It was her boss at the *Tribune.* Probably assigning her another burglary to report on before the morning. She checked her watch. If that were the case, she could be up all night. "Yes, this is Holly."

"I just got a tip from Seattle Homicide. A young female's body has been discovered in the woods in Riverview, near the West Duwamish Greenbelt Trailhead. I need you to head there now, and I want a full story by midnight."

A shiver of anticipation rippled through her. *Had Meg's killer struck again?* She stretched the phone cord to grab her coat off the chair at the kitchen table. "Got it. I'll be right there."

HOLLY

HOLLY'S HEADLIGHTS SWEPT over the white KOMO-TV news van when she parked her Honda Civic behind an unmarked detective's car at the trailhead. Holly scrambled out of her car, notebook and tape recorder in hand. A bright light shone on Stacey Evans, KOMO's evening news reporter, illuminating her Madonna-esque blond perm. Stacey held a microphone and spoke into the camera.

Holly swore under her breath, giving Stacey a wide berth so she wouldn't appear in the footage. The news channel must've gotten the same tip Holly had. So much for a breaking story tomorrow morning.

"An unidentified woman's body has been discovered in a wooded area in Riverview this evening by a jogger who reported a foul odor near a running trail." Stacey's solemn eyes, highlighted by blue eye shadow, bored into the camera. "The discovery comes less than two weeks after twenty-year-old waitress Jennifer Duran disappeared from a bus stop after leaving a friend's home in neighboring Burien."

Holly stopped at the sound of the woman's name. She'd been covering her disappearance, and on the drive, she'd said a prayer for Jennifer. Like the rest of the Seattle public, Holly had gotten caught up in Jennifer's disappearance and had been holding out hope that Jennifer was still alive. But right now, she had a job to do.

While the reporter continued to speculate, Holly strode up the dirt parking area toward the start of the trail, where a stone-faced uniformed officer had been posted beside the crime scene tape. He didn't look much older than her. Beyond the officer, several flashlight beams swept the woods, their lights cutting through the dark, dense forest. They were too far away for her to get a glimpse of what they were looking at. Not recognizing the officer, Holly pulled her laminated press ID out from her blazer.

The officer shone a flashlight on her ID, which also illuminated what looked to be a coffee stain on the front of his blue uniform shirt.

"There's no press allowed beyond this point," Officer Coffee Stain said.

"I'm Holly Sparks, primary crime reporter for the *Seattle Tribune*." She pointed to the dark-haired homicide sergeant combing the woods behind him who'd likely called in the tip. "We got a tip from Seattle Homicide."

Officer Coffee Stain glanced over his shoulder. "You still can't go back there."

"Could you let him know that I'm here?"

The officer flashed her a look of annoyance before shaking his head.

"Hey, Holly."

Holly spun. Her pulse surged when she recognized the tall, white-haired detective in a light gray suit striding toward her. His presence could only mean one thing.

"Hi, Andy."

Detective Andy Harris worked for King County Major Crimes, not Seattle Homicide, investigating serious offenses, including homicides that occurred outside Seattle's city limits. Like Jared and the sergeant Holly saw coming out of the woods, Andy was also on the Green River Killer task force.

"How you doing?" he asked when he got closer.

She'd met Andy five years ago, before becoming a reporter. He'd introduced himself as the detective assigned to Meg's murder while Holly sat, red eyed and clutching a tissue in the Major Crimes Unit's small waiting area—a moment she'd never forget.

"I'm good." Holly flicked on her tape recorder and held it between their chests. "Do you know who the victim is? I heard Stacey mention Jennifer Duran."

Andy frowned. He glanced in Stacey's direction. "They shouldn't be speculating anything. We haven't given them any inclination it could be Duran, because it's not." He exhaled. "I'm sure we'll be hearing from Duran's family now. I'll have a talk with her supervisor." He ran a hand through his white hair.

Holly looked behind her, unable to see anything in the woods besides swaying flashlight beams, which had moved farther away from the trailhead.

"Off the record?" Andy said.

She turned to face him, and he gestured to her tape recorder. She flicked it off.

Andy shot a look at the TV news reporter and lowered his voice. "It's hard to tell from the level of decomposition, but the clothes we found near the body match the description of a prostitute who was last seen getting into a car on Aurora Avenue last December. But until we know for sure, we can't release anything related to her identity to the public."

Holly nodded. "Got it. And you're thinking the victim

could've been killed by the Green River Killer? I assume that's why you're here." She didn't really need to ask—Andy's presence meant that they did. But she hoped he might tell her more.

He put his hands on his hips. "Well, it's too soon to say anything definitively. But most likely, yes."

"Cause of death?"

"Again, we won't know definitively until the autopsy. Despite the cold temperatures, the body has significant decomposition. But, off the record…"

"Of course."

"Her lack of any apparent major injuries makes it very possible she was strangled."

She studied Andy's eyes from the glow of a patrol car's headlights behind him. Without flicking on the tape recorder, she asked, "Do you know anything else?"

Andy folded his arms, lifting his gaze to the trail behind her. "Off the record, there is one thing that doesn't quite fit with the Green River Killer's previous murders."

Holly's heart skipped a beat. "What's that?"

"There are a few barefooted footprints near where her body was found, and her clothing was strewn around the woods nearby. It appears the victim was killed in these woods, not moved here after she died."

Holly's breath stuck in her lungs. *Just like Meg.* Meg was found partially hidden under an overgrown hedge, with evidence of a struggle around her.

"She also looks to have more defensive wounds than many of the suspected Green River Killer victims," he added. "But most likely she was just the first to put up a good fight. And her killing didn't quite go to plan."

"You said someone saw the victim getting into a car on Aurora Avenue. Do you know what kind of car it was?"

Andy pressed his lips together as if debating whether to answer. "It was a blue car, small, four-door, driven by a brown-haired, middle-aged man—with a child, a boy, in the backseat. However, the witness was a prostitute, and she was high at the time."

Holly's eyes widened, first from the mention of the blue car, then imagining a child witnessing their father brutally murder a prostitute from the backseat. Thinking of her nephew, out there somewhere being raised by strangers, caused a shiver to creep down the back of her neck.

"Do you have any idea who the driver might've been?"

Andy shook his head. "We did have a suspect, Gary Ridgway, who has brown hair and also has a young son, but he passed a polygraph last year. He also drives a maroon pickup, not a blue car. So, to answer your question, no. Nothing credible."

Holly turned to look beyond the crime scene tape and imagined Meg's killer chasing this woman through these woods after she escaped from his car.

"Hey. I know it's probably not my place," Andy said, "but I think you should tread lightly with Jared."

Holly whirled around at Andy's statement, jarred by the change of subject. She studied Andy's expression and sensed a fatherly protectiveness in eyes. "What do you mean?"

"He can be a real loose cannon sometimes," Andy said. "I've seen him lose his temper more than once, and it's not pretty."

Holly frowned, unsure of how to respond. Jared's words from earlier still stung, and she was considering breaking off their engagement, or at least postponing any wedding planning until she made sure his behavior earlier that night was a one-off. She and Andy had become friends over the years, but it didn't feel right to tell him about her doubts before she told Jared.

Especially when the two of them would see each other at work tomorrow. "Thanks," she said. "I'll keep that in mind."

"Sorry." His expression softened. "It's none of my business. It's just—"

"Hey, Detective!" a female voice called from the woods. "You might wanna see this."

"I gotta go." Andy patted her shoulder as he moved past. "That's probably all I can give you tonight."

Holly watched him go, letting Andy's comment about Jared slip from her mind as she mentally replayed what Andy said about the victim being picked up in a blue car, then killed in these woods, rather than her body dumped here postmortem.

Holly stared at the crime scene tape as Andy stepped over it. She was more certain than ever that the Green River Killer killed Meg. She could feel it: whoever killed this woman also killed her sister.

CHAPTER THREE

JOHN

JOHN OPENED THE lid to the kitchen garbage can but stopped before scraping what was left on his plate into the trash. In the next room, his dad hollered over the roar of Thursday night football playing on the TV. The Seahawks must have scored. John set his plate on the Formica counter and glanced at his dad in his recliner, making sure his father's attention was still glued to the football game before he lifted the *Tribune* out of the trash.

The front page was stained with sloppy joe sauce but mostly still legible. John held his breath as he scanned the headlines. Washington's inauguration of Governor Booth Gardner. The Green River Killer on the loose. Boeing experiencing downturns from the recession. Ever since his dad had attacked Sally and left her in those woods, John had been scouring the news, terrified Sally's body would be discovered, and his dad would go to prison. Even worse, get the death penalty.

Most days, John had time to read the newspaper after school in the hour he spent alone before his dad got home from Boeing. But Thursdays, John had chess club after school, and by the time he walked home afterward, his dad was already home. John glanced up at his dad before turning the page.

Sally's disappearance never even made the news—not like the twenty-year-old waitress who went missing earlier this month, whose disappearance had already been splashed across the front page three times. Even though the waitress wasn't a prostitute, the articles speculated she could be another victim of the Green River Killer.

In the days after his father attacked Sally, John worried his dad was the infamous Green River Killer. Then John went to the library and searched the *Tribune* articles from the summer of 1982. His dad had taken him camping on Mount Rainier for his fortieth birthday, the same week three of the Green River Killer victims had gone missing and were then found floating in the Green River.

The memory of Sally running petrified—and naked—through the woods, screaming for help, flashed in his mind. The image of him, standing there like a coward, doing nothing to save her, was seared in his brain. He forced the image away and tried to focus his thoughts on the newspaper.

John felt his shoulders relax after he read through the local crime section. Maybe Sally was still alive. A lump formed in John's throat, remembering her crooked, bright-lipstick smile. But then why didn't she go to the police? Maybe she was too scared. Plus, she'd have to tell them why she'd gotten into his dad's car. John was pretty sure they'd put someone like her in jail.

He looked up and watched his dad take a swig from his beer. Sally couldn't have been the first woman his father had attacked. How many had there been before Sally? Is that what his parents argued about before his mom died?

Mostly, John wanted to know why his dad killed Sally. But John was too afraid his questions might awaken the monster he'd seen chasing Sally through those woods. What had Sally done to turn his father into that evil beast? Ever since that day, John had been tiptoeing around the house, making sure he obeyed all his father's rules to the letter, careful not to slip up even once.

John turned and plugged the sink before setting his plate in the bottom and turning on the faucet. The monster John had seen in those woods wasn't the same father John knew. Thick, red-orange swirls of sloppy joe sauce curled through the water, twisting and unraveling like the confusing thoughts in his head. His dad could be harsh and strict, but John knew that his father cared about him. This made him wonder if Sally had done something bad to deserve what his father had done…like his mother.

"We bring you breaking news tonight after a body was discovered earlier this evening in Riverview by a jogger who noted a foul odor while running along the forested trails at Soundway Park."

John turned toward the TV, where a familiar blond newscaster filled the screen. He placed his palms against the counter.

"This discovery comes less than two weeks after the disappearance of twenty-year-old Jennifer Duran. However, police believe the victim has been deceased for closer to one month."

John's gaze darted toward his dad in the recliner. He appeared strangely calm, ankles crossed, taking another swig from his beer.

"Police *have* confirmed the body is female, but they are unable to provide an identification at this time. A source tells us it is possible the body could be that of a prostitute who went missing last month after being last seen getting into a car on Aurora Avenue."

John's heart beat into his throat. They'd found her. Sally was dead. His dad would go to prison. *I'll probably end up as a foster kid.* An even more horrifying thought ran through his mind. *What if the police find out I was in the car too? Would they arrest me for not telling anyone?*

John's fears changed to anger as he stared at the TV. *How could his father do this to him?*

"While the police investigation into this apparent homicide is just beginning, detectives did confirm this woman is most likely a victim of the Green River Killer, who is still at large and believed to have killed over thirty women in the last three years."

A hand clamped onto his shoulder. John jumped.

"Hey."

John spun around.

"Watch what you're doing."

His father turned off the faucet as water overflowed from the kitchen sink, spilling down the front of the oak cabinets. He handed John a towel, looking surprisingly calm after the mess John made. He'd been slapped for a lot less.

His dad smiled. "I could go for some ice cream. You?"

John nodded even though his sloppy joe had crept back up to the top of his throat.

His dad clapped his palms together after returning the stained newspaper to the trash. "Great. Clean this up and let's go out. How about Baskin-Robbins?"

"Sure," John heard himself say.

"Don't worry, John," his dad said as if reading his mind. "Everything's going to be fine. I'll grab our coats." His dad whistled as he waltzed out of the kitchen.

I've been worried for nothing, John thought as he wiped the water off the cabinets. When the police finally did catch the Green River Killer, they'd blame him for Sally's murder too.

A ripple of pride flowed through John. How smart his father had been. Much smarter than John had given him credit for. John pulled the rubber plug out from the bottom of the sink. As he watched the water go down the drain, he saw Sally's lipsticked smile when she'd grinned at him in the backseat. Then the image morphed, and her eyes took on a look of terror as his father chased her, naked, through the woods. John turned away from the sink, suppressing a shudder as he tried to erase the image from his thoughts.

Instead, he tried to make himself believe his father's words: *Everything's going to be fine.* Even as he tried, he knew he'd never be able to unsee that terrible moment. Sally's horror would be forever stuck in his mind.

HOLLY

HOLLY MOVED YESTERDAY'S copy of the *Tribune*, which was open to Meg's article on page three, to the edge of the kitchen table, along with the tall stack of letters she'd received since the article had been published. Meg's last high school photo before she dropped out was enlarged beneath the headline, "Refusing to Give Up: A Sister's Fight for Truth."

It had been a week since they'd found the latest suspected Green River Killer victim, now confirmed as nineteen-year-old prostitute Sally Hickman, and her case had already gone cold. With nothing new to report on Sally Hickman or the Green River Killer investigation, Holly had gotten permission for the first time to publish an article on Meg's murder.

Holly looked at the article, her name beneath the headline. It should have felt like a step forward, a victory—but instead, it was just words on a page, and her sister was still gone.

Holly shifted her attention from Meg's article to the one-hundred-page true crime book proposal she'd been working on over the last few months, detailing the brutal murder of popular late-night radio personality, Cassidy Ray. Two years ago, the *Tribune's* then-primary crime reporter had been busy writing a piece on a newly discovered Green River Killer victim when Holly got a tip that Cassidy Ray had been brutally murdered—bludgeoned to death with her Golden Mic award—in her Capitol Hill mansion. After Holly's article ran on the front page of the *Tribune,* the story became a national media sensation.

Covering the high-profile case launched Holly's career, quickly making her the *Tribune's* most-read reporter. Her byline soon dominated the *Tribune's* front page, pushing the male, veteran reporters farther back in the paper, until she'd taken their spot as the lead crime journalist. When a literary agent approached Holly about writing a true crime novel about the case, she'd happily agreed to submit a proposal, even though she knew the chances of getting a book deal were slim.

Holly glanced at Meg's smiling school photo in the open newspaper, then slid the proposal and sample chapters into the manila envelope addressed to her newly acquired New York literary agent. The pages detailed the radio host's deadly love triangle and the murder trial that followed, which resulted in Cassidy's assistant being found guilty of her murder, while Cassidy's boyfriend walked free, despite a public outcry. "Here's hoping."

Her phone rang, and Holly went to answer it before sealing the envelope.

"Hello?"

"Hey, sweetie. Happy anniversary."

Holly smiled. "Hi, Jared. Happy anniversary to you too." Today was one year from their first date, and Jared had insisted on celebrating.

She fingered the necklace he'd given her earlier this week, a sapphire encased in a gold heart, part of his apology for losing his temper over her Green River Killer "obsession." When she told

Jared she feared they'd rushed into engagement, Jared begged her not to throw it all away over his one mistake. Instead of breaking it off, she'd decided to give things more time. Since then, he'd been overly sweet to her, clearly feeling bad for his blow up. Except for last night, when he snapped at her for going on about the lack of leads in Sally Hickman's murder.

Maybe *snapped* was too strong, she thought. But she could tell when Jared asked her to give it a rest, he was growing irritated. And she let it go, not wanting to set off his temper. *It's the same thing Mom used to do around Dad: clam up, change the subject, make herself busy to stay out of his way, apologize when she'd done nothing wrong.*

As soon as the thoughts entered her mind, she forced them away. *This isn't the same thing.*

"I made us a dinner reservation at Vito's for seven," Jared said. "I'm still finishing up at work, so how about I pick you up in an hour?"

"Perfect." She checked her watch. It was just after five. If she hurried, she could take her book proposal to the post office before they closed. "I'll see you then."

"Also," Jared added before she could hang up, "my mom wants to know if we've decided on a date yet for the wedding. I told her we'd let her know soon."

Holly bit her lip. "I'm still thinking about it."

"That's what you said last week."

She glanced at the kitchen table. The truth was she'd been too consumed by her book submission and writing Meg's article to think about it at all.

"I've just been swamped with work lately." And planning a wedding felt like a chore she didn't have time for. But she couldn't tell Jared that. He'd been married once before, and they'd eloped, something he seemed to think contributed to the demise of their relationship. This time, he was set on having a proper wedding.

Holly gazed at the waning daylight out the window. She needed to leave in the next five minutes if she was going to make it to the post office before they closed. "Let's talk about it at dinner."

"Okay. Love you."

"Love you too."

Holly hung up, relieved he didn't press her any further about it right now. She folded the flap on the manila envelope and pressed the two metal prongs flat. She flipped it over and stared at the addressed envelope, thinking how surreal it was to be submitting a true crime novel to a New York literary agent. Growing up, she'd fantasized about becoming the next Danielle Steel, writing love stories in a notebook in her room with happily ever afters to escape her parents' arguments. It had been what she'd set out to do by majoring in English in college. But after Meg was killed, everything had changed.

Her childhood dream of having her name on a book cover had now been replaced with a burning desire to see Meg's killer brought to justice. The more Holly built up her credibility as a writer and researcher, the better chance she would have convincing detectives—and the public—that the Green River Killer murdered Meg. Hopefully, this book would do just that.

Her phone rang again, but this time she ignored it. Envelope in hand, she headed for the door. When she reached for the door handle, her answering machine sounded from the kitchen. She paused to hear who was calling.

"Hey, Holly. It's Sarah from the *Tribune*. Sorry to bother you at home, I know it's your day off."

Holly retreated toward her answering machine. Had they discovered another Green River Killer victim? Her recent article had made it no secret that Holly had a personal interest in the serial killer investigation. Holly stilled, her attention sharpened, as the *Tribune's* receptionist continued.

"But there's a woman here who's asking to speak to you. She read your recent article and says she knew your sister Meg. They roomed together at a group home the year before your sister died."

Pulse racing, Holly swiped the receiver off the wall. She'd been looking for Meg's roommate for years.

"Sarah?"

"Oh. Hi, Holly. I was just leaving you a mess—"

"Tell her to wait. I'll be right there."

CHAPTER FIVE

HOLLY

Holly was out of breath when she entered the *Tribune*'s downtown lobby.

"Is she still here?" she asked Sarah, who hung up her desk phone as Holly came through the revolving door.

Sarah stood, motioning to a woman standing in the adjacent waiting room. Holly assessed the woman wearing pleated acid-washed jeans and a matching jean jacket before approaching her. As a crime reporter, she was used to getting bombarded with all kinds of tips on high profile cases, most of which turned out to be bogus.

The woman came toward Holly with eager eyes. She looked a few years younger than Holly, which would make her the right age. If Meg were alive, she would be twenty-three. According to the woman who owned the group home, Meg had been only a few months older than her roommate. She stood nearly a head shorter than Holly, probably just over five feet tall. Her yellow-blond hair revealed an inch of dark brown roots.

"Holly?" she asked, gripping her purse with a white-knuckled grip.

Holly nodded. "You knew my sister?"

Meg's roommate's name was Callie, but Holly wanted the girl to say it first.

She swallowed. "I did. I'm Callie. We roomed together at the group home in 1979, the year before Meg… We were both seventeen. I'm so sorry about her…" She pressed her lips together and broke Holly's gaze. "Um. Her death."

Shortly after Meg died, Holly had visited Meg's group home, and the woman who ran the group home had said Meg's roommate was the only person close enough to Meg who might be able to offer information related to her murder.

"I tried to find you after Meg was killed," Holly said. "But the group home said you ran away shortly after Meg did."

A horn blared outside amid the downtown rush-hour traffic.

When Callie met Holly's gaze, there was pain in her brown eyes. "I was in a dark place. I lived on the streets for a few years, alternating between here and Portland. Making money however I could. Then I got arrested for drug possession and some other shit."

Holly studied the girl with compassion, knowing "some other shit" likely meant prostitution. Although they looked nothing alike, when Holly looked at Callie, all she saw was her sister. She felt a strange connection to the woman who'd known Meg and had to resist the urge to wrap the young woman in her arms.

"I ended up in a court-ordered rehab facility, which saved my life. I've been clean now for six months. I think of Meg often." Her voice faltered, and she cleared her throat. "How unfair it was that she died so young." She dropped her gaze to the floor. "And how that could've been me." She met Holly's gaze with wide eyes. "I didn't know her murder was still unsolved until I saw your article. And I might know something that could help."

"Hey, Holly." Josh, one of the *Tribune's* secondary crime

reporters, gave her a nod as he passed through the lobby, heading for the street.

Holly flashed him a curt smile, hoping he'd keep moving. Josh was a known busybody who spent more time bumming leads off other crime reporters than finding his own. Seeing Callie, he slowed as if waiting for Holly to introduce him.

Holly turned her back to him and leaned toward Callie. "There's a diner across the street." She lowered her voice. "Why don't we talk there?"

Callie nodded, and Holly waited for Josh to exit the revolving doors and turn left down the street before leading the way to the diner.

Right after they sat down at a booth, a middle-aged waitress appeared with an order pad and a pencil. "What can I get for you two?"

"Just coffee," Callie said, sliding into her seat.

"Same." Holly made sure the waitress was out of earshot before asking Callie what she was dying to know. "So, what is it you know that might be helpful?"

Callie placed her petite hands on the table and interlaced her fingers. "Well, Meg and I were tight, but she didn't tell me everything. We both came from screwed-up homes and were both acting out because of it."

Her words hit Holly like a dagger to the heart. *I should've been a better sister.*

"Anyway," Callie wrapped her fingers around her mug. "Before Meg got pregnant, and during most of her pregnancy, she was hanging out with an older dude."

"How much older?"

The waitress returned with two white mugs of steaming coffee.

"Thank you," Holly said after she set them on the table.

Callie grabbed two sugar packets off the condiment tray and poured them into her coffee. "Close to forty, I guess. So, like twice her age. At least." Callie stirred her coffee with a spoon before taking a sip. "I don't know that he killed her. Meg died about six months after I last saw him. But there was something about him that gave me the creeps."

Holly left her coffee untouched. This was the closest thing she'd gotten to a clue since Meg had been murdered. "Like what?"

Callie shrugged. "I can't really explain it. Just that something was off with him, ya know? He used to pick her up from school sometimes before she dropped out. He wore a wedding ring, and the few times I met him he would whip out a photo of his four-year-old son, like he was trying too hard to make me believe he was a normal guy. Oh." Callie paused to take another drink of coffee. "And Meg told me he was the one who knocked her up."

"*What?*" Meg had gotten pregnant from a forty-year-old man when she was seventeen?

"Yep. But he stopped showing up toward the end of her pregnancy, and I bet that's why Meg put the baby up for adoption, not that she was in any shape to raise a baby at seventeen anyways."

Holly took a sip of coffee, hoping the caffeine would help steady her whirling thoughts. *Meg might've been killed by the father of her child.* She took a deep breath.

"You okay?" Callie asked.

"Yes," Holly lied, spilling coffee onto the table when she set down her mug. "Do you know his name?"

Callie's gaze drifted out the window at the darkening downtown street. "I can't remember exactly, but I'm pretty sure it was Bobby, or Lou, or maybe Denny."

Holly frowned, hope draining from her lungs. "Those names don't sound anything alike." She studied the woman across from her. *What if she's making this all up?* Holly had seen enough in her years of crime reporting to be careful about trusting people who claimed to have case-breaking information.

Callie covered her eyes with her hands. "I hate that I can't remember, but I was using back then, and I didn't know Meg was going to get killed." Her voice broke. "I should've been a better friend." When she lowered her hands, her eyes were brimming with tears.

Holly reached out and placed a hand on Callie's. "None of us knew. You can't blame yourself for that." Holly choked back the emotion that swelled in her throat. *Easier said than done.* "You're helping Meg now."

Callie sniffed and wiped a tear from her cheek with the back of her hand.

"What did he look like, this guy?"

"Um. He was white. In good shape. Attractive, I guess, in a hot dad sort of way. Brown hair."

"That's good," Holly coaxed. "Do you remember how tall he was?"

Callie shook her head. "I never saw him get out of the car." Her eyes lit up. "Oh, but he had a mustache. I remember that."

"What kind of car did he drive?"

Callie cast a sideways glance toward the window as if straining to remember. Holly's stomach sank. *How can any of this be reliable if she doesn't even remember what kind of car they were in?*

Callie met Holly's gaze. "A white pickup."

"Are you sure?"

Callie nodded. "I'm sure."

"Do you remember the make?"

Callie pressed her chapped lips together. "No."

"That's okay." Holly patted her hand. "This is really helpful. Thank you."

Callie stared at the table. "I read your theory that Meg might've been killed by the Green River Killer. You don't think that could've been him, do you?"

Holly gazed out the window at the cars driving by. "I think anything is possible." Except, like Sally Hickman, Meg was last seen getting into a blue car, not a white pickup. Although, this mystery man could've had two vehicles, Holly supposed. Or bought a new car before he—

A bell chimed as the diner door opened. Holly looked toward the sound, surprised to see her fiancé striding toward them, wearing a scowl.

"Jared," she said when he approached their booth. "What are you doing here?"

He put his hands on his hips, ignoring Callie sitting across from her. "I could ask you the same thing. I went to your house, and when you weren't there, I went to the *Tribune*. Sarah told me she saw you go across the street. Do you even know what time it is?"

"Jared, this is Callie." Holly motioned to the woman across the table. "She knew Meg. And the father of Meg's child. Possibly even her killer."

Holly expected Jared to be amazed at this news like she'd been. Instead, his scowl deepened. He shot Callie a wary glance before turning back to Holly.

"Sweetheart, no offense, but if this woman had pertinent information related to your sister's murder, she would've come forward five years ago. I warned you this kind of thing might happen after your article came out, remember?"

Holly remembered. "But she was Meg's roommate. I tried tracking her down before—"

"Honey." The hardness in Jared's expression eased. "Don't take this the wrong way, but you're not a detective. You need to give it a rest. If the Green River Killer Task Force can't solve Meg's murder, then neither can you. Meg's murder was likely a random act of violence from someone she didn't know. If this woman—"

"Her name's Callie," Holly said.

Jared pursed his lips. "Callie. If what she knows is relevant then she should be telling Andy, the detective assigned to Meg's case, not you." He looked at his watch. "If we leave now, I can take you home to get changed and we might still make our reservation."

Holly's mouth fell open at how heartless Jared was being. Did he really think their dinner was more important than solving her sister's murder?

Holly dug a hand into her purse. Jared was right about one thing. Holly pulled out a business card and extended it to Callie. "You need to tell all of this to the detective who's handling Meg's case. His name is Andy Harris, and he works at King County Major Crimes. His office is on the second floor of the courthouse, less than a mile from here. You could also describe this man Meg was seeing to their sketch artist. Do you want me to go with you?"

Jared groaned. "Holly, what are you doing? We have to go. You can't go to Vito's like that." He motioned to Holly's sweatshirt.

Holly ignored him and locked eyes with Callie. "I'd be more than happy to if you don't want to go alone."

Callie shook her head. "No, that's okay."

"Are you sure?" Holly asked.

Callie nodded.

"But you'll still go see him, right?"

Jared huffed, but Holly didn't care. This was too important. If her fiancé couldn't see that, then she shouldn't be marrying him.

"Yes. I'll go." Callie flipped the card over in her hand. "I promise."

"It's our anniversary." Jared held his arm out toward Holly. "Let's go."

Holly shot her fiancé an icy glare. *"Just a second,"* she barked, surprised at the bite in her voice.

Holly grabbed a napkin off the table and used a pen from her purse to write down her phone number. "If you think of anything else, call me." She slid the napkin toward Callie. "Day or night."

"I will." Callie lifted the napkin before putting it into her jacket pocket.

"Is there anything else you remember about him?" Holly asked, ignoring Jared's impatient stare.

Callie gazed into her coffee. "No."

"Thank you," Holly said. "For finding me. And I mean it, please call me if you think of anything else, no matter how small."

"I will," Callie said as Holly left a five-dollar bill on the table for their coffees.

Holly didn't want to leave. Sitting across from Callie was the closest she'd felt to Meg since she died. But Callie had already told her what she knew. Holly hoped that the sooner she left, the sooner Callie would go see Andy. Reluctantly, Holly slid to the edge of the booth.

She started after Jared, who was already moving toward the door, when Callie's small hand wrapped around Holly's wrist.

"Wait," Callie said. "There's one more thing."

Holly stopped and turned.

"Meg told me that before they took her baby away from her at the hospital, she asked that his adoptive parents name him Tanner."

CHAPTER SIX

JOHN

March 1985

JOHN KNEW WHAT his dad was doing as they walked side-by-side through the damp woods beside Star Lake. His dad had been paying more attention to the news lately; in the evenings, John had seen him lingering over articles about the Green River Killer. And now his dad wanted to sniff out the famous killer's latest dump site.

When his dad had come into John's room that morning, John knew better than to argue. *It's time to get your head out of those books. The weather's getting warmer. Let's go fishing.* All John wanted to do this Saturday was finish reading *The Call of the Wild.* He'd already read it once, but the raw adventure of Buck's survival in the wild made John want to read it again.

John's favorite part was Buck's first kill, when he defeats Spitz, the lead dog, in a brutal fight for dominance. Buck hadn't wanted to kill Spitz, but he hadn't had a choice. It was kill or be killed. It made John wonder what made his dad kill Sally. Some kind of instinct, like what Buck felt? Or had Sally somehow deserved it? Maybe she'd tried to hurt his father.

But she'd seemed so nice. Her crooked smile from the front seat of his dad's car flashed in John's mind. Then an image of her, naked, running for her life out of those woods—away from his father. John eyed his father now, tromping through the forest. Why had he done that? There had to be a good reason, he decided, although he couldn't shake his dreaded suspicion that his father had done it for fun.

After they'd parked on a vacant lakefront lot, his dad had asked John to go for a walk with him through the adjacent woods before John had even gotten his line in the water. John hadn't been surprised. His father wasn't a fisherman. He was a hunter. And John had been keeping up on the news too.

His father obviously knew what he was doing, but it felt risky to come here. The latest Green River Killer victim had been discovered in these woods only three days ago. What if the police came back? John had realized his dad was using the serial killer to get away with murdering Sally, but did it bother his dad that the Green River Killer was all over the news, getting credit for killing not only his own victims, but Sally too?

John had seen the way his father looked at young women, even teenagers, when the two of them were out. He couldn't shake the feeling that his father would do to them what he did to Sally. He just hoped he wasn't around the next time it happened.

Then John was struck by a terrifying thought. What if his dad went down for all the Green River Killer murders and not the other way around?

John kept in stride with his father as he stepped over a fallen log.

He got the feeling his father was competing with the Green River Killer somehow, like it was all a game. John looked up at his dad, studying him as he crept through the woods. The woman the police had found a few days ago in these woods had gone missing the day after Thanksgiving, and John had been with his dad that whole day. They'd even gone to see *The Terminator* in the theater, so his father hadn't killed her. Still, maybe the Green River Killer didn't kill *all* those women the cops thought he had. Maybe his dad killed some of them.

Beside him, his father's footsteps were barely audible, despite him being over twice John's size. A branch snapped under John's shoe in the quiet woods, the sound reminding him of when he went into the forest and heard Sally scream. John winced at the memory. He'd been such a coward, running back to the car, leaving Sally to die.

John lowered his eyes to the ground, not wanting to look at his dad. A cold thought slithered in his head—*what if he does that to me?*

But no. His dad could get angry, could do terrible things, but he would never kill him. He wouldn't. John's throat felt tight, like he'd just swallowed a mouthful of dry cereal, as he forced himself to believe it. But if his dad wouldn't hurt him, then why had he hurt *her?*

John couldn't contain the question any longer. "Why did you kill her?"

His father stopped and extended his arm across John's chest. In a small clearing up ahead, two deer jerked their heads toward the sound. His dad kept his palm on John's breastbone as the deer stared at them before bounding in the opposite direction, the white underside of their black tails bouncing up and down as they disappeared into the woods.

"Good thing we aren't hunting," his dad said, ignoring John's question. "The secret to hunting is to not let your prey know you're coming. The element of surprise is a hunter's greatest weapon."

John stared in the direction of the deer, unsure of whether his dad was referring to hunting animals or humans.

His dad smiled. "Ready to fish?"

John swallowed over the growing lump in his throat. "Yeah."

Halfway back through the woods, in the empty grass lot adjacent to them, a car door slammed. John peered through the thinning trees. When he saw the vehicle that had parked behind his dad's blue Ford Fairmont, a wave of dread washed over him. It was a police cruiser. Bold green letters marked the side: *SHERIFF King County.*

John watched a muscular man wearing a navy-blue suit put his hands on his hips, exposing his silver badge. His stocky build and dark hair reminded John of Sylvester Stallone. He approached his father's car, studying the rear license plate.

His father placed a hand on the back of John's neck as they neared the edge of the forest. A cold knot formed in his gut at the thought of that same hand closing around Sally's windpipe. When the two of them reached the lakefront lot, the detective whipped his head in their direction then strode toward them.

"Let me do the talking," his father said in a low voice.

"I'm Detective Peretti from King County Major Crimes." He looked between John and his father without offering a handshake. Instead, he pulled back his suit jacket on one side, exposing his badge and holstered revolver. "Can I ask what you two are doing in those woods?"

"Just taking a walk," John's father said, lowering his steady hand to the top of John's back.

"Huh." The detective flexed his jaw, seeming to size up his father. "Did you know the body of a young woman was discovered in these woods only three days ago?"

His father didn't answer.

"We believe she could've been a victim of the Green River Killer," the detective added. He pointed behind him toward their parked cars. "You own this lot?"

His father shook his head. "No."

The detective's brown eyes narrowed. "Then you're trespassing. This is private property."

"Oh. Sorry, I didn't know that. I was just going to let my boy throw a line in the water. But in that case, we'll find another lake."

John looked up at his father, impressed by his calm demeanor. There wasn't a trace of a tremor in his voice.

"Let's go, John." His father started toward the car.

"Actually, I'd like you to come down to the precinct. Answer a few questions." The detective glanced at John before turning back to his father. "If you don't mind."

His father spun around. John had read enough to know that his father didn't have to go with the cop if he didn't want to.

"I don't mind at all," his father said.

John gaped at his dad. *What is he doing?* Panic gripped him. Was his father going to confess?

"You want us to follow you?" his father asked.

The detective looked triumphant. "That would be great."

John climbed into the backseat and waited until his dad closed the driver's side door before he spoke.

"Are you going to confess?" John kept his voice to a whisper even though the detective in the car behind them was already backing out onto the road.

His dad whipped around and put a hand on John's leg, just like he had after he'd killed Sally.

"Of course not. If I refused to go, it might look suspicious. There's nothing to be afraid of, John. I'll never get caught." He smiled. "If they ask *you* any questions, however, I need you to keep quiet. That is your right. So, say nothing. And I mean *nothing.* Don't let them trick you, because they'll try. Cops cannot be trusted. Understood?"

John nodded. He'd read about fifth amendment rights and knew what he meant. "Understood."

CHAPTER SEVEN

JOHN

"You seem tall for your age. You play any sports?"

John looked up from his book at the detective, who looked very different than the one who'd approached them in the forest. His young-looking face didn't match the white hair, reminding John of Steve Martin, but without the humor. He'd been sitting across from John in the small, windowless room for the last hour. His father had been taken to an interview room to speak with Detective Peretti, the man who'd found them at the lake, and another detective.

John shook his head.

"That's a shame," the detective said. He'd introduced himself as Detective Harris but told John he could call him Andy. "So, where's your mom?"

"She died," John answered, guessing the detective already knew.

"I'm sorry to hear that. How did she die?"

John thought of that night, three years ago. His mother's crumpled body on their concrete patio, her head lying in a small puddle of her own blood, was a sight he could never unsee. But John didn't gratify the man with an answer. The older detective was probably looking for a way to blame his mother's death on his dad. Instead, John lifted his faded, paperback copy of *The Call of the Wild* higher to cover his face. His leg jiggled against his chair.

"Whatcha reading, son?"

"*The Call of the Wild*," John said without looking up, even though it was clearly printed on the cover. "By Jack London."

"Huh. Your teacher making you read that?"

"No."

The detective shifted in his seat, causing his chair to creak. "I had to read *White Fang* in fourth grade. I don't remember it that well, but I know I wouldn't have read it on my own."

"You should've read *The Call of the Wild*." John turned the page. "It's much better."

The man chuckled. John lowered the book in time to see the detective's belly shake.

"I didn't know ten-year-olds were such literary critics."

John furrowed his brows at the detective before returning his attention to the book. *This guy couldn't get anything out of me if he tried.*

His stomach growled. He hadn't eaten since breakfast. What was taking his dad so long? There was no clock in this room, but it had to be at least early afternoon.

"You and your dad take a lot of walks in the woods?"

John thought of the sandwiches his dad had packed for them to eat at the lake that were still in the backseat of the car.

"You ever been down to the Green River, son?"

John's gaze shot up from his book. Ever since Sally's body was discovered, John had been stopping at the library most days after school, reading everything he could on the Green River Killer in the hope of understanding his father—and the laws about murder. Since John was under twelve, the detective shouldn't be questioning him without his father's consent. But if the police believed John had witnessed his father's crimes, that changed everything. But John knew enough to know he didn't have to answer. He'd memorized everything he could about the fifth and sixth amendments, and his teacher always said he had a memory like a steel trap.

John's stomach twisted, but this time it wasn't from hunger. Did they think his dad was the Green River Killer? Were they so desperate to make an arrest they'd lock his father up?

John set down his novel. He was about to say no, he'd never been to the Green River, when the door to the small room flew open. Detective Peretti, the Rocky lookalike who'd found them at the lake, stood in the doorway. John peered around him, looking for his father. But the hallway was empty.

Peretti turned to the older detective. "I'll take it from here, Andy."

"Actually, I was just asking the kid—"

"I *said* I'll take over now."

He sounded angry, and it reminded John of his dad when his temper threatened to seep out.

Detective Harris frowned. "Fine." He stood and turned to Peretti before opening the door. "But the kid's not talking. I already tried."

Detective Peretti smiled at John. "I had a great talk with your dad. He said I could ask you a few questions before you go."

Andy looked warily between Peretti and John, lingering in the open doorway.

"Oh." Peretti reached into his suit jacket pocket and withdrew a can of Coke and a Skor Bar. "Here. Your dad said you might be hungry." John took the candy bar—his favorite—and pop can. He looked up at Detective Peretti as he tore open the candy bar wrapper. "You sure my dad said you could question me?"

Harris spun around to face Peretti after he stepped into the hall. "Look, I don't think you should—"

Ignoring Harris, Peretti closed the door and turned the lock on the handle. "Yes, he did."

"Why are you locking the door?"

Detective Peretti took the older detective's place in the seat across from him. "Just to be safe. We have criminals here."

His dad's warning on the drive here echoed through his mind. *Cops cannot be trusted.*

"I had a great talk with your dad." The detective leaned forward, placing his elbows on his knees, which pulled his suit jacket tight around his biceps. "Has your dad ever picked up any women off the street?"

John bit into the chocolate-covered butter toffee.

Peretti cocked his head. "To give them a ride…or anything?"

John glanced at the locked door while he chewed. "Where *is* my dad?"

"He's just waiting while I talk to you."

"I know my rights." John popped the rest of the delicious candy bar into his mouth. "I don't have to answer anything."

Peretti smirked. "You been watching *Murder, She Wrote*, kid?" He sat back and crossed his bulky arms. "Well, you're right. I can't force you to talk to me. But helping the police is always the right thing to do. You want to do the right thing, don't you, John?"

John opened the pop can and took a swig. It was the first time the detective had used his name. John stared back at the detective in silence, his father's warning about police at the front of his mind.

"Have you seen the movie *The Terminator?*" the detective asked.

John stopped to think when the last Green River Killer victim had gone missing. The one who'd been found in the woods where his dad had taken him today. November 23rd. John studied the detective who waited eagerly for his response. *He's checking my dad's alibi.*

"Yes."

"Oh, yeah? Me too. I loved it." He grinned. "What was your favorite part?"

John didn't have to think about it. "When Arnold Schwarzenegger was naked and fought those guys three on one to take their clothes."

The detective's smile faded. "You see it at home?"

John shook his head. "The theater."

"Do you remember when?"

"The day after Thanksgiving."

The detective bit his lip. "And who'd you see it with?"

"My dad."

"Nice. Did you two do anything else that day? Like go for any drives?"

"No. We just watched football at home on TV."

"That's great." The detective attempted another smile, but it was forced.

John suppressed a grin.

Peretti withdrew a photo out of the inside pocket of his suit jacket and extended it in front of John's face. Every muscle in John's body went stiff.

It was Sally. She looked different in the photograph than when John had met her. She was younger with longer hair and less makeup. From the blue background behind the headshot, John guessed it was a school photo, probably from when Sally had been in high school. But it was definitely her. Seeing Sally's crooked smile and the same glimmer in her eyes that she'd had in the front seat of his dad's car made John's throat suddenly dry.

"Where's my son?"

John jerked his head toward his father's angry voice coming from the hallway. Detective Peretti held the photo closer to John's face.

"You ever seen this woman before?"

John's heart pounded so hard against his chest he was afraid the detective might hear it.

"Her name was Sally," Peretti added. "We know you were in the backseat when your dad picked her up in December."

A fist rapped against the door, rattling it against the hinges. John whipped his head toward the sound.

The detective put his thick hand on John's knee. "You know it's a crime to lie to the police, right? Your father wouldn't want that."

"I know he's in there," his father yelled. "Open this door!"

Peretti ignored John's father on the other side of the door and narrowed his eyes. "Tell me the truth. Have. You. Seen. Her?" He lowered the photo and brought his face closer to John's.

John's hands trembled. He clasped them tightly together. "No."

Rap. Rap. Rap. "Open the damn door!"

The detective frowned at John. "Don't lie to me, kid. You saw her. Your dad killed her."

John shook his head.

Peretti's demeanor darkened, his face contorting in anger. "He killed her in the woods while you sat in the backseat of the car. Or maybe you got out to watch? Tell me, kid, did you hear her scream?" He slapped the armrest of John's chair, making him jump in his seat. "Tell me *now*, dammit!"

Spittle from the detective's mouth landed on John's cheek. John closed his eyes, willing his mind to take him somewhere else. Anywhere but here.

Rap. Rap. Rap. The door handle jiggled from the other side, making the whole door shake. "Let me in or I'll kick the door down," his father shouted.

Peretti stood, flashing John a look of disappointment. As soon as he turned the lock on the handle, the door flew open. John's dad marched into the room with Detective Harris on his heels, his father's face flushed with anger as he looked from John to the detective.

His father snarled. "What the hell are you doing? I told you not to speak to my son." From the tightness in his jaw and the flare of his nostrils, John could tell his dad was fighting to keep his composure. He stepped toward the detective, pointing a finger at the more muscular man's chest. "How dare you question my son without me. And without my permission. He's a child. I came down here to be helpful, and this is how you repay me? Accosting my ten-year-old?"

Detective Peretti slid Sally's photo back inside his suit pocket while silently assessing his father.

"I was just bringing him a snack," the detective finally said, his voice calm. "I thought he might be hungry."

His dad lifted a hand toward John without taking his eyes off the detective. "Come on, John. Let's go."

As his father led him out of the room, John stole a glance over his shoulder at the burly detective. The moment their gazes locked, there was no mistaking the look in the detective's eyes: he knew what his father had done, and he knew John did too.

CHAPTER EIGHT

HOLLY

The faint scent of rain lingered in the air, mingling with the metallic tang of nearby traffic as Holly burst through the heavy double doors into the courthouse lobby. Footsteps slapped against marble and voices blurred together in a steady hum as she rushed through the crowd to the elevator. She clutched her notebook, fingers drumming against the worn cover. It had become her habit as a reporter to take it everywhere, so she'd never miss an opportunity to take down something that could be important.

She couldn't keep the grin off her face as she mentally replayed the phone call less than an hour ago from her literary agent.

She'd gotten the deal. A book deal. The words pulsed in her mind, quick and electric, as if they'd slip away if she didn't keep moving, keep breathing, keep herself from shouting it out right there in the lunchtime swarm.

Her advance was enough to replace one year of her salary at the *Tribune,* and she planned to give her notice so she could put all her energy into turning in the best book possible by her deadline with the publisher.

After hitting the button for the elevator, she tapped her foot against the stone floor. The doors opened. People filed out, and Holly stepped forward, bumping into someone on her left. She turned, seeing it was only a boy. He was older than her nephew she'd never met, probably closer to ten.

"Sorry," she said, smiling down at him when he met her gaze.

He peered up at her with large brown eyes, but he didn't smile back. Warmth moved up her chest, pooling in her throat as she thought of Meg's son. *Tanner.* That probably wasn't his name, but she liked to think it was and that Meg had gotten what was likely her final wish.

"Come on, son," a male voice called from behind her. The boy hurried after his father.

Holly slipped inside the elevator before the doors closed and tried to force the boy from her mind. If she saw Tanner in every boy she encountered, she would go crazy. She pressed the button for the fourth floor and lifted her head toward the ceiling as it ascended, still blown away that she was going to have her name on a true crime book published by a major New York publisher.

There'd been a time when getting a book deal like this would've been all she'd ever wanted. Now she saw it as a means to an end. Her true crime book would build a readership, amplifying her platform to raise awareness and pursue justice for Meg's murder. Just the thought of catching the guy who killed her sister caused a spark of excitement inside her.

After getting off on the fourth floor, Holly pushed open the heavy door to the Major Crimes Unit. The unit's gray-haired secretary looked up from behind the front desk and smiled.

"Hi, Dear."

"Hi, Colleen. Is Jared here?"

Before Colleen had a chance to answer, Jared's voice boomed

from behind the closed door to the office he shared with his partner across the hall.

"*I don't care, dammit,*" Jared shouted.

Colleen warily followed Holly's gaze.

"You should've held him back longer," Jared continued, his angry tone permeating through the wall. "I don't buy the alibi. If you'd just given me a little longer with the kid, I could've gotten him to talk."

Colleen returned her attention to Holly. "I don't think I should interrupt him right now. You okay to wait a few minutes, Hun?"

Holly forced a smile, wondering what Jared was so pissed about. "Sure." She sank into a folding chair against the wall as another male voice sounded from the other room.

"If we were holding the kid against his dad's will, any statement you got from him wouldn't be admissible."

It was Andy.

"We weren't charging him with anything," Andy continued. "You know I couldn't legally keep him away from his kid any longer. I kept him occupied for as long as I could."

"That's bullshit," Jared said.

Colleen's eyes met Holly's for an awkward moment before she looked away, making herself busy by rearranging an already neat stack of papers on her desk.

"He agreed to take a polygraph," Andy said. "What more do you want?"

"We shouldn't have let him leave. Now he's got time to get his story straight before he takes the lie detector test."

"You know there's nothing I can do about that."

"That's a load of crap."

The door flew open, and Jared marched out of the room. His jaw was set in a hard line, and there was an intense, piercing look in his eyes even though he wasn't looking at Holly. His narrowed gaze was set on the unit's main door. He strode right past Holly without so much as looking in her direction, slinging on his suit jacket as he stormed out of the unit.

Holly spotted Colleen gawking at the door before the secretary looked away, attempting to appear reabsorbed in her busywork at her desk. Holly got up and moved across the hall to the open office doorway. Inside, she found Andy leaning back in his chair with both hands on his white head of hair.

"Hi, Detective. Can I come in?"

"Oh. Hi, Holly." He heaved an audible sigh and sat forward, leaning his elbows on the desk. "Jared's not here. He just left."

"I saw."

Jared's desk sat snug against Andy's, cluttered with papers while Andy's was neatly organized.

She sank into Jared's empty swivel chair, trying to read Andy's expression. "What was he so upset about?"

"Well, you know Jared. It doesn't take much to get him riled up sometimes." He studied her for a moment, as if debating how much to say.

Holly thought of Meg and her still-at-large-killer while she tried to piece together what she'd overheard. Her chest wall stiffened. "Was it about the Green River Killer?"

Andy hesitated, and she berated herself for getting her own hopes up. *It couldn't be,* she thought. Like Meg's murder, the killings attributed to the Green River Killer had gone cold almost as soon as detectives had found their bodies. The Green River Killer task force hadn't had a serious suspect since last summer when Gary Ridgway had passed that polygraph with flying colors.

Harris exhaled through his mouth. "Off the record." He paused, holding Holly's gaze.

She straightened, nodding. "Off the record."

"Yes, it was."

Holly felt her eyes widen as excitement buzzed just beneath her skin.

"Jared caught a man and his son walking around the woods by Star Lake earlier today."

Holly stilled. The older guy Meg was seeing also had a son. She swallowed. "Where the last Green River Killer victim was found."

"That's right. And he drove a blue Ford Fairmont, just like the car another prostitute saw Sally Hickman get into on Christmas Day."

And Meg, Holly thought. Her heart thumped against her chest as she watched Andy pull out a smoke, wondering how she could keep him talking.

He extended the pack to Holly. She shook her head. "I quit."

Andy held it in the side of his mouth while he withdrew a lighter from another pocket. "Good for you."

Holly tapped her foot against the floor, the seconds it took him to light his cigarette feeling like an hour. *What if they've finally found him?*

Holly sat forward. "The older guy Meg was seeing also had a son. Remember what Meg's roommate said?" Like she'd promised, Callie had spoken with Andy, telling him everything she'd told Holly. But Holly had been disappointed Andy hadn't let Callie give his description to their sketch artist since there was no actual proof he was involved in Meg's death.

Andy put up a hand. "I remember. But lots of people have sons and own blue cars, Holly, including me. That doesn't make him the same guy."

"Does the suspect you interviewed have a mustache?"

Andy shook his head. "No."

"Brown hair?"

"Listen." Andy returned the lighter to his pocket. "He gave us an alibi for when several of the Green River Killer victims went missing, including three of the victims found in the Green River the summer of '82. We still need to confirm his alibis, but he agreed to come back later today to take a polygraph."

Holly's brows knitted together in confusion. "Coming back? You didn't arrest him?"

Andy turned his head away from her to blow out a long drag of smoke. "We couldn't. We have no hard evidence it was him. And he wanted to take his son home first."

That must've been what made Jared so mad. "When is he coming back to take the polygraph?"

Andy checked his watch and took another drag. "In two hours. However, if his alibis check out, he can't be our guy."

"What about Sally Hickman? Does he have an alibi for her murder?"

"It's not as solid, but he said he was at home watching TV with his son."

Holly caught a whiff of nicotine-laced smoke and resisted the craving for a long-familiar buzz. Instead, she pulled a stick of gum from her purse and folded it into her mouth, letting the minty flavor distract her from the urge.

"How long will it take?"

"The polygraph? Depends. If he's telling the truth, probably not more than an hour."

A surge of energy coursed through her veins. *What if it's him?*

Andy looked her over, seeming to register the gleam of hope in her eyes.

He gestured toward her, the cigarette smoking between his index and middle fingers. "Do not release any of this yet to the public, understand? He's cooperating, and we need to keep it that way. Plus, he might be innocent. But we'll know more after he takes the polygraph."

"What's his name? Does he go by Bobby, Lou, or Denny?"

Andy shook his head. "Holly…you know I can't give you that yet."

She sighed. It was worth a shot. "How long ago was he here?" Looking toward the interview room on the other side of the hall, she shivered at the possibility of the Green River Killer—and Meg's killer—being so close to where she was sitting right now.

Andy stubbed out his cigarette in the ashtray on his desk, leaving behind a faint spiral of smoke.

"Will you ask him about Meg?"

Andy cocked his head, giving her a look that said *we've talked about this before.* "Your sister is not a presumed Green River Killer victim. She wasn't a prostitute, and she was murdered nearly two years before his first victims were found in the Green River."

Meg was his first, Holly wanted to scream. "But what if Meg's death *is* related?"

A soft knock sounded on the opened door to Andy's office. Holly turned to see Colleen in the doorway.

"Sorry to interrupt, Detective. But the polygraph examiner is here, and he wants to know where you want him to set up."

Andy stood. "I'll show him."

Holly followed him out of his office. "Will you call me after it's done?"

He turned when he reached the hall. "I'll try, depending on how it goes."

Holly made her way to the elevator, her body on autopilot, mind whirling with the possibility of Meg's killer being captured later that day. She wished Andy had given her his name. The elevator doors opened on the first floor as her thoughts went wild trying to envision what he looked like.

Holly stepped off, remembering the boy who'd made her think of her nephew, the one she'd bumped into on her way up. Andy said the suspect had been with his son. Picturing the boy's face, Holly recalled the witness who'd seen Sally Hickman get into a blue car with a boy in the backseat. She closed her eyes, replaying the voice of the boy's father, wishing she'd turned around to look at him.

The skin on her arms prickled as the people moving through the busy courthouse lobby seemed to fall away. Holly froze, unaware of the elevator doors closing behind her. The lobby, full of subtle noises and movement, now felt unnaturally still, like a paused photograph.

In this very spot, she had been standing only a few feet from the man who could be the most prolific serial killer in American history. The man who might have killed her sister.

CHAPTER NINE

JOHN

Rain pattered against the windshield as his dad drove them home from the Major Crimes Unit. John pictured Sally sitting in front of him as she had on Christmas Day, then turning around and flashing him her red-lipsticked smile. The image haunted him, like an eerie rerun that never stopped playing, every time he rode in his dad's car.

John looked away and stared out his rain-streaked side window, watching the cars pass in a hazy blur. His dad hadn't said a word since they'd left the courthouse, making John worry that he'd be in trouble when they got home.

Fear pounded in his chest.

"Dad," John said, breaking the silence. He took a deep breath, deciding to ask the thing that had been gnawing at him for months. "What you did to Sally, would you ever…you know…do that to me?" His last word came out a croak.

"Of course not." After stopping for a red light, his dad twisted in his seat to face him. "You're my son. You're *part* of me."

The sharpness in his dad's eyes softened, replaced by something warmer. "I love you, John."

The tension that had been building in John's shoulders eased as he looked into his father's eyes.

"You know that, right?" his dad asked, patting his knee.

John nodded. He did know. *Sally must've done something to deserve what his dad did,* John thought. *Just like mom.*

"Good." His father faced forward. "Wow, do you see that? Gas is up to $1.20 a gallon."

The light turned green. John stared out his window. His father's reassurance—and swift change of subject—didn't make him feel any better. His gaze landed on a sign that said *Be Kind, Rewind* in front of a movie rental store as John longed for the kind of escape that came from getting lost in a movie, where the bad things weren't real, and everything made sense by the end.

&

"What's wrong?" his father asked when he came into John's room that night to tuck him in.

Normally, John read every night until his eyelids grew heavy. But tonight, he lay staring at his Transformer cars lined up in a neat row atop his dresser—the ones he hadn't played with since he witnessed his dad chasing Sally, naked and terrified, through those woods. Reading had become his only escape from the dark memory.

John searched his father's eyes. "I'm afraid you're going to go to prison," he said, finally blurting the thing that had been consuming him ever since they'd left Sally in the woods. After that Rocky-lookalike detective got in John's face today, he was now afraid they'd blame him too. He remembered a word from his research. Accomplice. That's what he'd be, an accomplice, and he'd go to jail. But he kept that part to himself, not wanting to sound selfish—or cowardly—to his dad.

His dad knelt beside his bed, resting his elbows on John's mattress. "That's never going to happen." His voice was confident and calm. "Remember what I told you on the way home from the precinct?"

His dad smiled.

"You said you're too smart for that," John said.

His dad nodded, pulling the blanket up to the top of John's chest. "That's right."

John stared at the popcorn ceiling. "I don't want you to leave me." His mouth went dry. He opened his mouth to speak but then closed it. *Like Mom.*

His dad placed a palm on John's chest. "That's never going to happen. You saw those detectives, especially the one who interviewed me—and tried to interview you. He's incompetent, letting his hot-headed emotions take control. He made assumptions, and that's his fatal flaw. Only seeing what he wants to see." His father tapped the side of his temple with his finger.

John turned toward his dad. "What happened when you went back to the Major Crimes Unit this afternoon?"

"I took a lie detector test."

John shot up in bed, widening his eyes at his father. "What?"

"Don't worry." His dad pressed his shoulders back against the mattress. "Relax. I passed it."

How was that possible? "Are you sure?"

"Yes." His dad smiled. "The trick is to make yourself believe what you're telling them."

John studied the glimmer in his dad's eyes and wondered how many times his father had lied to him. He knew his dad was capable of horrible acts, but John had always trusted his dad to tell him the truth. He stared at his father, thinking of all the times his dad said he'd been working overtime during the last two years. Had he really been at work?

"But I would never lie to you," his dad added, as if reading John's mind.

Seeing the concern on John's face, his father leaned over and kissed him on the forehead. "I promise, you will never have to worry about me being taken from you. I'll never do anything to jeopardize my freedom of being your father." He ran a hand over the top of John's head. "I'll never leave you, okay?"

"Because you're going to stop?"

John willed his father to say yes as his dad rocked back on his heels and stood beside John's bed.

"I'll do better."

John's stomach churned, wishing his father would've answered his question.

"Trust me," his dad added. "I'll never let those pigs get close to us again. They're never going to catch me, son. I've made sure of that."

John sank against his pillow. He'd underestimated his dad. He was smarter and more calculated than John gave him credit for. And now, he'd be smart enough to stop. *Maybe he's going to change.* He couldn't risk killing again when the cops already suspected him. Could he?

"How about we go on a trip?" his father asked. "I could take a week off of work. There are some places I want to scout out for hunting in the fall. Plus, it'd be fun to get out of town, don't you think?"

John wasn't sure. Maybe his dad wanted to go somewhere else so he could kill where the cops weren't on to him. "Where would we go?"

His dad's eyes brightened with excitement. "How about Alaska?"

⋘

John lay in the dark after his dad had left to watch TV. His father made Alaska sound like an incredible place: the Northern lights, polar bears, and snow. *Everything is bigger in Alaska,* his dad had said. *The animals, the mountains, the hunting grounds.*

John should have been excited. Parts of *The Call of the Wild* and *White Fang* took place in Alaska. Plus, John had never even been on a plane before.

But despite his dad's assurance, his mind ran wild imagining his dad going to prison and John growing up in a skeezy foster home. He replayed the fierce determination in the stocky detective's eyes today when he'd held out Sally's photo. *He knows what my dad did.* John turned on his lamp and plucked *The Call of the Wild* off the nightstand before his mind had a chance to dwell on it anymore.

Thirty pages later, John's thoughts drifted to what his dad had promised. Detective Peretti might know his dad had killed Sally, but he had no proof. Otherwise, Peretti would've arrested him already.

John replaced the Jack London novel on the nightstand before turning off the lamp.

Down the hall, his dad sang to himself "Shout" by Tears for Fears in the kitchen. It reminded John of his mom—always humming to herself—making him wonder what life would be like if his mom were still here.

John turned on his side, staring at the line of toys on his dresser. His father wouldn't take the chance of killing again. He couldn't. Not after the cops brought him in for questioning today. And not after promising John he'd never leave him.

At least, John hoped not.

CHAPTER TEN

HOLLY

THE SHRILL RING of Holly's phone cut through the otherwise quiet apartment as she unlocked the front door. She hurried to the kitchen.

"Hello?" She held her breath, imagining Andy on the other line, about to tell her they'd caught the Green River Killer, and that their suspect had confessed to killing dozens of women, including Meg.

"Hi, Holly. It's Andy."

Her heart rate spiked with anticipation as she pressed the phone to her ear.

"He passed," Andy said.

Holly closed her eyes and tilted her head toward the ceiling. "You're sure?"

"Yes, unfortunately. He's not our guy."

Holly's throat swelled, making it difficult to swallow. She wanted to tell Andy there'd been a mistake. They should redo the test. But she was too overcome to speak.

"Sorry, Holly. And listen, we're not releasing his name to the public. He cooperated with us and passed the lie detector test, and we don't have any hard evidence linking him to the Green River Killings."

"Can you at least tell *me* his name?"

A pause. "His first name was Louie."

"Lou was one of the names Meg's roommate gave me for the older guy Meg was hanging out with before she was killed." It had to be him. "Did you ask him about Meg?"

"I'm sorry. But it became clear after we questioned him regarding over a dozen murders that he wasn't the Green River Killer. And we had no evidence linking him to Meg."

"But Andy—"

"Holly, Meg's roommate admitted to being on drugs while she lived at the group home with your sister. The three names she gave me didn't sound anything alike. She couldn't remember; she was grasping at straws. I know it's disappointing. Hell, I wish he was our guy too. But he's not."

She heard voices in the background and was about to ask Andy if they asked him specifically about Sally Hickman when Andy added, "I've got to go. I'll talk to you soon."

He hung up before Holly could say goodbye. After replacing the receiver, she pressed her forehead against the wall.

Hours later, Holly stared at the map of Seattle and its surrounding area. It covered half the wall of her spare bedroom, marked with fifty-five *X's* where young women's bodies had been discovered, all of them strangled in the last five years. And all their cases were still unsolved. Beside the *X's*, she'd tacked notecards bearing the women's names, ages, and details of their deaths. Holly crossed her arms and stepped back, thinking about what Andy had said about the man who'd been brought in for questioning. He had an alibi for when the first three Green River

Killer victims were killed, as well as for when a recent Green River Killer victim went missing over Thanksgiving weekend.

She untacked the notecards and stuck them into two rows on the adjacent wall. Halfway through, she turned to the desk and rifled through the mess of typed pages to find a blank paper. Losing patience, she flipped over a typed page. Swiping the pen from above her ear, she scribbled a list.

SOME RUNAWAYS, SOME NOT

TEENAGERS - EARLY TWENTIES

LAST SEEN AROUND BUS STOPS

KILLED WHERE BODY FOUND (NOT DUMPED)

ALL MANUALLY STRANGLED

1980 – PRESENT

MOSTLY FOUND WITHIN SEATTLE CITY LIMITS

She tacked the list to the wall beside the first row of names on the left before making another.

RUNAWAYS, PROSTITUTES, OR LIVING ON THE STREETS

Holly paused, biting her lip before adding

–BUT NOT ALL

MOVED AND DUMPED POSTMORTEM

STRANGLED WITH BOTH LIGATURES AND MANUALLY

1982-PRESENT

MOSTLY FOUND OUTSIDE SEATTLE CITY LIMITS

Holly stepped back. She'd tacked Meg's name under the first list. Meg was last seen getting into a blue car at a bus stop. Her body had been found just south of Seattle city limits, but only three miles away from Sally's body. There were two victims left on the map that didn't completely fit on either list. One was Sally Hickman, and the other was Brooke Holtman. Both fit the criteria of Holly's first list except that they were prostitutes. And they each had shared something in common with Meg: Brooke Holtman had been last seen near a Seattle bus stop, and Sally had been last seen getting into a blue car.

Holly tacked their names under the first list, adding *AND SOME PROSTITUTES-BUT NOT MOST.* She crossed off *BUS STOP* and frowned. This didn't make sense. She rubbed her eyes. Her lists were blurring together.

The phone rang in the kitchen. Still holding the pen, Holly hurried across the small apartment to answer it, noting the city outside the apartment window had gone dark. *It has to be Jared.* She hadn't heard from him since he'd stormed out of the Major Crimes Unit that afternoon.

"Holly, it's Mack."

Her lungs deflated at the sound of her boss's gruff voice.

"I don't see your piece on my desk."

Holly's hand flew to her forehand. Her gaze darted to the binder containing a stack of articles and handwritten notes on the kitchen table for her true crime book about Cassidy Ray. Beside it was a pile of unopened write-ins she'd received that morning in her mailbox at the *Tribune.* She hadn't thought about either since getting home from work.

"I'm so sorry. I..." After the news from her literary agent and learning King County Major Crimes had brought in a Green River Killer suspect, she'd completely forgotten about her assignment to write a piece on the rising crime in Seattle's Chinatown district. She glanced at her watch and swore under her breath. Two hours till deadline. She hadn't even started it yet.

"I'm just putting the finishing touches on it." She had, at least, spent most of yesterday interviewing business owners in

Chinatown about the increase in break-ins and muggings the neighborhood was experiencing. Now, she just needed to compile all her notes into a succinct—and compelling—article. "Don't worry, I'll have it on your desk by ten." She stared at the open door to the spare bedroom she used as an office. With the time it would take to drive downtown to the *Tribune*, it was going to be close.

The *Tribune's* lead editor breathed into the phone. "Okay, good work. But next time I want it turned in earlier. Don't let all that success of yours go to your head. You still have a job to do."

"Understood," she said as the line went dead.

She sighed and trudged back into her office, preparing to crunch out a story over the next hour and a half before driving back downtown to turn it in. Before sitting at her typewriter, Holly gravitated toward the two victim lists on the wall. She tapped her fingers against her thigh before moving Sally Hickman, Brooke Holtman, and Meg to their own list. She also added Jennifer Duran, last seen at a Seattle bus stop, even though she was still missing.

She stared at the date Sally Hickman went missing, willing her mind to piece the puzzle together. Her gaze traveled to the second row of victims. Sally Hickman had been last seen on Christmas Day, a day after the *Tribune's* primary crime reporter ran a lengthy piece on the Green River Killer on Christmas Eve, highlighting the most recently discovered victim, found on December 19th.

Holly's eyes stopped on the tenth victim on her right-sided list. Her corpse had been discovered north of SeaTac airport last spring. While the victim had no criminal record for prostitution, police believe she had dabbled in it. The grim discovery of the eighteen-year old's body had made the *Tribune's* front page news. Brooke Holtman, the other victim who, like Sally Hickman, didn't exactly fit on either of Holly's two lists, had gone missing the very next day.

She stepped to the two-page typed list of young women who'd gone missing in the Seattle area in the last five years. One of the most recent was twenty-year-old waitress Jennifer Duran, last seen two weeks ago, whose disappearance had garnered extensive news coverage. Holly glanced at the date before checking the day the most recent Green River Killer victim had been discovered near Star Lake, where detectives had found the suspect walking around today with his son.

And then she saw it. Holly covered her mouth with her hand as she drew in a sharp breath. It was a crazy theory, but a pattern, nonetheless.

A sharp rap against her apartment door tore Holly from her thoughts.

HOLLY

HOLLY UNHOOKED THE lock and opened the door, realizing she should've checked the peep hole first. Fortunately, it was Jared.

"Hey." He ran a hand through his dark wavy hair as she stepped aside to let him in.

His eyes were bloodshot, but he was still wearing his suit. Her apartment was between his house and the Major Crimes Unit, so she doubted he'd been home yet.

Normally, she would've told him she couldn't see him when she had less than two hours to turn in a piece she hadn't started writing, but her heart raced with excitement at what she'd found. Five more minutes wouldn't hurt. Especially for something this important.

"I could use a drink," he said after she closed and locked the door behind him.

She pointed to the kitchen. "There's beer in the fridge."

"You got anything stronger?" he asked.

From his swagger toward the kitchen, she guessed he'd had a few already. Probably after finding out their only real suspect in the city's senseless slayings had passed a lie detector test. "There's vodka in the freezer."

He unholstered his gun and set it on the kitchen counter, like he did every time he came over. She got him a glass while he opened the freezer.

"You want me to do that?" she asked as he sloppily filled a generous pour into the short tumbler.

He shook his head. "Nah." He lifted the glass to his mouth. "You should move into my place. It's stupid to drive fifteen minutes out of my way to see you when you could live at my house."

She nodded, not up for an argument tonight, even though she had no intention of moving in with him yet. In less than a year, they would be married. Until then, she wanted to enjoy her freedom. And her space from Jared's mood swings.

She put a hand on his arm as he lifted the glass again. "I heard about your suspect passing the lie detector test. I'm sorry it wasn't him."

Jared winced after knocking back a big swig. "Don't be. It's not my problem anymore." He wiped the edge of his mouth with a sleeve.

"What do you mean?"

He swung the glass to the side, sloshing vodka onto the floor. "I'm off the task force."

"Why?" From what she'd gathered, Jared was the one who'd brought in their first suspect since a truck painter named Gary Ridgway passed a polygraph last May.

Jared's mouth twisted into a frown. "They said it's due to manpower, that they had to take someone off the GRK task force because we don't have enough staff for our other increasing homicides. But the truth is my sergeant hates me. He thinks I'm too abrasive or some shit." He pointed at Holly with a wavering finger. "But you can't tiptoe around a serial killer investigation."

Holly bet it had to do with him questioning the suspect's son today. Jared took another drink, and she wondered how aggressive he'd gotten with the boy. She knew Jared well enough not to ask—it would only worsen his mood.

"I want to show you something." Holly glanced at the binder on the kitchen table as she led the way to her office. She would tell him the good news about her book deal later. She heard him refill his glass before following her.

A flutter stirred beneath her skin as Jared stepped into the office behind her. "You know how the suspect you interviewed today had an alibi for some of the Green River Killer murders?"

Jared took a drink and stared at the wall.

"What if there are two killers?" she asked.

Jared shook his head. "That's an old theory. We know now that the Green River Killer has a pattern." He ran his gaze over Holly's long list of missing women. He lifted the glass toward the pages filled with names. "Some murders and disappearances that we're attributing to him may turn out to be unrelated. But the majority are connected." He stepped in front of the map marked with *X's*. "We're looking for a serial killer who's strangling mostly prostitutes and runaways. Some boyfriend might've offed his girl, and another might be the victim of a random mugging gone wrong, but there are not *two* serial killers out there."

She spun toward him. "Just hear me out." She pointed at one of the two rows of names on the far side of the wall. "What if these victims—mostly prostitutes, some runaways, bodies moved postmortem and all but one dumped outside of Seattle city limits, and killings that started in '82—are Green River Killer victims." She pivoted and pointed to her new list with only four names. "And *these* victims—two prostitutes and two not, *not* moved postmortem, and found mostly *within* Seattle city limits, killings starting in 1980 and last seen either at bus stops or getting inside a blue car, or both—were killed by someone else."

Jared threw his head back in annoyance. "Holly, you're not making any sense. Jennifer Duran is still a missing person. And the first Green River Killer victims were killed in the summer of '82."

"That's what I'm saying." She tapped the wall. "I think these women weren't killed by the Green River Killer. They were killed by a different serial killer, someone whose murders were wrongly thought to be done by the Green River Killer." Thinking of Meg, she added, "Or at least most of them."

Jared rolled his eyes and opened his mouth to speak, but Holly put up a hand.

"Sally Hickman and Brooke Holtman were both murdered one day after major news articles ran about the Green River Killer. I think these two killers might be feeding off each other. And the unidentified killer murdered those two knowing they would get attributed to the Green River Killer, not him. He's the smarter of the two, I'd bet." She stared at the lists, her mind spinning. "Possibly even a cop. Someone with inside information."

Jared scowled. "And you think you're smarter than me?"

Holly whipped around. In the short time she'd been talking, his face had contorted in anger.

"What? No—"

"You really think that after I get kicked off the task force, I want to hear about your Nancy Drew theories?" His face was red, and a vein bulged from his forehead.

She gaped at him. "That's not why I—"

He stepped toward her, spilling vodka onto the carpet. "Just because your sister was murdered doesn't make you a detective."

She recoiled from his words while he pointed at the wall.

"The Green River Killer is the only serial killer in this town.

And your sister wasn't one of his victims. She was a nobody stripper killed in a bad part of town because of the lifestyle she was living." He swiped a hand through the air. "Her case will probably never be solved."

Her throat swelled, and she blinked back tears. *He's had a bad day,* she reminded herself. *He's just not understanding what I'm saying.* "I'm trying to help. My theory would explain why your suspect today had an alibi for most of the Green River Killer murders, but not Sally's or Brooke Holtman's. It makes perfect sense," she continued, ignoring the sour look on Jared's face. "The killer is a genius, really." She gestured to her first column of victims. "He kills and makes it look like a Green River Killer murder, knowing he'd have an alibi for a lot of the Green River Killer murders. That you'd rule him ou—"

"Stop!" Jared shouted.

Holly stepped back, watching his chest heave as he drew in a deep breath. For the first time, he reminded her of her father. She ran a thumb over the engagement ring on her left hand, the metal suddenly feeling as though it were searing her flesh.

Jared knocked back the rest of his drink, then met her gaze, his expression softening. "Look, the guy we brought in today agreed to come back and take a polygraph. Andy still has to verify his alibi. Until then, he's still our main Green River Killer suspect. He's not going to pass the lie detector test."

"He already did."

Jared's eyes darkened. "How would you know that?"

"Andy called me."

He unsteadily closed the space between them, stopping when his face was an inch from hers. "Why would Andy call you?"

"He knows I'm trying to figure out who killed my sister."

"Yeah, I bet that's why he called." He narrowed his eyes, making her feel like an interrogation suspect.

"What is that supposed to mean?"

"Are you cheating on me?"

"Of course not." Andy was not only twice her age, but also married with two kids. She crossed her arms. She wasn't going to justify Jared's accusation by explaining herself. She stepped back. She needed Jared to go home. There was no reasoning with him tonight.

Jared started to pace, almost as if he'd forgotten she was in the room. "*I* should've been the one supervising that polygraph. Not Andy."

"That's what got me thinking about this," Holly said. "Maybe the questions they asked were about the Green River Killings and not specifically about Meg or Sally—"

Jared's hand struck the side of her face before she could stop it. Holly raised a palm to her stinging cheek.

"*Just shut up,*" Jared seethed, baring his teeth.

Her mouth flopped open as she stared at her fiancé in horrified shock. He'd gotten angry in the past, but he had never laid hands on her. His nostrils flared as more veins protruded from his red forehead. His eyes seemed to pierce through her, his pupils dilating with fury, like he was about to jump out of his own skin.

She staggered backward until her spine pressed against the wall, half-expecting him to apologize. Instead, he sneered at her, making the hairs on the back of her neck stand as a ripple of fear stirred beneath her skin, crawling down her limbs.

The phone rang. Jared cocked his head toward the kitchen. She sank against the drywall. *Thank God.* She slid past Jared, only to be yanked back when he grabbed her upper arm.

Jared brought his face to hers, the sweet smell of vodka on his breath making her stomach churn. "No one will believe you if you breathe a word of what just happened."

The phone kept ringing. She gritted her teeth and shook free of his hold. She marched toward the phone.

"Who is it?" Jared called after her. "Your boyfriend calling again to feed you inside info for your crazy obsession?" He scoffed. "I wonder how many times you had to sleep with him for that."

Holly whirled around. *"Get. Out.* We're done.*"* She slipped the engagement ring off her finger and tossed it toward Jared.

She realized her mistake as soon as the ring left her hand, when she registered the flash of fury in Jared's eyes. The ring bounced off Jared's stomach and hit the carpet a split second before Jared threw his empty glass at the wall behind her, and it hit the floor. She jumped at the shattering glass.

Jared pointed at his chest. "Andy should be calling *me*. Not *you*."

The phone stopped ringing when Holly had almost reached the kitchen, allowing her to hear her pulse pounding in her ears. Her gaze fell to Jared's gun in its holster on the counter. *I should've known better. I've seen his temper before. He's no different from my father. Maybe worse.*

"You're going to stop all this crazy shit when we get married," Jared continued as he followed her, the rage drained from his voice. "I'm not having people think my wife is a nut case. Plus, I don't want you working anyway after we have kids."

Holly spun to face him, her face hot with anger. "Did you not hear me? I'm not going to quit working. And I'm not marrying you."

He lunged across the room. Holly's back slammed into the wall before she had time to react. He grabbed her blouse with both fists.

"What the hell did you just say?"

As he shouted, she flinched from the spittle that flew against her face. The monster that consumed him moments ago had returned. The back of her skull throbbed from where she'd hit the wall. In a swift, effortless motion, he threw her to the ground. Jared shoved her face against the floor before she managed to flip onto her back. He kneeled over and raised a fist in the air when she kneed him in the balls as hard as she could.

He grunted, doubling over as she crawled toward the kitchen phone. She got to her knees when she neared the phone, reaching for the receiver when Jared's strong hand closed around her calf, pulling her backward across the linoleum. Her palms screeched against the floor in a futile attempt to resist his pull. She flailed her leg furiously as his fingers dug into her calf.

"Ahh!" She twisted and drove the heel of her other foot into his jaw.

He cried out in pain, releasing her leg to bring his hand to his face. "You bitch," he snarled. "I'll kill you."

She started to get up, but he tackled her to the ground. His hands closed around her throat, and she pressed her palms against his chest, then flailed, frantically trying to free herself as her airway collapsed from the vise-like grip. Her vision blurred. She opened her mouth to scream, but no sound came out. Adrenaline coursed through her, and she wondered if this was what Meg had felt before she died.

In a desperate blur, Holly's hand swept across the kitchen cupboard beside her. Her fingertips skimmed the surface until she hooked her fingers around the edge and yanked the door open. Jared grunted through gritted teeth as he tightened his grip on her neck. Her lungs screamed for air as her hand closed around a frying pan handle. She swung the pan at Jared's head with all her might. The handle vibrated in her hand as it struck the side of his skull with a dull, metallic *twang*, followed by a muffled crack.

He cried out in pain as his hands fell away from her neck. Holly dropped the pan and slid backward, out of his reach, as

Jared brought his palm to the side of his head. Ignoring the burn in her throat, she pushed herself to her hands and knees.

She swiped Jared's holstered revolver off the counter. She fumbled to unsnap the holster with trembling fingers. Jared groaned while getting to his feet behind her. She withdrew Jared's revolver with a shaking hand, then whirled around, arm outstretched, gun aimed at his chest.

Jared threw his hands in the air. "Holly, put that down before you hurt yourself." He stepped toward her.

Holly retreated until she hit the kitchen cabinets with the back of her legs.

Jared extended his hand toward the gun. "You don't even have the safety on."

Holly pressed her finger on the trigger and narrowed her eyes. "It doesn't have one. You told me, remember?" She raised the gun toward his face.

Jared stopped in his tracks, his face morphing into the man she thought she'd known all these months. "Sweetie. I'm sorry, okay? This was just a fight. Nothing more. I've had a bad day. And couples fight, okay? Put down the gun." Blood dripped from the edge of his mouth from where she'd kicked him.

Holly inched sideways toward the phone.

"Don't be ridiculous, Holly. I'm not a criminal. And look at what you've done to me. You'll look crazy if you call the cops on me. I *am* a cop!"

Holly lifted the receiver with her free hand, keeping her eyes and the gun trained on Jared. His gaze fell to the revolver as she punched three numbers into the phone.

He clenched his jaw, lifting his gaze to hers.

"9-1-1 operator, what's your emergency?"

Jared came closer, his voice low. "Holly, don't do it. You've assaulted a police officer. This won't end well for you."

Holly raised her arm, aiming the pistol at Jared's forehead as she pressed the phone to her ear. "My fiancé, Detective Jared Peretti from King County Major Crimes, just assaulted me. He tried to kill me. And he's still here in my apartment."

"Okay, Miss. Are you still in danger?"

Jared's gaze was unblinking and unwavering like a dark, icy abyss.

"I have him at gunpoint."

He stood still, seeing she was no longer helpless.

"Can I have your name, Miss?"

"Holly. Holly Sparks."

"Okay, Holly. Can I have your address?"

Holly rattled it off, holding Jared's dark gaze. The room felt smaller, the air thicker, with each passing second.

"Please hurry," she added. "He might try to take the gun from me. He's drunk, and his temper is out of control."

"A unit is en route. I'll stay on the line with you until they arrive."

It was then Holly spotted the frying pan in Jared's hand. His arm swung upward, holding the pan like a tennis racket. Holly squeezed the trigger. A blast erupted from the gun at the same time the pan impacted with the side of her face, and everything went black.

CHAPTER TWELVE

JOHN

May 1985

JOHN TRUDGED THROUGH the snowy woods next to his dad. A golden eagle soared above the treetops, its wings outstretched as it scoured the woods for prey. John quickened his pace, trekking ahead of his father while imagining he was White Fang running from his abusive owner.

"Not so fast," his dad said.

Begrudgingly, John slowed his steps, admiring the woods around them. They'd touched down in Fairbanks four days ago, and John was already dreading going home tomorrow. His dad had been right about Alaska. It was magical.

John inhaled a deep breath of cold forest air, relishing in the freedom of being so far from home. He surveyed the quiet woods, the only sound coming through the trees to their left, the rush of water from the Chena River. Being strangers in a faraway town where nobody knew them felt like a vacation from everything worrying him. He hadn't even thought about Sally since they'd arrived.

John silently vowed to return here one day when he was older. He pictured having a cabin in a remote forest with a cozy fireplace and a bookshelf filled with his favorite stories.

John felt the tug of his father's grip on his coat and spun. "What?"

His dad lifted a finger to his lips. "Shh." He stopped and leaned against the trunk of a spruce tree.

John lowered his voice. "What are we doing?"

"We're waiting."

John surveyed the white surrounding woods, wishing he'd brought the copy of *Ender's Game* that his dad had bought him for the trip. It wasn't what he normally read, but John had been surprised how much he was enjoying it, finding himself eager to get back to it in the evenings. He could see it becoming a movie one day.

John turned toward his dad. "Can I make a snowman?"

His father shook his head. "No. You could scare away the prey. We came here to scout out hunting grounds. We need to stay still, blend in with our own surroundings." He ran a hand down the rifle strap slung over his chest. "Patience is the key to being a good hunter."

Even though it wasn't hunting season, his dad insisted on bringing the gun anyway. For protection.

"The moment your prey becomes aware of you," his dad continued, "you've lost your advantage. That's why it's vital to remain concealed until you're ready to kill."

A deep growl emitted from somewhere in the forest ahead. John jerked his head toward the sound just as a massive brown bear emerged from the trees. It sauntered through the woods less than one hundred feet away, heading toward the river.

His father slipped his rifle off his shoulder and held it out for

John to take, pressing the butt against the front of John's shoulder before he wrapped John's hand beneath the base of the barrel.

"Line it up in your sights," his father whispered in John's ear.

John closed one eye as his father had taught him. His hand shook as he worked to keep the gun aimed on the moving bear's back.

"Now, shoot."

"What?" John lowered the gun to see his dad's hard-set gaze.

"Shoot," he repeated.

John's brows knitted together. "But it's not hunting season. You said—"

A guttural growl cut through the silent woods. John's lungs seemed to harden as the bear cocked his head toward them. It snarled, exposing large, yellowed fangs.

His dad snatched the weapon from John's hands and aimed it at the beast. The bear turned away and ran toward the river as the rifle's deafening blast echoed through the silent forest. John's ears rang as the huge animal dropped to the ground in a massive heap.

He turned to his dad, watching him lower the gun, then looked back at the lifeless brown mound of fur.

"It wasn't going to hurt us," John said. "It was running away."

"The second key to hunting is never to hesitate. When you have the opportunity to kill, you take it."

John studied the animal's corpse.

"Let's go. It'll be dark soon."

John tore his gaze from the bear and followed his dad, and for the first time on their trip, his thoughts returned to Sally.

CHAPTER THIRTEEN

HOLLY

HOLLY'S LEG JIGGLED as she sat beside Andy on the wooden bench outside the courtroom, waiting to be called. Thinking of Jared sitting inside the room behind them, pleading not guilty, made her stomach churn. She'd hoped it would be liberating to get out of her apartment and get this day over with, but now that she was here, under the same roof as her violent ex-fiancé, she felt overcome with the same fear that had ripped through her the last time she'd seen him.

"Ready?" Andy asked.

She smoothed the wrinkles on the front of her blouse that she'd donned at four in the morning after giving up on sleep. "No."

She stopped herself from imagining what it would be like to be on the witness stand alone, pointing Jared out to the jury as the man who tried to kill her. If she did, she might throw up.

She longed for a cigarette, but she'd thrown them all out after she'd quit. *Probably a good thing.* Once she started again, she might never stop. Instead, she settled for a piece of gum from the opened pack inside her purse.

She'd started smoking in college but then had quit after Meg had been killed. Growing up, Meg had been disgusted by smoking, calling it a dirty habit. After her sister died, every cigarette felt like a betrayal somehow. Holly imagined Meg looking down on her from wherever she was, despising her smoking.

She squeezed her eyes shut, the image of Jared's face—pale, blood blooming across his stomach—flashing behind her eyelids. Then her own body sprawled on the floor, the acrid tang of blood in the air, the siren's wail slicing through the chaos. She'd woken to flashing lights, police officers looming, the pounding in her head a deafening roar. Jared lay on the floor nearby, bleeding out from the gunshot to his stomach.

After emergency surgery, Jared had made a full recovery before being arrested for her assault.

According to her doctors, she'd made a full recovery too—until the panic attacks, nightmares, and insomnia set in. Now, two months later, she couldn't fall asleep without taking a sleeping pill, but she still dreamed of Jared. She didn't know which was worse: not sleeping or waking up in a cold sweat like she was reliving Jared's attack.

Her chest tightened, making her breaths quick and shallow. Her hands, damp with sweat, shook in her lap, and her heart raced like it might burst. She stood, knowing what was coming next. She had pills for panic attacks in her purse, but she didn't want to take one before getting on the stand. A panic attacked loomed, and she couldn't stop it.

She took a few steps forward and bent over, sucking in air while placing her palms on her knees.

A security guard walking by came toward her. "Ma'am, are you okay?"

Andy got up and put his hand on her back. "She's all right," he told the guard before turning to Holly. "It's okay," he said. "Just breathe. In and out. It's going to be fine."

Her breathing slowed as Andy led her back to the bench by her upper arm and helped her sit.

"Your testimony is going to put that sonofabitch behind bars so he can't hurt you—or anyone else—anymore."

Holly stared at the floor, remembering the statement Jared had given to the press after his arrest, claiming that he'd acted in self-defense after Holly had pulled his gun on him. "What if they don't believe me?"

"They will."

"I'm scared, Andy." Holly turned, meeting his gaze.

"I know. But as soon as you're done testifying, you'll never have to see him again. He can't hurt you from prison. Your testimony is the only way to make sure he pays for what he did to you. And to stop him from doing it again."

Her coffee burned like acid inside her stomach, and she felt like she might throw up on the marble floor. "I can't."

Andy put a hand on her shoulder. "Yes, you can."

She shook her head, her lungs twisting like a tetherball rope around her heart. She closed her eyes.

"I never told you this," Andy said. "But the woman Jared dated years ago dialed 911 from his house one night after they'd gotten into a fight. She claimed he'd shoved her against the wall in a fit of rage, but it was in '83 before the mandatory arrest law was enacted for domestic violence, so Jared wasn't arrested. They broke up afterward and nothing ever came of it." He sighed. "Jared claimed she'd lied. I wanted to give him the benefit of the doubt, but I'd seen his temper enough that I should've known better. And I should've told you."

Holly opened her eyes. "It's not your fault, Andy."

Beside them, the courtroom door opened with a creak. "Holly."

Holly turned to find the assistant DA's gaze on her.

"You've been called to the stand," she continued. "It's time to go."

Holly buried her head in her hands.

"She's coming," Andy said. "Just give us a minute."

"We don't have—"

Holly looked up to see Andy put a finger in the air.

"One minute," he said.

The assistant DA clenched her jaw, looking between Holly and the detective. "Fine. But no more."

As the attorney retreated into the courtroom, Andy moved in front of Holly and crouched into a squat so they were eye to eye. "Holly, I know this is hard. Meg never got the chance to speak up for herself in court. But you can. Meg would want you to testify, just like you'd want her to if she were still here."

Holly stared into his brown eyes, knowing he was right. Without a word, she stood to her feet. He nodded before opening the courtroom door for her.

"Here's our witness, your Honor." The assistant DA motioned toward Holly from the front of the courtroom after she stepped inside.

From the corner of Holly's eye, she saw Jared spin in his seat at the defendant's table. She could feel his menacing gaze on her as she moved toward the witness stand. She kept her eyes straight ahead.

"The prosecution calls Holly Sparks to the stand."

Holly lifted her chin, steeling herself for whatever Jared's defense attorney might throw her way on their redirect. Andy was right, Meg never got the chance to face her attacker in court. *This is mine.* Just like she'd never give up her search for Meg's killer, she had to fight for justice for herself.

No matter how much Jared or his attorney tried to intimidate her, she couldn't let him win.

CHAPTER FOURTEEN

JOHN

JOHN KEPT HIS gaze on the motel room TV, even though MacGyver had just finished, and thought about asking the question that had been running through his mind ever since they left those snowy woods.

Did it feel different today when you killed the bear than when you killed Sally?

"Here you go." His dad handed John the remote before sliding off the motel room's made bed. "I'm going to the bar to have a couple of beers."

John sat up, fingers gripping the remote. He opened his mouth to ask about Sally again, but the words stuck in his throat. His dad was already looking out the window.

"Can I come?" He'd finished *Ender's Game* and didn't feel like watching any more TV.

His dad shook his head. "Not tonight. I want you to get some rest. We've got another early morning tomorrow. There's another hunting ground I want to scout out before we take the red eye back to Seattle."

John's shoulders sagged with disappointment. Ever since they were questioned at the Major Crimes Unit, his dad had been pushing him away. Like his dad couldn't trust him or something. "But—"

"I said no." His father flashed him a dark look that sent a shiver through John.

He thought of that huge bear, dead in the woods. He hoped his father wasn't planning on shooting anything tomorrow.

"Tomorrow we're going to snowshoe, then I'm going to take you to Chena Hot Springs." His dad put a hand on John's shoulder and cracked a smile. "Sound good?"

John nodded.

His dad pulled a bag of M&Ms out of the grocery bag sitting in the corner of the room. "You can have these if you get hungry." He pointed at the digital bedside clock. "Don't stay up past ten."

John leaned back against the headboard. "Okay."

"I'll be back soon." His dad threw on his coat before going out the motel room door.

John scooted off the bed and went to the window, watching his dad stroll across the partially lit motel parking lot toward the bar across the street. Above the weathered wood building, *imberline Tavern* was lit up in green flickering neon lights. The *T* in *Timberline* was burned out. He'd only seen it during the day when the lights were off. John turned away from the window, picked up the remote, and flipped through the channels. He tried to imagine that he wasn't alone—that his dad was lying next to him, sharing his M&Ms while they found something to watch together. Even after a day like today, it felt like there was a chasm between them.

Last night he'd gone with his dad to the bar and had played darts while his dad drank two beers. *Why did tonight have to be different?* He tore open the bag of M&Ms, popping a handful into his mouth. John paused on an episode of *The Golden Girls*. His dad never talked about killing Sally, or what happened to his mother, or what he wanted John to be one day. Had his dad killed others too? Like that waitress Jennifer Duran? *How can I prove to him that I can be trusted?*

It's not like I don't know what he did. How could talking about it make it any worse?

He watched until the show went to commercial, then changed the channel.

A dark-haired news anchor filled the screen. She wore a royal blue blazer and sat behind a desk with a blown-up image of Fairbanks behind her. John set down the remote and lifted the bag of candy to his lips.

"The body of Jennifer Duran, the twenty-year-old waitress who went missing in Seattle earlier this month, has been discovered in a wooded area in the Seattle suburb of Burien. Jennifer Duran was last seen arriving at a bus stop after leaving a friend's house on foot at 4:00 p.m. on January eleventh in a West Seattle neighborhood. Detectives say they are investigating her death as a homicide, citing the at-large Green River Killer among their potential suspects."

The news anchor moved on to local news. John racked his brain as she announced that more snowfall was expected in Fairbanks that weekend.

There were several times in January that his dad hadn't gotten home from work until nearly six—two hours after Jennifer Duran was last seen.

But his dad *couldn't* have killed her, John reasoned, draining the last of the M&Ms from the bag. He would've had to leave work early to pick her up at 4:00 p.m. Plus, that had been after his dad had promised John he would do better.

The bear dropping dead with a *thump* in the woods assaulted

John's mind. The splash of blood on the snow next to its head. His father lowering the rifle. At least his dad had now shifted to hunting animals—not humans.

John flipped back to the episode of *The Golden Girls* and yawned. He looked at the clock. *9:15.* It felt later. Probably because it was 10:15 in Seattle. John turned off the TV and flicked off the lamp beside the bed. As he stretched out, a dull throb in his calves reminded him of the miles they'd walked today.

Without the noise from the TV, the country music playing from the bar's jukebox floated through the walls of the dark room. As his eyes adjusted to the dark, his gaze traveled to the motel room's door that led to the parking lot. A lot of boys his age were scared to be alone. But John didn't mind it. There was a peacefulness to it that John never quite had when he was with other people, even his dad. Especially his dad, sometimes, even though he wished he and his dad were closer. John closed his eyes and imagined himself alone in a remote cabin, surrounded by snowy woods like the one he walked through today, allowing sleep to overtake him.

∽

John woke to headlights shining through the motel room's blinds. He turned on the springy mattress and checked the clock. *2:05 a.m.* His dad's side of the bed was empty.

When the motel room door opened, John lay still, pretending to be asleep. His dad walked straight for the bed, his movements not sloppy, but coordinated, as he slipped off his coat and crawled into the bed beside John.

The world outside was quiet. The bar had to be closed. *Where had his dad gone with the rental car?* But he knew better than to ask. John turned on his side, willing himself to go back to sleep as his father's breathing morphed into snores.

John lay there a little longer before giving up and sliding out of bed, knowing if he continued lying there, it wouldn't be long before images of Sally—and that dead bear—consumed his thoughts. Wide awake, he moved to the window and parted the scratchy curtains, peering out into the night. He glanced back at his dad, still asleep, before quietly pulling on the clothes he'd worn yesterday that were lying on top of his suitcase.

His mind reeled, wondering where his dad had been tonight. What had he been doing? John turned for the motel door. He needed some fresh air to clear his mind. There was also something adventurous about going out on his own. Hopefully, after a cold walk, he'd be able to go back to sleep.

CHAPTER FIFTEEN

JOHN

"Hey. John. Wake up."

John opened his eyes. His dad sat on the edge of the mattress beside him. John rubbed his eyes as they adjusted to the bright daylight filtering in through the blinds.

"I've changed our plans. We're going to head back to the airport this morning."

His dad crawling into bed at two in the morning came flooding back to him. "What? Why?"

His dad ran a hand through his brown hair. "I want to see if we can catch an earlier flight instead of the red eye. That way you can get a good night's sleep in your own bed before school tomorrow."

Becoming more awake, John propped himself up on his elbow. "What about the hot springs?"

His dad's features relaxed. "I'm sorry. We'll have to do that next time when we come back in the fall to go hunting." He patted John's legs beneath the comforter. "I'm going to get in the shower, then we'll go."

John threw back the comforter and saw he was still in his clothes that he'd worn on his walk last night. Had his dad noticed? After the bathroom door shut, John turned on the TV. A dark-haired lady in a pink blazer and matching skirt appeared on the screen beside a large weather map covered in swirling shades of blue and white. She pointed to Fairbanks on the map.

"We're expecting more snow on the way for Fairbanks this weekend, with up to six more inches of snowfall by Sunday before we move into highs in the mid-fifties and even some patchy sunshine by the end of next week." She smiled and looked into the camera. "Paul, back to you."

The screen changed to a man sitting behind a news desk with the same backdrop of Fairbanks as last night's evening news. The news anchor stared into the camera with somber eyes.

"Breaking news this morning after a young woman's body has been discovered in a ditch off the Parks Highway. Detectives have yet to release her name to the public, as they are waiting to confirm her identity. But she is believed to have been last seen leaving the Timberline Tavern in the early hours this morning."

The shower water turned on. John shot a glance toward the bathroom.

"The victim was discovered partially clothed, despite the below freezing temperatures. Authorities have confirmed they are treating her death as a homicide and are asking anyone with any information to come forward."

John was barely aware of the shower turning off as the news went to a commercial. When his dad emerged from the bathroom a minute later, John still stared at the screen. Heart pounding, he flicked off the TV. As he looked at his father, a strange numbness came over him. It started in his fingertips, making them feel heavy and distant, as though they no longer belonged to him.

"Ready?"

John followed his father outside to their rental car in silence, his gaze cutting across the street to the Timberline Tavern. In the daylight, all the letters were visible on its sign. He pictured the dead woman leaving the bar last night before climbing into his dad's car.

Behind him, the car door opened. "Get in, son."

John turned to his dad, who held open the passenger door.

His father's look of impatience morphed into concern. "What's wrong?"

John averted his gaze from the bar and met his father's warm eyes. He worked to relax his shoulders, afraid his dad could sense the emotion raging inside him. "Nothing." He trudged toward his father who rested a hand on John's shoulder before he sank into the passenger seat.

Through the frosted windshield, John watched his dad's outline move around the front of the car. He climbed behind the wheel to start the engine before stepping out to run an ice scraper across the windshield. Warm air blew out of the car's heater, and as John shifted in his seat, something bumped against his tennis shoe. He reached down, fingering what felt like a shoe on the floor.

He lifted it up. It was a woman's sneaker. Baby blue. The brand name *Keds* was etched into the sole.

His heart froze, as if time itself had stopped.

His dad sank into the driver's seat beside him. John felt the blood drain from his face as he turned to his father, still holding the shoe.

"I don't know what this is doing here," John heard himself say.

His dad snatched the shoe from John's grip and set it on his thigh. "Must be from someone who rented the car before us."

John sat in silence, staring at the dirty mounds of snow piled along the side of the road as his dad drove toward the airport while keeping the shoe on his lap. About two miles from their hotel, John spotted three patrol cars parked on the shoulder of the highway, with yellow crime scene tape stretched across the adjacent ditch and running across a clearing, connected to one of the trees that marked the edge of the woods. A blue and white van marked *CORONER* was parked in front of the patrol cars.

As they drove past, John craned his neck to get a look at the scene. He couldn't see the body, but he spotted a man in a dark suit carrying an evidence bag to his car. When John recognized the light blue Ked inside the clear plastic bag matching the one on his dad's lap, he thought he might puke.

He inhaled audibly, then glanced at his dad to see if he'd noticed. But his dad peered past John out the passenger window as they sped away from the scene.

"Wonder what happened there," his dad said.

John gulped. They passed a sign that read "Parks Highway" as John's M&Ms from last night rose to the top of his throat. John already knew that's what highway they were traveling on. The newscaster had said so that morning. He avoided his dad's gaze as they continued toward the airport, knowing there was no way he could hide what he knew if he looked his dad in the eye.

John gripped the door handle as his dad pulled into the empty parking lot of a Dunkin' Donuts.

"Let's grab some breakfast."

A Fairbanks patrol car pulled into the lot and parked in the spot beside John. John froze as the officer got out of his car. His dad grabbed the shoe and slid it inside an empty McDonald's bag from the backseat before getting out.

"Morning, Officer." His dad nodded to the cop.

John held his breath, afraid his father was about to confess. Then his dad stuffed the bag into a covered garbage bin outside the entrance, coming around the car and opening the door for John.

I should say something, John thought. *Now's my chance.* Guilt swept over him, chilling him to the core. As he climbed out, he kept his gaze on the pavement.

His dad bent over and gripped John squarely by both shoulders, forcing him to meet his gaze. "Don't worry. Everything's going to be fine." He smiled, tussled John's hair, and led the way into the Dunkin' Donuts.

John followed his dad in silence. *I sure as hell hope so.*

His dad placed a hand on his stomach as he strode toward the building's entrance. "Man, I'm starving." He held the door open for John.

John moved through the doorway, and a warm, sugary scent hit him. The cop stood at the register, and a young, redheaded woman greeted them from behind the counter. John stared at the donuts in the display, mentally replaying his dad coming back to the motel in the middle of the night, waking John from his sleep.

He knows where that shoe came from, John thought. *He has to.*

John turned to his dad as he flashed the woman behind the counter a charismatic smile, making her blush. John couldn't help but be impressed at his father's lack of reaction to the shoe and crime scene they'd passed on the highway. His father was an even better actor than John had given him credit for.

PART 2

CHAPTER SIXTEEN

HOLLY

March 1990

"As the gavel fell, sentencing Richard Kane to life in prison without parole, the courtroom exhaled a collective breath that felt both hollow and heavy. For the neighbors on Queen Anne Hill, who once admired the picture-perfect couple in the Tudor on 4th Avenue, the trial had revealed the cracks beneath the façade of normalcy. But for advocates fighting to make domestic violence visible, Diane Kane's story became a rallying cry—a tragic emblem reminding all of us why silence is no longer an option."

Applause filled the packed downtown bookstore as Holly closed the hardcover copy of her newest true crime release, *Behind Closed Doors.*

"Thank you," Holly said into the microphone before stepping aside to allow her publicist, Laurie, to take her place behind the podium. "Thank you so much."

Holly worked to stifle the yawn that threatened to emerge.

Thanks to Laurie, Holly's life for the last three weeks had become an endless parade of readings, interviews, and book signings. Her books would be nothing without her readers—and Holly was grateful for each one of them—but she'd forgotten how energy-zapping these kinds of events were for her. And this was her biggest book tour so far.

In the last four years, four of her books had been published, each hitting the *New York Times'* Bestseller List. As every advance grew larger, her publisher expected Holly to do more promotion. It was a balancing act, trying to keep up with her writing deadlines and the demands that came with her success. Over the last few weeks, she'd fallen behind on the new true crime novel she was writing. Yesterday, she'd broken down and asked her publisher for an extension—something she'd never done before and hoped she would never have to do again.

"Holly, I think I speak for everyone when I say that was an incredibly moving reading." A second round of clapping erupted from the crowd gathered inside the main floor of Pike Street Bookstore.

Holly blushed, smiling as her gaze fell across the tightly filled room. Sometimes, she felt like pinching herself. Was this really her life? She was in a crowded room full of strangers who'd come to hear her read words from her own book that was being made into a TV series. A lump formed in her throat as she scanned the strangers' faces, wishing her sister could be here. Despite Holly's success as a true crime author, she was no closer to finding out who had killed Meg.

Laurie paused, waiting for the applause to dissipate before adding, "Holly will now be signing copies at the table near the back of the store. We've got quite a large crowd here today, so we ask that you have your cameras ready if you'd like to take a photo with Miss Sparks and be mindful of allowing time for those in line behind you."

Holly moved through the aisles to the back of the store, thinking again of the message her mom had left on her answering machine that morning. The last time her mom had stayed with her was when she got home from the hospital after Jared's attack, when her mom had been terrified of losing her only living daughter. But after Holly recovered, her mom had gone back to Spokane and continued their old relationship, making up excuses why she couldn't visit. This time it was that Holly's stepdad didn't like to be alone, so she couldn't make the signing. It was always something. But Holly knew the real reason was there were too many painful reminders of Meg in Seattle for her mom.

Holly was still moving toward the signing table when a tall man striding toward her caught her eye. His white hair was in sharp contrast to his black trench coat, shoulders beaded with raindrops that still pattered against the bookstore's roof.

"Andy." Her mouth lifted into a smile. When he got closer, she greeted him with a warm hug. It had been over a year since she'd last seen him, though she called him periodically with questions related to her true crime writing and to find out if there were any breaks in Meg's case, which, sadly, there never were. "Thank you for coming. You didn't have to." She shook her head. "I know how busy you are."

A shadow crossed Andy's face, replacing his easy grin with something heavier. "Actually, I came to tell you something. I thought it should be in person."

The room around her seemed to freeze, like a VHS tape on pause. She searched his blue eyes. Andy still served on the Green River Task Force, although the team was smaller than it used to be now that the GRK's killings were much less frequent. Had they finally caught the Green River Killer? Meg's killer?

Holly had never convinced Andy that Meg was a Green River Killer victim. Like Jared, Andy clung to the belief that Meg had simply been in the wrong place at the wrong time—another casualty of random, brutal violence. Holly disagreed. While she hadn't ruled out the Green River Killer as her sister's murderer, she suspected another predator was out there, and Meg could be one of his victims. Frustratingly, Andy didn't buy that theory either.

Laurie grabbed Holly's elbow, her French-manicured nails glinting in the fluorescent light. "You've already got a huge line at your signing table."

"Just a second," Holly said, keeping her eyes on Andy. "What is it?"

Laurie cast a worried glance over her shoulder. "The crowd's getting antsy."

Holly lifted a finger to her publicist. "I'll be there soon. Just give me a few minutes."

Laurie pursed her lips, shooting Andy an annoyed glance before leaving them alone.

"It's Jared."

The floor swayed beneath Holly's feet.

Andy watched her publicist walk away before turning back to Holly. "The parole board approved his early release."

The room seemed to drop in temperature, an invisible chill sweeping through the air.

"We're ready for you, Holly," Laurie called from the back of the room, annoyance permeating her voice.

Holly kept her eyes on Andy, mentally reliving the moment in the courtroom when she pointed to Jared as her attacker, the man who'd tried to choke her to death. From the pure hatred that seeped through his eyes as he stared back at her from behind the defendant's desk, there was no doubt in Holly's mind he wished he'd finished the job.

Laurie's voice sounded again from the rear of the store. "Maybe it will help if we all call Holly's name together. Ready everyone?"

Holly swallowed, ignoring the chant of her name from the growing line readers that wrapped around the bookstore. *Holly. Holly. Holly.*

"When does he get out?" she asked.

"He already is. He got out yesterday."

CHAPTER SEVENTEEN

HOLLY

HOLLY STARED AT her computer screen beside the main floor window of her Lake Union houseboat. She could afford more, but she liked the feeling of being on the water. At least she used to, when she knew Jared was behind bars in a maximum-security prison. Now, she wished she lived in a high-rise condo with twenty-four-hour security.

She took a drink from the large glass of wine she'd poured after getting home from her book signing. In the last hour or two, she'd written three sentences. Something fluttered outside her window, and her body stiffened. She jerked her head to see a seagull landing on the adjacent dock.

She closed her eyes and pinched the bridge of her nose. Less than three weeks remained before she had to turn in her manuscript portraying the life and death of Roxy Vega, the lead singer of the up-and-coming Seattle rock band, The Screaming Violets. In November of 1988, Roxy's body had been discovered in a dumpster of a Seattle alley. After a night out with friends, she'd been on the way back to her apartment when she'd been brutally beaten and strangled to death by a homeless ex-felon.

Holly checked her word count and took another drink from her wine. She was never going to finish her draft if she kept letting her mind wander to her ex-fiancé. Ever since Andy told her about Jared's release, she'd been on high alert.

Her gaze drifted to the rust-red pipes and towers of Gas Works Park, the skeletal remains of the old gasification plant across the lake as a float plane came down for a landing. Holly lifted a crime scene photo off the stack of papers beside her keyboard and found the handwritten notes she'd taken yesterday after replaying her recorded interview with Roxy's mother.

Holly started to read her words when an image of Jared being led out of the courtroom after his sentencing flashed in her mind. She envisioned his menacing grin as if it were yesterday. Even though he'd been convicted of first-degree assault, he'd wanted her to know it wasn't over. She hadn't won.

She imagined Jared's face, which then morphed into the shadowy face of the elusive Green River Killer.

Jared, the Green River Killer? A thousand questions swirled in her mind. Even though it seemed an outrageous thought, it had crossed her mind before. There had long been speculation that the Green River Killer was a cop: someone with authority who women trusted wouldn't hurt them, someone calculated and knowledgeable enough to know how to avoid detection. Had Jared joined the task force to manipulate the evidence? Maybe that was why he lost it in Andy's office that day.

After Jared went to prison for assaulting Holly, the presumed Green River killings became infrequent, so much so that Holly wondered if the handful of murders attributed to him since Jared went to prison could've been done by a copycat, or simply unrelated. But she'd chalked her suspicions up to having too many true crime stories floating around in her head.

Now, with Jared out of prison, her suspicions didn't feel foolish. Had he killed Meg? Had she been engaged to her sister's murderer?

The floor rocked from the float plane's wake, but Holly hardly noticed. She positioned her hands on the keyboard and turned back to the screen.

Stop letting Jared get to you. That's in the past. Right now, you need to focus.

Behind her, a kitchen cupboard smacked against its frame, making her jump. She spun in her seat, half-expecting Jared to be standing in the kitchen, wearing the same evil grin as the last time she'd seen him.

But her kitchen was empty. Her heart thudded against her chest. She chided herself for being so jumpy. Her cupboards had shifted from the wake of the float plane. It happened all the time.

She turned back around to face the computer. *Jared doesn't know where I live.* She kept her phone number and address unlisted from the White Pages. But could Jared have a connection on the force who he could convince to give him her address?

Her fingertips rested atop the keyboard as she exhaled out her mouth. She'd typed three words when she suddenly remembered. *The article.* How could she have forgotten?

She snatched the cordless phone off the desk and punched in the number she knew by heart.

"Hello?"

"Laurie. It's me."

"I was just about to call you. I've got great news. I just got off the phone with—"

"We need to cancel that article in *People* magazine. They can't run it."

"Cancel?" Laurie scoffed into the phone. "You're kidding me, right?"

"No."

"Are you drinking?"

"No." Holly's gaze fell to the glass of wine on the desk. "Well, yes, but not like that."

"Why on earth would you want to cancel? This is the kind of publicity most authors would kill for. Aside from Stephen King, you're the only author I know of to get a feature article like this."

"They can't run it. What if Jared reads it and sees where I live?" Holly stood, pacing the small space between the desk and the kitchen. She should never have let Laurie talk her into allowing *People* to take her photo inside her houseboat for the feature article. At the time, they both thought Jared would remain behind bars for another three years, but she should have been thinking about the future.

"It's too late, I'm afraid. It came out today. I slipped a copy into your bag at the bookstore, remember?"

Holly didn't. She'd been too preoccupied by the news of Jared's release.

"Shit." Holly moved to the couch and felt inside the messenger bag. She withdrew the March issue of *People*, recognizing the Menendez brothers on the cover, who'd been shockingly arrested for their parents' slaying earlier that month. *Murder in Beverly Hills* was printed in bold yellow letters above a photo of the Menendez family mansion. Holly's heart sank at the smaller headline in the upper right corner: "Holly Sparks: Making Waves on a Seattle Houseboat."

"No, no, no." Holly cradled the phone with her shoulder as she flipped past the featured article showing a Menendez family photo beside an image of the two brothers sitting in a courtroom as they were arraigned for their parents' brutal murder. Once she'd thumbed to the right page, her mouth fell open at the full-page image of her Lake Union houseboat's exterior with Gas Works Park visible across the water. Anyone familiar with Seattle could figure out the location of her houseboat. Holly gritted her teeth at the title: "CRIME ON THE WATER: Lake Union Houseboat Author Makes a Killing."

"Did you find it?" Laurie asked. "It's a great piece, right? We couldn't have timed it better with those Menendez brothers on the front."

"I didn't say they could photograph the outside of my houseboat."

"I know, but—"

"Laurie, this is my *life*." Holly tossed the magazine onto the couch. "I can't stay here. As soon as Jared gets in line at a supermarket, he'll know exactly where I live."

"I get it, but that was what, five years ago? Don't you think the guy's gotten over it by now? If he got an early release, maybe he's reformed."

Holly breathed into the phone. Laurie didn't get it at all. "Have you even *read* any of my books? Jared's had five years to stew over my testimony, which sent him to prison." Laurie hadn't seen the way Jared looked at her in the courtroom. "Trust me, he hasn't gotten over it."

"Okay. I hear you. I'm flying to LA tomorrow, but I can help you start looking for a place on Saturday."

"I can't wait that long." Holly turned toward the window. Dusk had settled over the gray sky, which was growing dark nearly as fast as her apprehension.

"You're welcome to stay here with Ken and the girls while I'm away."

Holly imagined trying to write at Laurie's kitchen table in the suburbs, Roxy Vega's crime scene photos splayed over the table for Laurie's four-year-old twins to see. Plus, Laurie's name was listed in the magazine article too. Unlike Holly's address, Laurie's *was* listed in the White Pages. But Holly didn't want to scare her by saying so.

"That's okay. I'll get a hotel until we find something." Holly looked at the computer monitor, envisioning herself lugging it to a hotel room. But what choice did she have? "Thanks though."

"Oh, wait!" Laurie exclaimed when Holly was about to hang up. "I just remembered. Ken's parents just moved out of their house in Tacoma. They're downsizing to a condo and planning to rent out their house after they get rid of their extra furniture. I'm sure you could stay there. That way there wouldn't even be a paper trail. You know…just in case."

Holly swallowed. *Just in case Jared tries to kill me.* She peered out the window, checking for movement on the dock. Around the edges of the shore, houseboats and buildings glowed softly as night fell over the city.

"It's a big house. Four bedrooms. Plenty of room to write."

Holly looked at the magazine on the couch. "All right. Thanks, Laurie."

"I'll call them tonight."

Holly hung up and returned to her seat in front of the desk. The lake had gone quiet, aside from the water lapping against the side of the houseboat and the soft jazz playing from her next-door floating neighbor. She finished the wine in her glass.

She wasn't going to let him get to her tonight. He'd already upended her life once. She had work to do. She had neighboring houseboats within a few feet on either side. *I could easily call for help if I needed to.* They would hear her scream if Jared tried to break in.

But it didn't make her feel any better. She'd lived in an apartment the night he'd tried to kill her, and sharing a wall with another unit hadn't stopped him. Wishing she had a gun, she forced her thoughts to her interview with Roxy Vega's mother.

Holly yawned despite being wired from the news of Jared's release. The two cups of coffee she'd drunk before opening a bottle of wine hadn't helped much. She forced herself to painstakingly finish the chapter before she allowed herself to check the time. It was after eleven, which meant it had taken her twice as long to write the remaining five pages as it normally did. She got up and stretched her arms over her head. Sometime in the last few hours, the neighbor's music had turned off.

As she went to double check that the front door was locked, her gaze landed on the grim-faced Menendez brothers pictured on the cover of *People,* the magazine still lying on the couch. A shiver ran through her thinking of their parents, murdered by their sons in their mansion in Beverly Hills, which was thought to be the safest place in the country. Holly wondered what it had been like for their parents, falling asleep on their couch watching TV, only to be awakened by their sons standing over them, the blast from the shotgun barrels stealing the parents from their slumber.

Assured her deadbolt was locked, Holly made for her upstairs bedroom, gripping the cordless phone in her hand. She started up the stairs, then stopped and retreated toward the kitchen.

If there was one thing she'd learned from writing true crime, it was that the victims who weren't afraid to fight back, scream, or run were the ones who most often got away from a dangerous predator. Holly withdrew her sharpest knife from the butcher block on the counter and turned back for the stairs.

If Jared *did* come for her, she wasn't going down without a fight.

CHAPTER EIGHTEEN

HOLLY

"THINK THIS WILL work?" Laurie stepped back from the desk where they'd set up Holly's computer in Laurie's in-laws' home office.

Holly knelt over a plastic tub and peered inside. She traced a finger around the edge of the shoebox her sister, had left behind at the group home, staring at its contents: a cheap bracelet Holly gave Meg for her tenth birthday, an AC/DC cassette tape, a movie stub from *Caddyshack*, and the sealed adoption contract Meg had signed six months before her murder.

The box was a poor stand-in for the warmth of her sister's voice and the comfort of her laugh, but it was all Holly had left. Even though her stay was temporary, leaving Meg's things at her houseboat felt wrong, like she was abandoning her sister all over again.

Holly stood and stuck her hands in the jeans' pockets as she gazed out at the top of the Narrows Bridge, visible through the upstairs window through the tall evergreen woods that separated the neighborhood from the Sound. As dusk deepened, the bridge shimmered to life, its lights piercing the twilight sky.

"It'll be great." The neighborhood was nice, more upscale than what Holly had pictured. When she'd followed Laurie to the home at the end of a cul-de-sac earlier that day with her Honda Civic packed with clothes and all she'd need to finish her true crime novel, Holly felt at ease seeing the manicured yards and large two-story homes that looked to all have been built in the last decade. She hadn't expected to have a view of the Narrows Bridge from her office window. But Holly missed her houseboat already; it felt strange to be in such a big house compared to her small place on Lake Union.

"Need any more help?" Laurie asked, glancing at the two boxes on the floor.

Laurie had spent the last several hours helping Holly move her clothes, computer, and boxes of notes into the upstairs of the large suburban home.

"I'm good."

Holly followed Laurie's gaze to the boxes filled with marked-up maps of King County—each X the location of a body that had been discovered, the suspected victims of the Green River Killer. Under the maps lay piles of newspaper clippings and Holly's ever-growing list of young women who'd gone missing in the Seattle area, along with her shorter list of suspected Bus Stop Killer victims, which included Meg. She planned to put them on the office wall out of habit since she'd never written without having them nearby. She'd always hoped that by keeping them up, something might come to her in her subconscious as she worked.

"I think my in-laws have an old bulletin board in the garage," Laurie said. "You want me to get it so you can hang some of this stuff up?"

Holly tore her gaze from the boxes and managed a smile. "I can find it later. You've done so much already."

She'd wait until Laurie left to unpack those. Her publicist had voiced on more than one occasion that she worried Holly's fixation on her sister's unsolved murder was excessive, and those of the Green River Killer. Laurie didn't know the half of it. She'd never told Laurie about her growing theory there was a second serial killer at large around Seattle, The Bus Stop Killer, and that he'd killed Meg and a handful of others.

"Well, in that case, I'd better go," Laurie said. "I promised Ken I'd be home to help with dinner and bedtime with the girls."

Laurie swept her teased bangs to the side, blending them in with her feathered strawberry blond hair. She cast Holly a motherly look, even though they were less than ten years apart. "You going to be okay here?"

Holly wondered if Jared could've been lurking in the parking area to her houseboat and had followed them here. She imagined him breaking a window in the night, wrapping his thick fingers around her neck as she slept. She envisioned waking up in a strange bed, Jared looming over with the same crazed look in his eyes that he had when he—

"Holly. Hello?" Laurie snapped her fingers. "You need anything else before I go home?"

Holly blinked the thoughts away and forced a smile. "I'll be fine. Just need to get back to work." *And get my mind off Jared.*

Laurie crossed her arms. "You seemed like you were somewhere else there a moment."

Holly shrugged. "Just the creative mind, I guess."

Laurie furrowed her brows, looking skeptical as Holly glanced at the night falling outside the window. She hadn't written anything today. Her literary agent had called this morning letting Holly know that her publisher had agreed to an extension. Holly was meant to send in her manuscript this Friday, but they'd given her two more weeks. She needed at least double that, but she would take what she could get.

Holly turned to the desk, where the pile of notes, Roxy Vega's thick casefile, and her tape recorder filled with hours of interviews lay beside her keyboard. It was going to be a late night.

"Thanks for all your help today," Holly said as the two of them made for the staircase.

As Holly had lugged her computer monitor and hard drive up the strangers' staircase earlier that day, she couldn't help feeling she'd overreacted. Maybe Laurie had been right, and Jared was reformed.

"And please thank your in-laws for letting me move in on such short notice," Holly added as she followed Laurie down the carpeted stairs.

"They were happy to help." When Laurie reached the bottom of the staircase, she turned toward her. "My mother-in-law is a huge fan of yours. She's read all your books and was *thrilled* to know you'd be staying here." Laurie cocked her head and placed a hand on Holly's forearm. "A little too thrilled, if you ask me. You might need to worry about *her* stalking you now and not just Jared."

Laurie laughed. Holly frowned.

"Sorry." Laurie shook her head. "I was just trying to be funny. But seriously, she wanted to come over and show you the house, but I told her we would be fine by ourselves. Trust me, you'd never get her to leave. She would've yacked all night about your books, and I know you're on a deadline. But after you turn in this new book, she would love to meet you."

"I'd love to meet her too." After hugging Laurie, Holly opened the front door. "Give my love to Ken and the girls."

"I will. I put the garage door opener on the kitchen counter, and I dropped the house keys into your purse."

"Thanks."

Laurie pulled the hood of her sweatshirt over her head as she stepped onto the porch. "One more thing. The phone is in the kitchen, and it's on a party line."

"Those still exist?"

Laurie laughed. "This cul-de-sac is miserly and stuck in the seventies." She lifted a finger in the air as she started down the porch steps. "So, watch out. If you pick up the phone at the wrong time, you'll be stuck listening to Carol from two houses down rehashing the latest *Murder, She Wrote* to her sister."

Holly smiled. "Good to know."

"Oh." Laurie spun around as Holly started to shut the door. "I almost forgot. I told the next-door neighbor, Clint, that you're moving in so he doesn't think you're squatting here or anything." She winked and pointed to the house on her left. "If you need anything, I'm sure he'd be happy to give you a hand." She grinned. "He's also single."

Holly rolled her eyes. She'd hardly dated after everything that happened with Jared. Instead, she'd buried herself in her work. "I'm perfectly capable of living on my own without needing a man's *help*."

Laurie put up a palm. "Look, I'm just saying, it wouldn't hurt you to have a man around for a change."

Holly let out the closest thing to a laugh she'd experienced since learning of Jared's release. "I hate to break it to you, but you might be more stuck in the 70s than this cul-de-sac."

Laurie's brick-red lipsticked mouth curled to a smile. "You might change your mind after you meet him. He's very easy on the eyes."

"Thanks for sharing, but now let me get back to work."

"Hey." Laurie stepped back toward the door before Holly could close it. She placed a manicured hand over her chest. "As your publicist, I'm in no spot to complain about you working so hard—and I know you're on a tight deadline." Laurie met Holly's gaze, the usual spark in the publicist's eyes dimming to a quiet intensity. "But as your friend, just remember, you need to go out once in a while. You're thirty-one years old, beautiful, with no responsibilities of motherhood or marriage holding you back." Laurie dipped her head. "I worry about you sometimes, always cooped up with morbid crime scene photos. I probably shouldn't say this, but…trust me." Laurie lifted her gaze to lock eyes with Holly. "There's more to life than work. Meg would've wanted that for you. To move on, have a life, maybe even a family one day."

Holly opened her mouth to tell Laurie that her work *was* her life, but Laurie held up a hand again.

"I know you're on a deadline," Laurie added. "But once you're done, you should go on a vacation."

"I'll think about it."

In the glow of the front porch lights, Laurie flashed Holly a knowing side glance. "No, you won't. I've seen that look before. But when you're old and alone, wishing you had someone to spend your lonely days with, don't say I didn't warn you."

"Unless I'm dead, I'll still be writing books." Holly smiled. "Plus, I have you."

Laurie pursed her lips and started down the concrete porch steps. "That's depressing."

"Is it? I think it sounds wonderful."

"You're weird," Laurie called when she reached her minivan. "Oh," she added after opening the driver's side door. "I picked up your fan mail from your PO Box this morning like you asked. It's in the kitchen."

Holly knew she should be thankful—the letters were proof that her books mattered to someone—but the thought of that stack of envelopes on the kitchen counter sent a sharp pang of anxiety through her chest. Years ago, she'd promised herself to respond to every letter she got from her readers unless it was hate mail, which she'd gotten her share of too. But right now, fan mail was one more demand when she had no time to spare. "Thanks, Laur."

After locking the deadbolt behind her, Holly leaned against the door. Being alone forever didn't scare her. She'd already lost the most important person in her life. What *did* scare her was Meg's killer walking free forever.

Holly trudged into the kitchen and immediately spotted the unopened envelopes on the counter. Seeing the stack wasn't as high as she'd feared, her shoulders relaxed. She sifted through them. There were only eight.

I'll open half tonight and half tomorrow. Then I'll respond after I mail in my manuscript. Sometimes, getting an encouraging note from a reader helped her get out of a writing slump—something she could use tonight.

She tore open the top envelope, noting her name and address were typed instead of handwritten. There was no return address in sight. She unfolded the paper inside, letting it fall to the counter after she read the short, typed poem.

Roses are red and violets are blue,
Your stories are thrilling, but I'm watching you.

CHAPTER NINETEEN

HOLLY

AN HOUR LATER, Holly pushed her cart of bagged groceries toward the Albertson's exit. She'd called Laurie and told her about the poem as soon as Laurie had gotten home. Unlike Holly, her publicist wasn't convinced it was Jared, reminding Holly that she'd gotten weird hate mail before. Laurie's words echoed in Holly's mind. *Not everything is a mystery waiting to be solved.*

Holly didn't consider herself 'famous,' but the letter could've been sent by some crazy fan like in *Misery*, the Stephen King novel that was being made into a movie. But in her gut, she knew it wasn't a fan. She hoped Jared only wanted to scare her, not finish what he started.

After hanging up with Laurie, she'd been too disturbed by the poem to write. To fill the time, she'd run out to get groceries at a store less than two miles away, hoping the errand would clear her mind to work on her novel when she got back.

She exited the grocery store through automatic doors, passing a twentysomething blond woman on her way in. Their eyes locked momentarily as the young woman pulled back the rain-soaked hood of her jacket. A cool drizzle hit Holly's cheeks as she pushed her nearly full grocery cart out into the parking lot.

Too bad you can't have groceries delivered, she thought, pushing the cart through a puddle to get to her Civic near the back of the parking lot. She glanced at the bags of food, reminded of her mother's words: *You should never go shopping when you're hungry.* At least it was mostly healthy, aside from the bag of Cheetos she'd seen on the end of an aisle and couldn't resist.

In the time she'd been in the store, the parking lot had thinned out. Holly spotted her Honda. The cars that had been parked around it when Holly had gotten to the store were now gone. She shivered from the damp air and the raindrops bleeding through her thin sweater, wishing she'd thought to bring her rain jacket when she dashed out of the house. She quickened her pace, eager to get back to work.

After unloading the bags into the trunk, Holly looked around the dimly lit lot for where to return her cart. She strained to see in the dark. She'd tried to find a spot under a streetlamp, but those spaces had all been taken when she'd arrived. She closed the trunk, spotting a cart return a few spaces up.

Headlights rolled down the row as Holly pushed the cart. She stepped aside, giving the car room to move past as she walked back to her car. But the vehicle didn't accelerate. It crept behind her, illuminating her from behind with its bright beams.

Holly turned, squinting from the light. It looked to be a car, not a truck, but it was too dark for her to make out much beyond that. She walked faster, acutely aware of the engine's hum behind her. When she reached her car, she hurried to the driver's side.

She dug a hand into her purse for her keys, glancing up at the headlights, willing the vehicle to keep moving. Instead, it stopped, idling behind her Civic, blocking her path out of the parking spot. The figure behind the wheel looked male, but the darkness made it impossible for her to be sure. *Could it be Jared?* She wasn't going to linger long enough to find out.

She frantically felt for her keys, cursing herself for having so many lipsticks. The driver's door of the idling car opened as Holly's fingers closed around her key chain. Holly thought about screaming for help as the figure stepped out, but there was no one in the nearly empty parking lot to hear her.

She withdrew her keys and fumbled them, missing the lock on her first attempt and scratching her key against the door. The stranger moved toward the front of his car as Holly thrust her key into the lock. She shot a glance at the dark outline of a man before she flung open the door and climbed inside, pushing down the door lock as soon as she closed the door.

She kept her gaze on the unmoving figure in the rearview mirror as she shakily inserted the key into the ignition. Heart pounding, she pulled forward through the empty bay in front of her as the man got back into his car. Holly gripped the wheel with both hands and peeled out onto the street, glancing over her shoulder to see the car still idling in the parking lot. She sped through a yellow light just as it turned red, holding her breath as she floored the gas pedal.

By the time she'd reached the neighborhood gate, the drizzle had turned to rain, drumming against the windshield in a rhythmic cascade. She collapsed against her seatback. *It had to be Jared.* Which meant he likely knew she was staying nearby. She checked the rearview mirror as the gate slid open. There was only darkness. She thought of Andy's offer to help her get a restraining order, berating herself for not getting a look at the car's license plate. She couldn't even say for sure that it was Jared, even though she knew it had to be.

She pulled through the gate as soon as it opened, then waited for it to close behind her before turning onto the street that led to her cul-de-sac. Even if Jared had followed her to the neighborhood gate, he wouldn't know which house she was staying in.

As she pulled into the driveway, she felt around the passenger seat beside her purse for the garage clicker. She didn't want to leave her car outside for Jared to recognize. Not finding it, she flicked on the dome light as she idled in front of the garage. She thought she'd grabbed it on her way out of the house, but in her rush, she must've left it on the kitchen counter.

"Shoot."

She found the house keys inside her purse and left the engine running while she jogged to the front door, bowing her head in the rain. She unlocked the door, and her nerves started to calm as she moved through the house to the kitchen where the garage opener lay on the counter.

She grabbed the clicker and hurried outside. When she opened her driver's door, a hand clamped onto her shoulder. She screamed.

She whipped around in the glow of the exterior garage lights to see the wide, surprised eyes of a man as he threw his hands in the air.

He took a step back, offering her a disarming smile. "I'm sorry. I didn't mean to scare you," he said over the rain. "I called out to you, but you must not have heard me. I'm Clint." He pointed to the house next to hers. "I live next door."

"Oh." Holly exhaled, placing a hand over her heart. He was attractive, she noted, his broad shoulders filling out his plaid button-down shirt. She swallowed. "Hi. Um. I'm Holly."

"Laurie told me you were moving in. The author, right?"

She nodded, trying to hide her annoyance. Laurie always had to overshare. She wondered what else Laurie had told him.

He wiped a damp piece of hair to the side of his forehead. "I won't keep you in the rain. I was just taking my garbage out and thought I'd let you know that tomorrow is garbage day." He gestured behind him to a trash can on the curb between their two houses.

"Thanks."

"No problem." He backed away, flashing her another friendly smile. "Nice to meet you, Holly."

His shirt, now wet from the rain, clung to his muscular upper body as he turned to his house. Holly climbed into her car and opened the garage.

She waited for the garage door to fully close before getting out to retrieve the groceries from the trunk. She relaxed her shoulders at knowing Clint was next door, glad now that Laurie had told him she was moving in. He would, after all, know the normal comings and goings of the neighborhood and be more likely to spot a strange vehicle—or someone who didn't belong.

Once inside, Holly caught her reflection in a decorative mirror hanging in the hallway. She cringed. The rain had made her mascara bleed beneath her eyes, and her wet hair clung limply to the side of her head.

Hopefully it had been too dark outside for Clint to get a good look at her, she thought. Because Laurie had been right. He *was* easy on the eyes.

CHAPTER TWENTY

REBECCA

Rebecca smiled at the woman leaving Albertson's as she stepped through the automatic doors, even though she felt like crying. She'd had a lot of practice pretending she was happy. On autopilot, she grabbed a shopping basket and wandered around the grocery store in a fog.

She'd told Neil they were out of milk, but really, she just needed to get out of their apartment. He'd offered to drive her tonight, but she assured him she was perfectly happy taking the bus. She wandered the aisles, thinking of her boyfriend at home, watching *Married with Children,* waiting for her return. He had no idea his girlfriend was having a mid-life crisis while she meandered through a grocery store like a sleepwalker, half-lost in thought, and half-lost in general. *Can you even have a mid-life crisis at twenty-five?*

Rebecca turned down the frozen food aisle, wondering if she should bring back some ice cream. She scanned the freezers of ice cream, guilt pooling in her stomach for wanting more than the life she was living. Even though her pay at the hair salon wasn't a lot, it was steady. Her boyfriend was sweet to her, if boring at times. He worked hard and treated her well. *So what if Neil doesn't laugh at all my jokes and doesn't want to go out as much I do?* He was loyal and kind.

Her mother's voice rang in her ears. *What more could you want?* She dropped a pint of Häagen-Dazs into her basket and made for the check-out line.

When she reached the front of the store, she spotted a copy of *Vanity Fair* with Kathleen Turner wearing a white dress on the cover. Rebecca looked away, feeling her throat swell with regret. When she'd graduated from beauty school, she'd planned to stay in Tacoma for only a year or so until she saved up enough to move to LA and pursue her dream of acting. But here she was, five years later, working at Supercuts and dating Neil, who had no desire to move to California. She didn't even like doing hair, but she hadn't planned on it being her lifelong career.

Rebecca added a roll of Mentos to her basket in the check-out aisle before paying, thinking it was probably already too late for her to get her start in acting. She should've moved to Hollywood right after high school, despite her parents encouraging her to stay in Tacoma and "get a real job."

She trudged through the parking lot in the rain to wait for the bus to take her home. She sat on the bus-stop bench, rain pattering against the shelter's roof, and pulled a Mento out of the roll. A bus sped by on the opposite side of the street with an advertisement for *Ghost* on the side, "Coming to Theaters This Summer."

She chewed the mint as the bus sped away. *If I'd gone to LA instead of taking my parents' advice, that might've been me wrapped in Patrick Swayze's arms on the side of that bus, not Demi Moore.* But now she'd never know.

I've got to stop blaming my parents for what my life has become.

If she wanted to be a Hollywood actress, there was only one person stopping her: herself.

Rebecca shivered and zipped her jacket to the top of her neck as a car pulled out of the Albertson's parking lot. Suddenly, she didn't want to go home. The idea of walking back into her apartment felt like she would be giving up on her dream all over again.

Rebecca checked her watch in the dim light from the streetlamp. The bus came about every twenty minutes. She'd been sitting here for at least five, so it shouldn't have been too much longer.

Headlights slowed coming toward her on the street, but they were too low to be a bus. The car came to a stop in front of her, its tire rolling into a puddle beside the curb. The passenger window rolled down, revealing the shadowy figure of a man behind the wheel.

"You need a ride?" he asked.

Rebecca shook her head. "I'm just waiting for the bus."

"Looks wet out there."

She glanced at the roof over her head. "I'm all right."

The man made no attempt to pull away. Rebecca felt a flicker of fear stab at her chest, thinking of the Green River Killer still at large. Then she remembered he only killed prostitutes, not hairdressers waiting at a bus stop.

"Okay. Well, I'm heading up to Everett. I could drop you off anywhere between here and there if you need a ride."

Rebecca thought of her friend Barbara from high school, a free spirit and artist who lived on Whidbey Island across the Sound from Everett. Unlike Rebecca, Barbara was doing what she loved and had a gallery on the island where she sold her paintings.

Her bus arrived and pulled to the curb in front of the car with the same ad for *Ghost* on its side. *Am I really going to spend the rest of my life with Neil, living in this city and doing hair?*

Growing up, she'd told herself she wasn't going to live a typical ordinary life like her parents, like most people. Not that there was anything wrong with that, it just wasn't for her.

The man in the car started to roll up the window as the bus doors opened with a *whoosh*.

"Wait." Rebecca stood from the bench and grabbed her grocery bag. She stepped toward the car. "Can you take me to the Mukilteo ferry? I'm going to see a friend on Whidbey Island." She needed to get away, clear her head, rethink her life. Barbara would understand better than anyone else.

"Sure," the man said through the half-opened window. "Hop in."

CHAPTER TWENTY-ONE

HOLLY

HOLLY LEANED HER elbows onto the desk and rubbed her eyes. She'd been staring at the blank page for over half an hour. She stood and stretched her arms overhead. She needed coffee if she was going to keep working for several more hours. Outside the office window, the late-afternoon sun peeked out from behind the clouds above the Narrows Bridge.

Yawning, she made for the stairs. She'd tried to work when she got home from the grocery store last night but had been too shaken to focus. Giving up, she'd gone to bed early, hoping the rest would clear her mind. Instead, she'd lain awake all night, tossing and turning in an unfamiliar bed, her mind running wild trying to decipher the face of the dark figure in the parking lot. It had to be Jared.

He could've attacked her if he'd wanted to. Had he only wanted to scare her? Or maybe he'd been worried someone might see them or hear her scream. But if Jared knew where she was…

She'd called Andy at King County Major Crimes when she'd gotten up this morning to tell him she wanted the restraining order against Jared. But her call went to his answering machine. He still hadn't called her back. Walking into the kitchen, she glanced at the microwave clock. It was after four.

She grabbed the glass coffee carafe and turned on the kitchen sink when a knock sounded at the door. She jumped, nearly dropping the carafe. She turned off the water and left the pot in the sink, then made her way to the front of the house.

She squinted through the peephole. It was Clint. She exhaled, chastising herself for being so jumpy before opening the door.

"Hey," he said with a smile. He wore a different plaid shirt than he had yesterday, checkered blue instead of red, and held a pair of hedge pruners. "I normally prune the hedges around back every spring for Norm and Maurine, but I wanted to make sure you were okay with me going into your backyard."

"Oh, sure." She hadn't noticed the dimple on Clint's chin last night; he was even more attractive in the daylight.

"Okay, cool." He extended her a rolled-up newspaper wrapped in plastic. "And this was in your newspaper box."

"Thank you." Her fingers brushed his when she took the paper, making her blush.

He shot her a crooked, friendly grin as he started for the side of the house.

As she closed the door, it struck her she hadn't put on any makeup this morning before she started writing. She could only imagine what she looked like after a night of practically no sleep.

She caught her reflection in the hallway mirror on her way back to the kitchen and cringed, attempting to smooth her unruly hair. *Did I even look in the mirror this morning?* She'd been so preoccupied by last night's encounter that she couldn't remember. Holly slipped the plastic bag off the newspaper and tossed it into the trash.

The phone rang on the kitchen wall when she set the *Tacoma*

Herald on the counter. Her shoulders sank with relief as she turned to answer it. It must be Andy, calling her back.

A restraining order might not stop Jared, but getting served with the order would hopefully give Jared pause if he was thinking of trying anything again—especially if he knew doing so could be a violation of his parole and land him back in prison.

"Hello?"

"Hey, it's me."

Recognizing Laurie's voice, Holly sank against the wall. "Oh, hey."

"I just called to check in," Laurie continued. "Everything okay at the house?"

Holly bit her lip, seeing Clint outside the kitchen window. His back was to her, and his shirt was pulled taut around his muscular arms as he trimmed one of the large hedges that lined the yard, starting at the top.

"Yeah, great," Holly said, turning from the window. She decided not to tell Laurie about what happened in the grocery store parking lot. Laurie would probably insist on coming to stay with her. While her publicist meant well, Holly couldn't concentrate with Laurie talking on the phone with PR outlets all day.

"How's your writing going?"

"Good," Holly lied.

"Did you meet the neighbor yet?"

"I did."

Holly cocked her head toward the window. Clint laid his hedge pruners on the grass to peel off his plaid shirt, revealing a fitted white undershirt.

"And?"

Holly continued to stare as Clint tossed his plaid shirt on the ground and bent over to pick up the pruners. "And nothing."

"Okay. Well, if you get lonely one of these nights, I'm sure he wouldn't mind if you came over for a drink. I may have even hinted that you could use some human contact, so don't be surprised if he invites you over."

Holly's jaw dropped. "Laurie! Human contact, really?"

"Don't worry. I didn't say it like that."

Holly breathed into the phone, watching Clint move around the side of the hedge. He turned to face her house, and she spun away from the window.

"I should get back to work." Holly cradled the phone in the crook of her neck as she unrolled the paper on the counter. Seeing the front-page headline, she froze.

HAIRDRESSER MISSING FROM ALBERTSON'S BUS STOP

Laurie sighed into the line. "Okay. I just wanted to check in and make sure you were settling in okay."

Holly scanned the article. Her breath stuck in her lungs when she got to the end of the first paragraph. *Rebecca Lopez, twenty-five, was last seen getting into a sedan near the bus stop in front of the Tacoma Albertson's on 43rd Street just after 9:00 p.m.*

"Were you able to figure out the hot water in the upstairs shower? I know it can be finicky."

The article blurred in Holly's vision. That was the same grocery store she'd been to last night, less than fifteen minutes after she'd left. Holly blinked and kept reading. The missing woman failed to return home to her boyfriend last night and didn't show up this morning at the hair salon where she worked. Detectives were seeking information from the public related to her disappearance.

Holly's heart thudded against her chest. *Jared.* Could it be possible that he had taken her? Was he trying to show her what he was capable of?

No, she thought. *It couldn't be. He had a violent temper, but Jared wasn't a killer.*

"Holly? You still there?"

Or could it? She closed her eyes, recalling the veins bulging out of Jared's forehead after he'd wrapped his hands around her throat five years ago. She pinched the bridge of her nose. Either way, she had to tell Andy.

A knock on the window made her whip around. Outside, Clint gave her a thumbs up, which must've signaled he was done with the pruning. Holly forced herself to return the gesture, her mind somewhere else.

"Laurie, I have to go."

"Hol—"

"I'll call you later."

CHAPTER TWENTY-TWO

HOLLY

WHEN HOLLY ENTERED the King County Major Crimes Unit, a young blond woman Holly didn't recognize looked up from behind the front desk. "Can I help you?"

"Is Detective Andy Harris here?"

"He is." The secretary flicked her gaze to Andy's office door, now farther down the hall than it used to be. "Can I ask your name?" The blond regarded Holly warily.

Holly looked down at her Levi's and hooded sweatshirt. She hadn't wasted any time worrying about her appearance after hanging up with Laurie.

"I'm Holly. Holly Sparks. He'll know who I am. Can you tell him I'm here?"

The woman straightened. "Holly Sparks, like the author?"

"Yes." Holly leaned forward to peer inside the open door to Andy's office.

The secretary's blue eyes lit up. "Oh my gosh." She stood, flashing Holly a broad smile. "I'm Tara. I'm a huge fan of your books." Still smiling, she smoothed the front of her sweater.

"Oh, thanks." Holly forced herself to return the woman's smile as she spotted Andy's white hair inside his office. He was bent over his desk filling out paperwork.

Tara followed Holly's gaze. "I'll go see if he's available."

Holly exhaled as Tara turned down the hallway, relieved she wasn't going to start chattering about Holly's books. Andy needed to know about last night.

"He says to go on in." Tara stepped to the side of Andy's office door.

"Thanks."

"So nice to meet you," Tara gushed as Holly stepped through the doorway into the space Andy now had all to himself.

Holly nodded politely. "Likewise."

"Hey, Holly." Andy leaned back in his chair and intertwined his long fingers atop his head.

From the dark circles beneath his bloodshot eyes, Holly guessed he hadn't slept much more than she had last night, if at all.

"I got your voice message a little while ago. Everything okay?"

Holly shook her head. She hadn't told him anything about last night in her voicemail, only asked Andy to call her.

Andy motioned to one of the two padded folding chairs opposite his desk. "Sit down."

Holly plopped onto the one closest to the door.

"Sorry I hadn't called you back yet," Andy said. "The last twenty-four hours have been pretty nuts." His eyes appraised hers. "Everything okay?"

"No." She cleared her throat.

He raised his eyebrows, waiting for her to elaborate.

Her heart hammered against her chest as she recalled the figure creeping toward her last night in the parking lot.

She swallowed. "It's Jared."

Andy's eyes widened in alarm. "What happened? Did he hurt you?"

She shook her head and pulled the envelope containing the threatening poem from her purse, unfolding the typed paper on Andy's desk. "No, but I got this. It was sent to my PO Box where I get fan mail. There was no return address, but it has to be from Jared."

Andy dropped his gaze to the poem and pulled a pair of reading glasses from his pocket. He looked up after reading the poem. "You've gotten hate mail before, haven't you? Weren't you telling me last summer that you got a slew of nasty letters from some woman in Nebraska?"

"Well, yes." Holly crossed her legs, trying to mask her frustration. *How can he not see this is from Jared?* "But that was different. She was the aunt of a convicted killer I'd written about. She didn't try to hide who she was. And they weren't vague threats like this."

"Okay. I can have this dusted for prints."

Relieved, Holly sat back against her seat. "Thank you."

"If you get another letter like this, try not to touch it and put it in a Ziploc."

She berated herself for getting her fingerprints all over it. She should've known that from all her true crime writing, but she'd been too rattled to think clearly. "And Andy, last night"— she dropped her gaze to her hands in her lap— "I went to Albertson's—that same Albertson's where that hairdresser from Tacoma was last seen at the bus stop. You know, the one who's gone missing?"

He nodded.

"And a car followed me to my parking spot. Then it stopped, blocking my path. A man got out of the car and came toward me until I locked myself inside and drove away."

Andy brought a hand to his chin. "Did you see his face?"

She met his gaze. "No. But I'm sure it was Jared. He was stalking me."

"Did he follow you after you drove away?"

"No, that's what I'm saying. It was just before 9:00 p.m. I think he killed that woman. I think he could be The Bus Stop Killer."

Andy's gaze drifted toward the office window. He stared pensively at the darkness beyond it. She'd known Andy long enough to know that he was debating how to answer her.

"We've talked about this before. There is no Bus Stop Killer. Plus, it couldn't have been Jared," he finally said. "He has an alibi for last night."

Holly stiffened in her chair. "How do you know that?"

Andy got up and closed his office door. "Last night, I had someone sitting on the house where Jared is living—plainclothes, unmarked car," he said on his way back to the desk. "Jared is staying with an old informant of his from his time in the Narcotics Unit."

"I remember Jared talking about him once. Tommy something, right?"

Andy nodded. "Tommy Reed. Another low life. So, it doesn't surprise me they're still friends. Anyway, my surveillance detective got pulled before midnight for a big narcotics operation that's carrying out a bunch of search warrants in multiple houses across King County. But he was watching the house from about 5:00 p.m. to 10:00 p.m. There were two men inside, and one looked to be Jared. And he didn't see anyone come or go." After sitting, Andy rolled his chair toward his desk.

The short surveillance on Jared's residence did nothing to convince Holly of Jared's innocence. He could've left the house before five and not got home until after ten.

"The man in the parking lot last night, did you see his face?" Andy asked.

"No, it was too dark."

Andy folded his hands on the desk. "Then how do you know it was him?"

Holly sighed. "I—I don't know. Just a feeling, I guess." She locked eyes with Andy, realizing how stupid she must sound. "Wait." She put up a palm, confused. "Why did you have an undercover watching Jared?" Fear wound around her lungs like a vine. Was Andy so worried Jared would come after her that he deemed around-the-clock surveillance necessary? She wasn't sure if that reassured or unsettled her. She knew how rare twenty-four-hour police surveillance was—after all, even Ted Bundy's watch had been cut short due to budget cuts. Despite Jared's history, she was surprised Andy had managed it at all.

Andy withdrew a pack of cigarettes from his shirt pocket, the same brand he'd smoked for years, and placed one between his lips. Knowing she didn't smoke, he returned the pack to his pocket before reaching for the lighter on the desk. He took a drag before holding the cigarette a few inches from his mouth.

"Before Jared went to prison for what he did to you..." He lowered his voice, glancing at his closed office door. "Jared was a suspect in the Green River Killer murders."

Holly stared at him in disbelief.

"That's the real reason Jared was taken off the task force, not because of his temper. Although, that hadn't helped."

Her jaw dropped. "But you never..."

"I know. And I'm sorry. I wanted to tell you, but we didn't know anything for sure." He gestured to Holly with the hand that held the cigarette. "And then he went to prison."

Holly stood to pace in the small space as Andy took a long drag of his cigarette. She turned toward him, gripping the back of her chair with both hands, and studied Andy's expression, realizing why he still suspected her ex-boyfriend of being the most prolific serial killer in American history.

"And the rampage of killings stopped," she said. "There have been only a few in the last five years you've attributed to being possible victims of the Green River Killer. Nothing like the fifty plus victims you suspected he murdered between 1982 and 1984." She tried to read Andy's eyes. "You still think it could be Jared?"

He frowned. "I don't know."

"What made you suspect him?"

"One of the initial FBI profilers believed the Green River Killer was someone with authority, possibly a cop. Jared had been overly eager to join the task force, and you know better than anyone how volatile his temper could be. In early '85, a prostitute gave a witness statement saying she saw one of the Green River Killer victims getting into a car matching Jared's personal vehicle, along with Jared's description."

Holly's stomach churned. She'd almost married that man.

"Before joining the task force," Andy continued, "Jared had been visiting one of the body dump sites after victims had been discovered. After that prostitute's witness statement, I started to wonder if Jared's interest in the cases could be more personal than professional."

Holly groaned, tilting her head toward the ceiling. "How is this even possible?" She looked at Andy. "How could you never have *told me?*"

He blew a puff of smoke out the side of his mouth. "I wanted to be sure before I said anything to you. But there's something else I never told you. You're not going to like it, and I don't want you jumping to any conclusions. But at this point you might as well know."

Holly stared at him in silence.

Andy dragged his gaze toward the window. "Jared was seen more than once at the strip club where Meg worked."

Holly stood from her chair. *"What?"*

Andy put up a hand. "It was *after* Meg was killed and before the two of you started seeing each other. I have no idea if he ever went there while Meg was working. In fact, I doubt that he did."

Holly turned away from Andy, her movements stiff as she circled behind her chair before tightening her fingers around its back. She racked her brain, thinking of all the times she'd mentioned to Jared about Meg working at that seedy strip club. Never once had he given any indication that he'd been there. The floor tilted beneath her feet. *Had Jared seen Meg working there? Had he…was it possible…* She took a deep breath.

"I'm sorry I never told you."

Holly's eyes brimmed with tears when she met Andy's gaze. "You should have."

"You're right. But I'm ninety-nine percent certain that Jared isn't the guy we're looking for. Meg worked at that place for, what, only four months? Most likely, she and Jared never crossed paths." He scratched the back of his head. "Jared's an asshole, but that doesn't make him a serial killer."

"You didn't see the look in his eyes when he tried to kill *me.*"

Andy's expression softened. "I'm not saying he isn't capable. Just that I don't think he's the killer we're looking for. While Jared's been in prison, there have been a number of women who've gone missing who fit the victimology of the Green River Killer."

Holly already knew this from Andy keeping her informed of the investigation over the years. "But they haven't been found. Without bodies, you have no idea how they were killed. Some of them might even be alive. Plus, they were all involved in prostitution, which is a high-risk lifestyle on its own. You're only assuming they were victims of the Green River Killer." Holly lifted a hand to her neck, remembering the feel of Jared's meaty hands closing around it. What if Jared was the Bus Stop Killer? There hadn't been any murders fitting that profile around Seattle since Jared had been locked up.

Andy's cigarette flared as he took a long pull before stubbing it out on his ashtray. "We don't know anything for sure."

"That's what scares me, Andy."

His tired eyes met hers. "Me too."

CHAPTER TWENTY-THREE

HOLLY

HOLLY SHIVERED AS she moved through the darkened parking garage, reflecting on what Andy had told her. Given Jared's supposed alibi for last night, and the fact she hadn't seen the man's face in the Albertson's parking lot, Andy didn't think she should file a restraining order—yet. Although, unlike Andy's surveillance guy, Holly wasn't convinced Jared had been the one he'd seen inside that house.

She dug a hand into her purse in search of her keys, cursing herself for not cleaning out her bag after last night. She took a cursory glance around the parking garage before climbing into her Civic and locking the door. On the drive home, her mind reeled, thinking of Jared.

Rain splattered against the windshield as she sped along I-5. She increased her wiper speed. *Could Jared really be the Green River Killer?* She recalled him standing in the home office of her old apartment, looking at her wall, listening to her theories about the man she believed had killed her sister. She shuddered at the thought of having been intimate, physically *and* emotionally, with Meg's killer.

Instead of continuing toward Tacoma, she found herself exiting off the interstate and heading for the Green River. It had been years since she'd come down here, but she knew the area well from the time she used to spend combing the woods nearby in the years after the first Green River Killer victims had been discovered, hoping she might see something, or someone, that could lead to finding her sister's killer. The industrial area was more built up than it was in the mid-eighties, but even still, it was quiet this time of night. Passing cars became less frequent the farther she got from the interstate.

As she neared the Green River, she imagined Jared driving these same streets in the middle of the night with a dead body—or two—in his trunk. A pair of bright headlights shone in the rearview mirror, interrupting her dark thoughts. The car encroached closer on her tail, its beams flooding her mirror with a blinding light.

"Just pass me already," Holly said over Janet Jackson's "Rhythm Nation" playing on the radio.

There were no cars in the oncoming lane. Instead of passing her, the car flicked on its high beams and surged closer to her bumper. Holly lay on the gas as she passed the sign for the Strander Boulevard Bridge over the Green River.

She squinted from the blinding lights shining in her mirror. "What's your problem?" A part of her was tempted to brake check them, but she had no desire to ruin her car, or to be forced to get out in the middle of nowhere with some road-raged maniac. It was Friday night, and they were likely drunk.

Finally, the car swerved into the oncoming lane as Holly sped toward the bridge. Glancing out the window, she saw the vehicle move beside hers, but, of course, it was too dark to make out the driver. She eased up on the gas, but the car slowed to match her pace.

At first, she thought he was drunk or a weirdo, but now she realized she might be in real danger. She dared another glance, expecting the car to accelerate, but it stayed beside her. As she took in the sedan and the hooded figure behind the wheel, a cold certainty ran down her spine. This wasn't a drunk driver. This was her stalker from last night. The hairs pricked up on the back of her neck.

The driver looked in her direction, but it was too dark and rainy for her to make out the face. With both hands gripping the wheel, Holly returned her attention to the road as she crossed onto the bridge. She forced a deep breath into her stiff lungs. *Just stay calm.*

A metallic screech erupted from the side of her car as the sedan slammed into hers, forcing her toward the short, concrete barrier to her right. She jerked the wheel to the left, but it was too late. Her scream was drowned out by the guttural howl of twisting steel and the high-pitched shriek of her tires clawing at the asphalt as she stomped on her brakes.

Despite her white-knuckled grip as she turned the wheel to the left, her Civic careened toward the low barrier at the bridge's edge.

The passenger side smashed through the concrete, busting through the barrier. The force of the other car pressing against hers propelled her front tires over the side until her headlights shone through darkness. Holly lifted away from the seat, feeling momentarily weightless until the front of the car dropped, pulling her against the seatbelt.

The rear tires slid off the bridge, and her weightlessness returned. Out the windshield, the river blurred as she soared toward it. Her headlights reflected on the dark, flowing surface. Holly opened her mouth to scream but nothing came out as her undercarriage hit the water with a deafening splash. Holly's temple smacked against the steering wheel. She shot out her arms to brace herself against the dash as water enveloped the windshield.

CHAPTER TWENTY-FOUR

HOLLY

WATER SLOSHED AGAINST the windshield as the headlights sunk beneath the surface, illuminating the dark, murky water. Not seeing the river bottom, her muscles tensed with fear.

Frigid water rushed over her feet, soaking through her sneakers. She fumbled to unlock the seatbelt, but when she pressed a thumb against the release button, it wouldn't budge. Water rose to her shins as she frantically pushed on the release mechanism.

"Shit."

It released with a *click* as water crept over the base of the windshield. She tossed the seatbelt to the side. Thank God. She was free. Now, she just had to swim out. Before she could move, her headlights shut off, leaving her in darkness as more water filled the car.

Holly hyperventilated, more from terror than the cold, as water spilled over the seat. Her frantic mind latched onto an article she'd written once for the *Tribune*, a tragic story of a minivan containing a mother and two children that had accidentally driven into Puget Sound while attempting to drive onto a ferry. At the end of the article, she'd given some safety tips on how to escape a submerged vehicle. She'd learned not to open the car door, as it would flood the vehicle with water and cause it to sink faster.

Holly pressed the button on the door to open the window. Nothing happened. She swore. Water rose to her waist. The river's surface lapped against the top of the driver's side window. Her lungs seized with panic.

She felt the car being dragged backward and downward from the river's torrent. Only this wasn't a ride. It was certain death if she didn't get out soon.

How deep is this river? But her mind was too panicked to think.

Screw it. The car was already flooding with water. She just needed to escape. She reached for the door handle and pushed. But it didn't budge. She frantically jiggled the door handle while pushing her shoulder against the window.

She'd locked it for safety after climbing inside at the Major Crimes Unit. She felt the door for the power locks and pulled the lever up with her finger. She tried the handle again. Nothing. The water must've short-circuited all the electrical power.

"Ahh!" She slammed a hand against the side window in panic.

Her breathing quickened as water rose over her chest. *Calm down*, her mind screamed. *You have to focus. Think.*

She leaned over and felt for the glove compartment, now submerged. She pulled it open and swept a hand inside for something she could use to break a window. But all she felt were soggy registration papers, a notebook, a couple of cassette tapes, and a pack of gum.

Then she remembered. *My umbrella.* She cursed herself for not thinking of it earlier. She always kept one on the floor of the backseat. She twisted and reached behind her as water encircled her neck.

She sucked in a breath and lowered her face underwater as she skimmed the backseat floor with a hand. Her lungs burned as her fingers swept the carpeted mat, not finding it. She turned and got to her knees on the seat, taking a gulp of air from the few inches remaining at the top of the car.

She leaned forward, submerging her head again to feel beneath her seat until her hand closed around the umbrella. She sat tall, taking as deep a breath as her freezing lungs would allow from the shrinking pocket of air beneath the roof.

She turned and thrust the umbrella's metal handle into the driver's side window with all her might. It splintered with a *crack* but didn't break. She swung it against the window again, hearing another crack. Then a third time.

Water rushed in, filling the top of the car after the umbrella broke through the glass. Holding her breath, Holly used both hands to bust a larger hole in the glass with the umbrella. As soon as the hole felt big enough, she swam through the opening, ignoring the pain from a shard slicing her wrist.

She was halfway through when she was pulled backward by her sweatshirt. Air escaped her mouth as she frantically tugged at the fabric. It was stuck.

Holly felt for the zipper and unzipped her hoodie, sliding her arms out one at a time. Now free, she propelled her arms through the water, kicking her legs once they were out of the car. Her lungs screamed for air as she swam through the dark, freezing water. She broke the surface and gasped for air.

Now on the opposite side of the bridge from where her car had gone into the water, she used the light from a nearby streetlamp and swam for the shore. Numb from the cold, her body was slow to respond to her commands when she reached the overgrown riverbank. Her teeth chattered and her whole body shivered as she trudged up the hillside, thick with foliage, and looked back at the river.

It struck her how close she'd come to never making it out. It would've taken only a few more minutes. *I'm lucky to be alive,* she thought as she continued up the hill. She thought of the young women who'd been dumped in these waters by the Green River Killer, who were beyond having a chance to escape. When she reached the top of the hillside, a wild blackberry bush pricked her bare arm, but her skin was too cold to feel any pain.

She trudged toward the road, exhaling with relief to see the dark sedan was nowhere in sight. *It had to have been Jared inside that car.*

Less than a block away, a white pickup pulled out of an industrial building's parking area and turned toward her. Holly stepped into the road, blocking its path and waving her numb arms over her head. She recalled a witness statement from one of the early Green River Killer victims who had seen the prostitute get into a man's white pickup the last time she'd been seen alive.

She lowered her hands as the truck slowed. What if she'd escaped Jared only to walk right into the hands of the Green River Killer? Wouldn't that be ironic. Then, with a shudder, she thought back to what Andy told her earlier: that Jared and the Green River Killer could be one and the same.

The truck's headlights blurred in her vision as a man stepped out. Holly was vaguely aware that she was swaying on her feet as the man came toward her.

"You okay, Miss?"

The world seemed to spin, like the road was moving beneath her. She stuck out her arms to steady herself before collapsing on the pavement.

CHAPTER TWENTY-FIVE

HOLLY

LAURIE CROSSED HER arms, turning toward her in-laws' couch where Holly lay. "You know, I've been telling you for years you needed to get a new car. I don't understand why you were still driving that beat-up Civic anyway. That thing should've been retired years ago."

Holly managed a small smile, a dull ache forming in her chest as she thought back on the car that had been submerged in the river.

Laurie glanced around the living room. "Is there anything else I can do before I go?"

Holly set her alarm clock on the coffee table beside the *TV Guide* before lying back on the pillow Laurie had brought down from the upstairs bedroom. "I'll be fine. Just need a short rest. Then I'll get back to work on my manuscript."

Her recollection of last night's ambulance ride was fuzzy, but she faintly recalled giving the medics Laurie's name and number. Laurie had arrived at the Valley Medical Center soon after Holly was brought to the ER and hadn't left her side since.

Laurie frowned in the early morning light that filtered through the gap in the floral curtains. "You need more than a short rest. You've been up all night. Not to mention you nearly died last night. You shouldn't even be thinking about work right now."

"I have a deadline." Holly yawned. "Plus, I took a few naps in the ER. You, of all people, should understand. You're my publicist."

"I'm also your friend." Worry lines appeared between Laurie's full brows. She crossed her arms. "Maybe I should stay."

"No, really, I'm fine." Aside from having mild hypothermia and needing six stitches from the gash where she'd hit her head on the steering wheel and sliced open her palm swimming through the broken window, she was unscathed from her near-death encounter. She'd spent most of her time in the ER waiting to have a scan to ensure she hadn't sustained any head trauma, which she hadn't. And Holly needed the quiet of an empty house to write.

She was already behind, so she couldn't afford to lose a whole day sleeping. Roxy Vega's life—and death—was already being made into a movie. And her publisher was set on releasing Holly's book six months before the movie premiered to maximize sales. It was part of the contract she'd signed, and she'd already been paid her advance. But it wasn't about the money. She wasn't about to let Jared ruin her career or her reputation as an author. This was a competitive business. If she couldn't come through for the publisher, someone else would.

"I'll sleep better if the house is empty," Holly added.

Laurie pursed her lips. "You mean write more."

Laurie knew her too well. Holly turned on her side, pulling the knit blanket Laurie had draped over her up to her shoulders. "Don't worry. I promise to get at least a few hours of sleep first."

Laurie sighed, her signal she was giving up on the fight. "You should be sleeping all day after what you went through, not just a few hours. You're lucky to be alive, you know."

Holly closed her eyes. "I know." She opened them a minute later, sensing Laurie was still looming over her.

"Do you need any cash?"

"Cash?" Then Holly remembered why Laurie was asking. Before leaving the hospital, Holly was told that a recovery team would retrieve her car and purse from the Green River, but they were waiting for the water level and current to decrease. It would likely be three weeks before she got her driver's license back. Once the insurance confirmed her Honda was totaled, they would give her the money to replace it. Holly had enough in the bank to buy a car in the meantime, but she didn't have time to shop for one until she turned in her manuscript. "I've got a spare checkbook upstairs."

Laurie leaned over the couch and pulled the curtains all the way closed. "I still don't get why you don't want to sleep in the upstairs bed."

Because I'd sleep too long. And I need to get to work. "I like it here," Holly said, closing her eyes again.

"All right, I'll leave you be. As long as you promise to rest and call me if you need anything?"

"Promise," Holly mumbled.

"Ken is picking me up, so I'll leave you our spare car. The keys are on the kitchen counter. It's a very unsexy station wagon, but it'll get you around. I asked Ken to bring a baseball bat for you to have for self-defense. I'll put it in the entryway. I never thought I'd say this, but you might want to think about getting a gun."

Laurie's footsteps sounded toward the front door as Holly imagined her car sitting at the bottom of the Green River, making her shiver.

"I have a spare key, so I'll lock the door behind me after I grab the bat," Laurie called.

"Thanks, Laurie."

While the hospital had called the Tukwila police to take down a report of the car that had driven her off the bridge, Holly had called Andy from her room in the ER to find he was still at the office. He'd driven down immediately and listened alongside the officer to what had happened after she'd left the Major Crimes Unit. The Tukwila detective had taken down her report, and while it wasn't technically Andy's case, he'd promised to pay Jared a visit to find out if he'd been involved. In the meantime, Andy had arranged to have a Tacoma squad car periodically patrol her neighborhood for any sign of Jared or other suspicious activity.

She recalled the determined look on Andy's face in the ER, confident he would figure out who'd done this to her. He'd squeezed her hand before leaving the hospital, assuring her he would find whoever was responsible.

She heard Laurie's van roar to life before it pulled away from the house. She could only hope Andy was right.

❧

Holly could tell as soon as she opened her eyes that she'd slept much longer than she'd intended. While it was still daylight, there was no longer any direct sunlight shining through the curtains behind the couch. She sat up and reached for her alarm clock on the coffee table. 3:46 p.m.

The alarm that she'd set for 10:30 a.m. had been turned off, and instead she'd slept for over eight hours.

"Laurie," she grumbled, replacing the clock on the coffee table.

She got up and moved through the home's main level to the

kitchen to brew a pot of coffee. While irritation pooled in her chest at Laurie turning off her alarm, she couldn't deny how much better she felt. This was the most rested she'd been since she'd moved in.

Holly glanced down, feeling a bit conspicuous wearing the neon pink sweater and pastel lavender jeans Laurie had brought from her own closet for Holly to change into at the hospital. It was a far cry from the gray sweatshirt and ripped jeans Holly routinely wore when she wrote.

She placed the coffee pot under the faucet when movement outside the kitchen window caught her eye. Next door, Clint stepped onto his front porch, dressed in his usual plaid shirt and jeans. As the coffee pot filled, she watched him stride down his driveway. He continued past his mailbox and headed toward her house, making her heart skip a beat.

Water overflowed from the coffee pot as Holly leaned forward to get a glimpse of Clint starting up her drive. She swore, leaving the overflowing pot in the sink after turning off the faucet, then rushed to find the closest mirror. She darted into the powder room and let out a groan.

She ran her fingers through her mess of brown waves, then tried to smooth her bangs, grimacing when they refused to obey. She swiped her fingertips over the mascara smudged beneath her eyes. She'd been too exhausted to shower when she got home from the hospital, even though she needed one after her swim in the Green River.

The doorbell rang. Holly scurried out of the bathroom, searching for where she had left her purse.

"Coming," she called, scanning the kitchen countertops, then the entryway table for her handbag. A lip gloss would undoubtedly be easier to find inside than her car keys. With a sinking feeling, she remembered it was inside her car at the bottom of the Green River.

She recognized Clint's tall frame beyond the frosted glass beside the front door. She smoothed the front of Laurie's ridiculously bright sweater and took a deep breath before opening it.

"Oh. Clint. Hi." She smiled, trying her best to look surprised.

"Hey."

His hazel eyes locked with hers, and her dizziness from last night returned. She gripped the door tighter to keep from swaying on her feet.

"Laurie asked me to check on you. Make sure you're feeling all right and"—one side of his mouth lifted into a smile—"not working too hard."

Of course, she was. Holly wasn't sure whether to be livid or grateful. Maybe a little of both.

"She told me about your accident last night," Clint added, his expression turning serious. "That must've been quite a scare."

"Oh, it was nothing."

His eyes widened.

"I mean, not nothing. Just…" She shifted her feet, her face hot. *Why can't I talk?* "It was a shock, yes, but I'm fine. Just making some coffee, actually, before I get back to work."

He leaned against the pillar at the top of the porch stoop. "Getting driven off a bridge into the Green River doesn't warrant a day off?"

"I have a deadline. Really, I'm fine. I've been resting all day." Thanks to Laurie.

"Okay, cool."

He flashed her a devastatingly effortless smile that left her unsteady, as though the floor beneath her had turned to air.

"Well." He stood straight. "Just let me know if you need anything."

"You want some coffee?" she heard herself ask when he started down the porch steps.

He turned. "Sure, that sounds great."

She held the door open for him as he stepped inside, hoping he couldn't hear the flutter of her heart. She glanced upstairs at her office while he took off his shoes. She really did need to get to work, but it was already four. What was one cup of coffee going to hurt now?

CHAPTER TWENTY-SIX

HOLLY

"CREAM OR SUGAR?" Holly asked.

Clint, standing on the other side of the kitchen island, shook his head. "No, thanks."

Holly handed him a mug of freshly brewed coffee before pouring creamer into her own. "Want to sit in the living room?"

"Sure." He followed her through to the front of the house.

Holly moved the blanket to the side of the couch and took a seat. Instead of opting for the armchair, Clint settled in beside her. He turned toward her with a look of concern in his eyes.

"Do the police know who ran you off the bridge last night?"

Holly imagined Jared's face, twisted in rage behind the wheel as he rammed his car into hers. She shook her head. "Not yet."

He put a hand on her knee. "Sorry, we don't have to talk about it."

His palm felt warm through her jeans. She met his gaze, and he pulled it away.

"I won't stay long," he said, lifting the mug to his lips. After taking a sip, he added, "I know you've got work to do, and my son is getting a ride home soon from baseball practice. I told him I'd be home when he got back."

She hadn't realized he had a son. Laurie hadn't mentioned it, and she hadn't seen anyone other than Clint at his house. Although, she'd been living next door for only a few days. He'd probably been at school. Or even at his mom's house. "How old is he?"

Clint sighed. "Fifteen. Going on twenty-one."

"I have a nephew close to that age. Well, sort of. He's eleven."

"Ah." Clint shifted in his seat to face her. "So, you'll know soon how teenage boys can be. It's a handful."

Holly opened her mouth to say she'd never met him but thought twice, knowing it would lead to her sharing what was probably too much information for a first date. *That's not what this. He's only here because Laurie asked him to come.*

"What's your son like?" she asked before taking a drink from her coffee.

"He's a typical teenager. Dying to get his driver's license even though he doesn't turn sixteen until next year. The other night, I caught him sneaking out with my car. Needless to say, he's grounded this weekend."

Holly studied him as his gaze fell to his mug.

"It can't be easy being a single parent," she said.

Clint looked up, shaking his head. "Not always, but he's a good kid. He normally doesn't get into much trouble. He's a big reader and loves true crime. In fact, he's a big fan of your books."

"Really?" She felt flattered and surprised that her books would spark the interest of a fifteen-year-old boy. Most of her readers were much older.

Clint nodded.

"Well, tell him thank you. I have a copy of *In Cold Blood*, the first ever true crime novel, upstairs. He's welcome to borrow it if he hasn't read it." She smiled. "That is, if you're okay with him reading while he's grounded."

"I'll tell him, thanks. He loves English." Clint lifted his mug. "Although, I keep telling him that an English degree isn't going to pay the bills." His face faltered. "No offense, you probably have one. And if you do, don't tell him or he might stop believing I know everything." Clint winked.

Holly laughed. "I switched my major from English to journalism partway through college, so no offense taken."

Clint lowered the mug to his lap and stared pensively at a painting of Mount Rainier hanging on the wall. "What got you interested in true crime?"

Holly opened her mouth to tell him about Meg when the sputter of an engine sounded down their cul-de-sac. Clint stood and cracked open the curtains. Holly followed his gaze, seeing a green Bronco pull into Clint's driveway.

"Sorry." He turned. "That's my son getting dropped off. I better go so he doesn't wonder where I am."

Holly followed him to the kitchen after he insisted on taking his mug to the sink. "Thanks for the coffee," he said after putting on his shoes.

"Anytime."

Clint stood in the entryway for a lingering moment, making her wonder if he was going to kiss her before he reached for the door.

"Oh." He turned around after stepping outside. "I'll tell my son about borrowing that book. I'm sure he'll be thrilled."

"Great." Holly returned his smile before he hurried down the porch steps, feeling stupid for thinking a completely ordinary pause was something romantic.

She blew out a breath after closing the door, placing her palms against her temples as she climbed the stairs. It was time to stop thinking about her own life and focus on Roxy Vega's, who—like Meg—could no longer speak for herself.

Halfway up the staircase, the phone rang in the kitchen. Holly thought about letting it ring, but it was probably Laurie, and if she didn't answer it, Laurie would drive over to make sure she was okay. And Holly didn't want any interruptions once she finally immersed herself in work.

She trudged down the stairs, planning what she would say to her publicist slash overly concerned friend. Laurie needed to stop asking Clint to check on her. Not that she minded her handsome neighbor coming over, but it should be on his own terms, not because Laurie asked him to.

The phone was still ringing when she reached the kitchen, where the smell of coffee lingered in the air. Holly pulled the receiver off the wall, glancing at Clint's house through the side window and seeing the Bronco back out of Clint's drive. Clint and his son must've already gone inside.

"Hello?"

"Holly, it's me."

Andy. Her pulse quickened.

"I went to see Jared earlier with Detective O'Malley, who took down your report, and thought you should know what we learned."

She swallowed, bracing herself for him to tell her Jared was in custody for trying to kill her a second time. "Okay."

"Jared and his roommate have an alibi for last night, and it's stronger than their alibi from the night before. They said they were at a bar downtown watching the Mariners opening game only a few blocks from the Major Crimes Unit, from about 6:00 p.m. to 10:30 p.m. They both have receipts for a few beers time-stamped to match what they told us.

"Jared's roommate drives a dark gray Toyota Camry, which I

checked for damage while we were there. I didn't see any. Jared, however, owns a black Ford Escort that he had put in storage when he went to prison."

A flush of heat crept up her neck. *That had to be the car that ran me off the bridge last night.*

"But it wasn't at the house. According to Jared, he hasn't driven it since getting out. His driver's license expired while he was in prison, and Jared claimed he's working to get his license and registration renewed before driving it again."

Holly pressed her arm against the wall and cradled her forehead in the crook of her elbow. It had to have been Jared last night. "Wait. Can't you get a warrant for wherever Jared is keeping the car? It has to be damaged from hitting my car last night—that's why he's hiding it."

Andy breathed into the line. "It depends."

Holly noted the tiredness in Andy's voice, just as she'd seen in his eyes yesterday.

"First, we need to verify Jared's alibi with more than just a receipt. I went to the bar to see if any of the bartenders could verify Jared's statement, but the guy working last night called out sick today. I just got a lead on my double homicide, so I gave Detective O'Malley the bartender's home address so he can speak to him. Since your case isn't technically my jurisdiction, it'll be better if he follows up anyway, in case this goes to trial. But I asked him to keep you informed."

Holly turned and sank against the wall. "It was Jared, Andy. It had to be him."

"I'm suspicious of Jared too. But if Jared's alibi checks out, then we won't have enough probable cause for a warrant. That's why I asked O'Malley to speak to the bartender. If the bartender *can't* verify that Jared was at the bar during the time of your accident, then yes, I think he'd have enough cause to search Jared's vehicle. But if he can…we have to consider that Jared wasn't the one who did this to you last night."

Holly wound the phone cord around her finger. "Okay," she said, feeling only slightly reassured. Jared couldn't have been at the bar when her car went over the bridge. What if the bartender just *thinks* he was? If Jared went there before and after, how could the bartender really be sure? Especially if the place was busy.

The skin on her arms prickled. That would leave Jared free to come after her again.

Before Jared worked for King County Major Crimes, he was a detective on the Narcotics Unit and often worked undercover. She remembered Jared telling her once that he had some friends in low places who owed him favors. He might've also made some new ones in prison. *What if this bartender is one of them? What if that's why Jared went there, knowing he would vouch for him being there all night?*

"How are you feeling, by the way?" Andy asked.

She bit her lip, imagining what Jared had planned for her next.

"Holly? Are you feeling okay?"

"Oh. Sorry. I'm um. Better. Thanks," she lied.

"Good. Hey, I gotta go, but I'll talk to you soon. Get some rest."

"Thanks for calling, Andy."

She heard the edge of fatigue in his voice and knew he probably hadn't gotten any sleep last night after coming to the hospital and helping take down her report. Holly replaced the receiver after Andy hung up.

She went to pour another cup of coffee, thinking about Jared's alibis for the last two nights. When Detective O'Malley had taken her report last night in the ER, she couldn't be certain the car that had driven her off the bridge was the same car she'd seen in the Albertson's parking lot the night before, only that they were both sedans. She was sure the car that ran her off the bridge had been black, but it had been too dark in the Albertson's parking lot for her to make out the exact color of the car that stalked her.

Andy's words replayed in her mind. *We have to consider that Jared wasn't the one who did this to you last night.* She refilled her mug and noticed her hand trembling. *What if Jared was telling the truth?* She replaced the carafe and pressed her palms against the counter. The thought that Jared might be innocent clawed at her, unsettling in a way she hadn't expected. *I should be relieved if it wasn't him.*

But if Jared didn't drive her off the bridge, then who did?

CHAPTER TWENTY-SEVEN

HOLLY

HOLLY TURNED UP the volume on her Walkman over the rain pelting against the roof and closed her eyes. Roxy Vega's first hit single, "Anarchy in Neon," played through her headphones. She tried to envision what it must've felt like to be the young singer, on the uprise of punk rock fame, strolling along a downtown street in the middle of the night after leaving her friends at a bar near Pike Place Market.

Rap. Rap. Rap.

Holly opened her eyes and paused the cassette. Had she heard something? Streaks of rain blurred the window that looked out over the Narrows Bridge. It had been raining on and off all day, just like it had the day Roxy Vega died.

She was about to press play when she heard it again.

Rap. Rap. Rap.

She pulled off her headphones, then crept slowly down the stairs, her shoulder sliding along the wall. Laurie always called before dropping by. Holly paused at the bottom of the steps, straining to make out the figure beyond the frosted glass. The outline looked taller—and thinner—than Jared's stocky frame.

The stranger stood still, no longer knocking, as if they'd sensed Holly was on her way to the door. She got to her tiptoes and peered through the peephole. The tension dissipated from her shoulders. It was a teenage boy. Probably looking for money for a school fundraiser.

He turned and started down her porch steps.

Holly opened the door. "Can I help you?"

He spun. He was a good-looking kid. Tall, wavy brown hair and hazel eyes. He smiled.

"Hi. Sorry to bother you. I just came to see about borrowing that book."

Holly's brows knitted together. "Sorry?" He must have had the wrong house.

He glanced sideways in a look of confusion. "I live next door. I'm Clint's son—"

"Oh!" Holly's hand flew to the side of her head. "Yes. Of course." Sometimes it was hard to pull her mind out of the story she was writing to reenter her present reality. She wondered on occasion if that was why she wrote. "Come in." She opened the door wide.

The young man's expression softened. She could see it now—the boy's resemblance to his father. Same hair, lankier than his dad but a similar build.

"Sorry," she added when he stepped inside. "I meant to find it for you. I've been writing all day. It's just in a box upstairs."

"I'm a huge fan of your books. I've read them all. *The Last Broadcast* was my favorite."

"Thank you. Me too. That was my first."

He stood in the entryway when she started up the stairs, looking unsure about stepping farther into the house. Halfway up, she glanced over her shoulder. "Come on up if you'd like. It might take me a few minutes to find it. As long as you don't mind the mess of a writer's office."

A flash of excitement showed on his face. "I won't mind at all." He slipped off his Nikes and glanced at the baseball bat leaning against the entryway wall. "You play baseball?"

Holly followed his gaze, slightly embarrassed at the bat Laurie had given her to use as a weapon. "Oh, no. That's for… um…self-defense."

"Oh, right," he said, politely acknowledging her reason as if it were a normal explanation before following her up the steps.

"So, you read a lot of true crime?" she asked when she reached the top of the stairs.

"I read a little of everything. But yeah, I've been getting more into true crime the last few months. Aside from your books, I really liked *Helter Skelter* and *The Onion Field*."

"Then you're going to love *In Cold Blood*." She stepped into her office and moved toward one of the two boxes on the floor beside the desk. She opened the first, seeing her stack of notebooks and cassette tapes of countless recorded interviews about Roxy Vega. "It must be in this one." She moved to the second box, finding the book near the top, along with her dictionary and *The Chicago Manual of Style*. She stood to give it to him, but the boy wasn't looking at her.

He stood, open-mouthed, gazing at her office wall.

Holly followed his gaze to the map and the list of suspected Green River Killer victims, organized by the locations where they'd gone missing and where they'd been found, along with the state of their corpses upon discovery. Even though Holly had never been able to prove her theory, she still kept a list titled *BUS STOP KILLER?* with a small group of women's photos underneath, including Meg's. This morning she'd added a newspaper clipping to the growing list of victims she was increasingly worried Jared was responsible for. It featured a photo of Rebecca Lopez, the twenty-five-year-old hairdresser who'd gone missing after leaving the nearby Albertson's. There were also several photos of body dump sites that she'd clipped from newspaper articles over the years, some of which she'd written herself.

"I'm sorry," she said. *How had I not thought about my murder wall before inviting him upstairs?* "I forgot I had all of that up." Her obsession over her sister's murder had become normal to her. It was only in moments like these that it struck her that it wasn't—especially to a teenager.

He stepped toward the wall, his eyes wide with fascination. "What's all this?"

"It's um…research." Holly's theory that there were two serial killers at large—not one—and that one of them killed her sister, seemed like too much to explain.

He turned away from the wall. "I read an article you wrote about your sister's murder. I'm sorry."

"Thank you." Holly cocked her head. The article she'd written for the *Tribune* where she'd mentioned Meg's killing had come out in 1985. "How did you find that?"

His mouth lifted into a half smile. "The library."

"Ah." She nodded and held out the book. "Here you go."

He accepted the book, flipping it over to the back cover.

"This is the first true crime novel ever written." Holly pointed to the author's photo. "Truman Capote is credited with creating the genre. This is also the only true crime he ever wrote. Before this, he was known for writing *Breakfast at Tiffany's.*" She tapped the back cover. "But this is much better." She looked up to meet the boy's gaze. "Have you read *To Kill a Mockingbird?*"

He cracked a grin. "Three times."

"Harper Lee and Truman Capote were childhood best friends, and she helped him with his research."

"Cool." He let the book fall to his side.

"Is your dad also a big reader?"

He shrugged. "No, not really."

"Your mom, then?"

His gaze shifted back to the wall. "Maybe. I'm not sure." His Adam's apple bobbed. "She died when I was seven."

"I'm so sorry. I assumed your parents were divorced."

"That's okay." He met Holly's gaze. "I don't remember that much about her. Mostly just what my dad tells me."

Holly studied him, feeling bad for bringing it up. "It's hard to lose someone you love." She wondered how his mother had died. Her gaze travelled to the *X* on the wall where Meg's body had been found.

"Well, I better go," he said. "I promised my dad I'd help make dinner, and I've got some homework to do." He looked down at the faded paperback in his hand. "Thanks for the book. I should have it back to you sometime this weekend."

Holly waved a hand through the air. "Take your time."

"It was nice to talk to someone about books," he said as Holly followed him down the stairs. "My friends are only into video games."

"They're missing out."

He nodded, throwing her a lopsided grin. "Definitely."

Holly paused halfway down the staircase. "If you liked *Helter Skelter*, I have another book you might like called *Till Death Us Do Part*. It's written by that same attorney. If you have a minute, I'll run up and see if I can find it."

"Sure." He nodded. "Thanks."

"Be right back." Holly bounded up the stairs, only to return a few minutes later without having found it. "I looked through the boxes I packed, but it must still be at my houseboat. Sorry."

"That's okay. I'm excited to read this one." The boy stood tall after tying his shoelaces when Holly reached the bottom of the stairs.

She appraised the well-mannered teenager as he opened the front door. Clint had done a great job raising such a nice kid as a single parent. It couldn't be easy to do alone.

"Thanks again for the book," he said before stepping outside.

"You're welcome."

He turned, reaching into the front pocket of his hooded sweatshirt. "Oh. I almost forgot." He pulled out a mass market paperback copy of *The Last Broadcast*. "Would you sign this for me?"

Holly blushed. It didn't matter how many books she'd signed; she still felt flushed whenever someone asked. "Sure." She took the book as he pulled a pen from his pocket and held it out to her.

Her cheeks felt hot when she opened it to the title page but for a completely different reason. "Oh, my gosh. Sorry, I don't think I got your name?"

"It's John."

"John," she repeated as she signed the book to him. She smiled, closing the book and handing it back. "It was nice to meet you."

CHAPTER TWENTY-EIGHT

JOHN

JOHN SEPARATED THE navy-blue curtains and peered out his upstairs bedroom window, watching Holly return to work. His bedroom gave him a clear view into Holly's office window. It had been hard for him not to react when he'd seen the photo of the woman who'd disappeared from Albertson's a few nights ago tacked to her wall. What if his dad had picked her up and killed her after John went to bed that night?

What worried John more was the list of names Holly had written beneath *Bus Stop Killer*. John had never heard that nickname before. Not everything on Holly's wall was right, but she was a hell of a lot closer to the truth than the police were. It had taken all his willpower not to show his amazement—and fear— after seeing those familiar faces laid out like that.

John studied the true crime author as she pulled a pair of headphones over her head and began to type. Holly Sparks was a problem. His dad had been much more careful about his kills over the last five years, and it seemed so had the Green River Killer. How had this crime writer connected the dots to Sally and

Jennifer Duran when even the cops couldn't figure it out? What if she somehow connected them to his dad? It made his heart hammer in his chest like a trapped bird.

John vividly recalled the moment when he asked his dad if he'd killed Jennifer Duran. It was right after they'd gotten home from Fairbanks where John had seen the news in the motel that the Seattle waitress's body had been discovered. His father had admitted it, and it had been the last time he'd spoken to John about his kills.

John lowered his gaze to Holly's kitchen window on the first floor, glad now that he'd done what he did. He knew Holly was staying next door only temporarily, hiding out from her abusive ex-fiancé. But every day she stayed in that house posed a risk to him and his dad.

John had read all of Holly's books before she moved into Norm and Maurine's home, and he recalled coming across her author's note in *Behind Closed Doors,* where Holly recounted being brutally attacked by her ex-fiancé, a detective for King County Major Crimes in the spring of 1985, the same time his dad had been brought in for questioning. Yesterday, John had gone to the library to search through old news articles until he'd found an article detailing how the King County Major Crimes detective had been sentenced to prison for the first-degree assault of his fiancé, crime reporter Holly Sparks.

When John had seen the five-year-old photo of Detective Jared Peretti, he'd nearly fallen out of his chair. He'd never forget the face of the Sylvester Stallone lookalike who'd stuck Sally's photo in John's face, shouting at him to confess while John's father had banged on the door to the room. It was ironic yet satisfying that the asshole detective had gone to prison, not his father.

John returned his attention to the window of Holly's upstairs office, looking beyond the writer seated at her desk to the lists of murder victims and map that covered the wall. Dread coiled in his gut like a cold, tightening vise. John couldn't let her uncover what had really happened.

He thought back to their conversation in Holly's office, wishing he hadn't told her about his mom's death. *What if she starts looking into that too?* He should've just let her believe his parents were divorced. *She won't,* he reassured himself. *She has no reason to look into what happened to my mom.*

Part of him wanted Holly to know, and that scared him.

Even though no one could know the truth besides him and his dad, it bothered John that they never talked about it. Ever since that trip to Fairbanks, John had felt his dad shrink away from him. It drove John crazy that they never talked about what happened to Sally, Jennifer Duran, or the woman found in that ditch in Fairbanks.

His father's growing distance had made John feel like he'd done something wrong. But deep down, John knew his dad had nothing to be upset with him about. When they'd gotten home from that Fairbanks trip, John had asked his dad why he was acting so different.

I showed you some things about me too soon, his dad had said. *Maybe I was wrong. I should've waited until you were older.*

John had tried to assure him it wasn't too soon; he'd *wanted* to know who his dad really was. But his dad had pulled away, nevertheless. They felt like strangers now, pretending to live a normal, mundane life under the weight of long-kept secrets, though John knew they weren't normal at all.

And here he was, fifteen years old, and his father still treated him like a child. How long would it take for his dad to see him as an equal? As a man?

John heard the faint ringing of Holly's phone on her downstairs kitchen wall. She slipped off her headphones and tilted her head toward the noise. John backed away from the window so she wouldn't catch him watching as she rose to her feet.

From the shadows of his room, John kept his eyes on the house next door until he spotted Holly entering the kitchen and picking up the phone. A stack of mail lay on the counter beside her. She'd be gone soon. He just needed to be patient.

John crossed his room, picked up the phone off the nightstand, and held it to his ear. He recognized Laurie's voice on the line talking to Holly. Thankfully, his dad and their cul-de-sac neighbors were still sharing a party line. Normally, John found it annoying when the line was tied up because his father and their neighbors stayed stuck in the past to save a few pennies. But John had never needed to keep tabs on any of their neighbors before.

He sat on his bed and moved the mouthpiece toward his neck so they wouldn't hear his breathing. *Man, did Laurie love to hear herself talk.*

Since he was grounded, he wouldn't be going anywhere for the rest of the night. John lifted his borrowed copy of *In Cold Blood* off the foot of the bed and turned on the bedside lamp. Being forced to stay at home wasn't really a punishment when he had a good book. He wondered how long Laurie would keep Holly on the line. He probably wouldn't learn anything useful by listening, and he was dying to start the book Holly had loaned him.

His dad didn't understand his love of reading. Said he'd gotten it from his mother. Lately, it seemed to be another thing that widened the chasm between them. John reclined against his headboard and opened *In Cold Blood* to the dedication.

John's ears perked up, hearing Laurie say his dad's name on the other end of the line. He set the book down on the bed beside him and gave Holly's phone call his full attention.

CHAPTER TWENTY-NINE

HOLLY

"I JUST WANTED to check in and make sure you were doing okay after everything," Laurie said.

"I'm fine." Holly looked around the empty kitchen, trying not to let her disappointment show in her voice. She'd been hoping the phone call was Andy with an update on Jared's alibi from the night she went over the bridge.

One of Laurie's twins squealed in the background, followed by an ear-piercing scream. "Ken," Laurie yelled. "Can you come give me a hand for a second? I'm on the phone."

Laurie's daughter's crying grew fainter as Holly imagined Ken carrying her out of the room.

"Sorry," Laurie said. "How's the manuscript coming? I'd like to think you're taking some time to recover, but I know you better than that."

"It's coming," Holly said, slumping against the kitchen counter. "But I may not finish if I have to keep taking breaks answering the phone."

"That's why I'm calling. To make sure you *are* taking some

breaks. Speaking of that," Laurie added. "Have you seen Clint today?"

Holly groaned, lifting her gaze toward the neighboring house. "No. And please, stop telling him to check on me like I'm some kind of damsel in distress. It's embarrassing."

"But also nice, right?"

Holly contained a smile. Maybe, but she wasn't about to give Laurie the satisfaction of saying so. "You didn't tell me he was a widower. Not that it really matters. I just assumed he was divorced."

"I thought I did. It's quite tragic, actually. She killed herself when their son was only seven. Jumped off their third-story balcony in the middle of the night. Clint found her body the next morning. My in-laws woke to Clint screaming for help after he discovered her lying dead on the back patio. I'm surprised Clint can still live in the house."

"That's awful." She recalled the distant look on John's face in her office when she'd assumed his parents were divorced. What a horrific thing for him to go through.

"I know."

Holly's gaze drifted to the French doors at the back of the kitchen. "Isn't his house two-story? I haven't seen a balcony anywhere."

"There's a daylight basement. Clint took the balcony down shortly afterward and put a window there instead. I can't blame him; it must've driven him crazy having to look at it after what happened. According to my mother-in-law, Clint's wife Diana wasn't right in the head, even though she seemed like a normal, doting mom. Clint said she'd never gotten over her baby blues after their son was born. Probably had undiagnosed postpartum depression, which wasn't really recognized back then. In fact, the day before Diana killed herself," Laurie continued, "she came over and told my mother-in-law how nice it was knowing her and told her she was going away for a while. Maurine thought she was going on a trip. Then, after she learned what happened, she realized the woman must've been saying goodbye. Maurine still feels terrible about the whole thing and blames herself for not knowing what Diana was intending to do. I can only imagine what Clint must've felt like."

Holly felt a shiver pass through her as another high-pitched scream cut through the background of their call. Poor Clint. He must've felt guilty too, being her husband.

Laurie sighed. "Anyway, I also wanted to tell you I left a stack of mail from your PO box on your kitchen counter. I picked it up like you asked but forgot to tell you after taking you home from the hospital. But you've probably seen it by now."

Holly's gaze dropped to the stack of unopened letters on the table. "I did, thanks." She'd gone through the envelopes after finding them to make sure none looked like the one Jared had sent. Thankfully, none had.

Holly heard some commotion on the line as she sifted through the envelopes again, her mind still on Clint's wife committing suicide. One of Laurie's twins shouted something Holly couldn't make out.

Laurie let out an exasperated sigh. "I have to go. Lily just spilled a gallon of milk all over the floor."

The line went dead before Holly could say goodbye. She started to hang up when a crisp, white envelope sticking out of the stack of fan mail made her blood run cold. Her name and address were typed on the front with no return address. She dropped the phone on the counter and lifted the envelope. She hadn't remembered seeing it before when she'd checked the mail. Her fingers trembled as she ripped it open.

She drew in a sharp breath after unfolding the paper and reading the typed words.

Roses are red, violets are blue, the locks on your doors won't keep me from you.

She covered her mouth with a hand, letting the paper fall to the counter. She spun around and dialed Andy's work number.

"Come on, pick up." It was Sunday, she realized. Andy might not be back at his office until tomorrow.

He answered on the second ring. "Detective Harris."

"Andy, it's Holly." She paused to take a breath. "I just found another note. From Jared. But this one's threatening. It says…" She closed her eyes, not needing to see the words again to recite them. "The locks on your doors won't keep me from you."

"Where did you find the note?" Andy asked, his voice calm.

Holly turned. "I just found it on the counter with a bunch of fan mail."

"So it wasn't delivered to the place where you're staying, right?"

"I—I'm not sure how it got here." She lifted a hand to her forehead. "Laurie brought over my mail from my PO Box, but I went through it yesterday and I don't remember seeing this envelope with the others. It's possible I could've missed it, but what if…" She nearly choked at the thought of Jared breaking into her house in the night, watching her sleep before planting the note in the kitchen.

"Are there any signs that someone broke in?"

She glanced around. "No, not that I know of, but—"

"Hang on."

There was muffled murmuring on the other line.

"Okay, I'm coming," she heard Andy say.

"Holly?"

"Yeah?"

"You're in a gated neighborhood, and there's no way Jared should know where you are. If you bring the note to me tomorrow, I'll have it dusted for prints."

She stared at the typed letter from Jared on the counter. *Tomorrow? What if that's too late?* "Why not tonight?"

"The print lab isn't staffed on Sundays. There won't be technicians working again until the morning. But I wouldn't get your hopes up. The only prints lifted off that first poem you got were yours."

Holly's heart sank. *Of course, Jared hadn't left his prints on the poem. He was an ex-cop.*

"In the meantime," Andy continued. "I already have a patrol car monitoring your neighborhood. I also pushed through your restraining order given you being run off that bridge. I'm afraid there's not much more I can do at the moment. If you feel unsafe, maybe you could stay with a friend?"

Holly bit her lip. Aside from Laurie, she didn't have any. And she couldn't risk drawing Jared to Laurie's home with her two young daughters.

"It's okay. I'll stay here for now."

"Holly, I'm sorry, but I have to go."

She could hear the fatigue in the detective's voice. She pinched the bridge of her nose and took a deep breath, trying to remain calm. *He's doing all he can.*

"Andy? What about Jared's alibi from the other night with Tommy Reed? Were you able to confirm it?" Holly glanced at the waning daylight beyond her window.

"Not yet. I asked Detective O'Malley to give me a call tonight to update me. I'll let you know."

"Okay, thanks."

"Don't let him rattle you. It's going to be okay."

Holly stared at the note after hanging up. She strained to remember if that envelope had been there yesterday when she'd flipped through the mail. If it had been, why hadn't she noticed it?

Now, she couldn't clearly recall it *not* being there either. She lifted her fingertips to her temples. *Maybe I just didn't see it.* After running her off the bridge, it was hard to imagine Jared breaking in to leave a note. If he'd been in this house, she'd likely be dead.

She glanced at the sun setting beyond the window and thought of the long night ahead.

A knock at the front door made her nearly jump out of her skin. She whipped her head toward the entryway, then pulled a steak knife from a drawer before moving to the front of the house. It was too dark out to make out the person standing on the front steps, only that it looked like a man.

Her shoulders sagged with relief after she checked the peephole. It was Clint.

He smiled in the glow of the porch lights, looking his usual handsome self. When she opened the door, he held up a bottle of red wine.

"Hi." His cheerful expression faded, the spark in his eyes dimming with worry. "Are you okay? You look like you've seen a ghost."

Her heart still hammered against her ribs. "I'm fine," she said, trying to convince herself as much as her handsome neighbor.

His gaze fell to the knife in her hand.

She followed his gaze. "I was just…um." She lifted the knife. "Cooking."

"Oh." His expression relaxed. "What are you making?"

"I hadn't decided yet."

His brows knit together. He studied her as if waiting for her to elaborate or say she was kidding. When she did neither, he lifted the bottle again. "Well, John has retreated to his room with that book you loaned him, and I didn't feel like drinking alone." He shook his head. "That came out wrong. Not that I share wine with my fifteen-year-old." He ran a hand through his hair.

Was he nervous?

"I just thought it'd be nice to share this with someone." He cracked another smile.

She glanced at the bottle, unable to shed from her mind the image of Jared creeping around her house.

"I know you're on a deadline," he added, seeing the hesitation in her eyes. "So feel free to say no, although if you don't mind me saying so, you look like you could use a drink."

He cast her a lopsided grin, and she opened the door wider for him to step inside.

"Yes, I could."

Plus, she felt safer with Clint here anyway.

CHAPTER THIRTY

JOHN

Hearing the front door close, John set the phone on his bed and moved to the window. He expected to see his dad's car headlights pulling out of the driveway. It wasn't unusual for him to run to the store in the evening to grab beer or something else they'd run out of. But instead of headlights, John saw the motion-activated porch lights turn on at the house next door. When he saw his dad on Holly's porch, his mouth fell open.

Was that wine in his hand? After a short exchange, she let him inside.

"Shit." What was his dad doing? He didn't even like wine.

John watched his father trail Holly into the kitchen and set the bottle on the counter beside the stack of mail. Holly turned and retrieved two wine glasses from the cupboard. From his upstairs window, John narrowed his eyes at his father.

He should've left this alone. I already had it handled.

John hadn't actually spoken with his dad about the ex-crime reporter's presence next door, but it went without saying that a true crime author obsessed over her sister's unsolved murder was a problem. They didn't need her turning over the wrong stone.

Thankfully, John had overheard that loudmouth Laurie talking to his dad the other day about the cryptic note Holly had received from her ex, which had given him an idea. He'd met Laurie only a few times, but he'd figured out she loved gossiping about other people's problems. And that she had the hots for his dad.

Holly set the glasses beside the bottle and laughed at something his father said.

John scoffed. Making her fall for him wasn't going to solve anything. They needed her to leave, not stay. His father loved the line in *The Godfather Part II* when Michael Corleone said, "Keep your friends close but your enemies closer." John disagreed. Keeping your enemies close was a risk, especially when you had things to hide.

John crossed his arms and watched Holly tuck a wave of hair behind her ear before searching through a kitchen drawer. Was his dad actually falling for this woman? She was pretty, but there were lots of pretty women who didn't have walls covered with photos of murder victims.

Holly lifted a corkscrew from the drawer. She reached for the bottle when John's dad extended his hand. John's pulse spiked as she handed him the corkscrew.

Is he going to kill her? John stared out the window, wanting to scream. *Doesn't he know how dangerous that would be?* They weren't the only people living on this cul-de-sac. What if someone saw his dad go inside her house? It could be the end of their life together. His dad would go to prison, and John would go to some godforsaken foster home.

As his father unfolded the bottle opener, John debated whether to sprint downstairs. *If he hurried…* But then it was too late. His father plunged the corkscrew into the cork, effortlessly opening the bottle before filling the two glasses with wine.

John exhaled the breath he'd been holding as Holly reached for a glass. *I should've known better. My father isn't reckless. If he were, we wouldn't still be living here.* A lock of Holly's dark hair fell in front of her eye again.

His dad closed the distance between them, tucking it behind her ear before she could do it herself. They stared into each other's eyes for a moment, and John didn't look away until after his father lowered his mouth to hers.

John moved away from the window, hoping his father wasn't making a mistake. If he was, it would be up to John to fix it.

HOLLY

Clint pulled his mouth away from Holly's, leaving behind a lingering heat that made her breath catch. She could still taste him on her lips. Her pulse spiked from the long kiss they'd shared. She opened her eyes to find him taking a step back.

"Sorry." He shot her a half smile. "I'm not very good at this. I haven't dated much since my wife passed."

Neither had she since Jared's attack, but it was too soon to tell Clint about that. She didn't want to scare him away.

Instead, she asked, "How long ago was that?" She didn't want to let on that she already knew.

"Eight years ago."

"Wow."

Clint lifted his wine glass. "I know, I'm old."

Holly smiled, shaking her head. "That's not what I meant." She dropped her gaze to the floor as Clint took a sip of wine. "I lost my sister ten years ago. Sometimes it feels like forever, and other times I can't believe it's been that long."

Clint set his glass on the counter before leaning against it. "I know what you mean."

He reached for her hand, and Holly shifted her focus toward his long fingers intertwining with hers.

"I'll never forget the look in my wife's eyes right before she died," he added.

Holly lifted her gaze to meet Clint's. "I thought you found her in the morning."

Clint's brows furrowed in confusion. "How did you know that?"

Holly felt her face flush. How could she explain without admitting that she and Laurie had been talking about it? Clint's eyes searched hers, waiting for her answer.

"Laurie told me about your wife's death."

Clint's expression darkened as he pulled his hand free from hers.

"Sorry." Holly cringed. "It's none of my business."

Clint pressed his lips into a thin line, exhaling sharply through his nose. "I should go."

Her heart sank at his words. She didn't want him to leave, but she also didn't want to make things worse.

"I'm sorry," Holly repeated, following Clint to the door.

"Goodnight," he said after stepping outside, his voice clipped and low.

Holly held back a second apology as he started for his house, hating herself for being so careless with her words. "Goodnight."

After closing the door, she leaned her forehead against it. "Shit."

She turned for the kitchen and took a drink from the wine Clint had poured her, gazing out the window toward Clint's house as she tried to calm her racing thoughts. She set down her glass and spotted Jared's note on the counter with the stack of mail, reminded that she had bigger problems than her love life. She took another drink, then headed back to the front door to turn the deadbolt before going upstairs.

She tried to let herself feel reassured by Andy's words. *Jared doesn't know where I am. He's just trying to scare me.* But she couldn't let him get under her skin. *I'm safe,* she tried to convince herself. She had to stay strong.

She glanced in the direction of Clint's house one last time before going into her office. She'd apologize to Clint again tomorrow. Hopefully, he would forgive her nosiness.

In the meantime, she would write until exhaustion claimed her.

Holly woke with her forehead stuck to her arm and the memory of Clint's mouth on hers. Her recall of Clint's kiss gave way to a sinking dread as the events that followed came rushing back. She sat up in the desk chair, squinting from the morning light coming through the window. She wiped the drool from the side of her mouth and checked her watch. It was after ten.

What time had it been when she'd finally fallen asleep? She'd written three chapters, and it had been dark out for several hours when she'd closed her eyes for what was supposed to be only a few minutes. She stood and stretched her arms overhead before going downstairs to brew a pot of coffee.

Her gaze lingered on the front door on her way to the kitchen. She swallowed, remembering Clint leaving last night. She replayed his cold reaction, the way his demeanor darkened the moment he learned she and Laurie had discussed his wife's death. Holly hadn't meant any harm—surely Clint knew Laurie had a habit of oversharing. Why had he been so upset?

Grief can do strange things to people, she thought as she entered the kitchen. She, of all people, understood that.

Jared's threatening poem lay open where she'd left it on top of the stack of mail. Seeing it made her stomach churn. As soon as she consumed some caffeine, she needed to take it downtown so Andy could have it processed for prints. It would probably be for nothing though. If Jared had been smart enough not to leave any evidence on his first note, he certainly wouldn't leave his prints on a more threatening one.

She grabbed the empty coffee pot and moved to the sink, deciding to knock on Clint's door later today. She hadn't felt this way about anyone since Jared, and she wasn't going to give up over a misunderstanding. Hopefully, Clint would feel the same way.

She looked out the window as she held the coffee pot under the faucet, spotting a car she didn't recognize in Clint's driveway. As she turned on the water, a pretty brunette emerged from Clint's front door. She appeared to be about thirty, maybe a few years younger. The woman laughed before she hugged someone goodbye who stood just out of sight. His face was blocked by the doorframe, but Holly spotted his familiar plaid sleeve. His hand slid down the woman's back and lingered on the back pocket of her jeans before letting her go. The woman smiled as she trod down Clint's porch steps through the rain and hopped into her car.

Holly turned off the faucet, keeping her gaze trained on Clint's house. His front door closed as the woman sped out of the cul-de-sac. Holly stared out the window. Last night, Clint said that he'd hardly dated since his wife passed. Had he gone home and called an old flame? Or gone out and picked someone up at a bar? Or had he been lying and really had a girlfriend?

Her mind reeled with questions as she finished making coffee in a daze. Minutes later, after filling a mug, she studied Clint's home. It was a Tuesday. Shouldn't he be at work?

It doesn't matter, she thought. *Clint is no longer my business.* And apparently, he never was. She'd been stupid to think he felt for her the way she had for him. She tore her gaze from the window and stared at Jared's typed note. Picking bad men did run in her family. She used kitchen tongs to place the note into a press-seal plastic bag before heading upstairs to change.

CHAPTER THIRTY-TWO

JOHN

THE TASTE OF his teacher's strawberry ChapStick lingered on John's lips as he pressed the button to open the garage door. Seeing rain hit the driveway as the door began to lift, he ran back inside to grab his jacket. When he returned, the door was fully raised, and he spotted his new nosy neighbor creeping slowly past his house in the station wagon that had been parked in her drive the last few days.

John stepped behind the hot water tank, wondering if she'd seen his English teacher leaving. He peered around the tank to see Holly had stopped in front of his driveway and was staring into his garage. *Shit.*

John stayed still until she accelerated down the street. He glanced in the direction of the house next door. *I have got to be more careful.*

He climbed into his dad's spare car that would be John's once he got his license. It wasn't legal for him to be driving alone, but he wanted something else for lunch than what they had in the fridge. And with his dad at work while John was on spring break, he'd have to go to the store himself. But driving without a license wasn't what worried him about Holly Sparks spying into his garage.

At the start of the school year, he and his teacher had connected over their shared love of classic literature, but she'd been the one to come on to him. After that, things had heated up fast. While John knew it was wrong, he'd let the affair continue. But he needed to put a stop to it before someone found out.

From a young age, his father had instilled in him the belief that cops could not be trusted. But he should've taught John not to trust women either.

John started the Ford Fairmont's engine and threw it into reverse. It had been a mistake letting his teacher come here. He couldn't take the risk of someone seeing her again. Especially Holly Sparks.

When John got to the end of his street, he spotted Holly's station wagon peeling out of their gated neighborhood onto the main road.

Where is she going in such a hurry? Wherever it is, it can't be good, he thought as the station wagon disappeared from his view.

He eased his foot off the gas pedal, wanting to keep a good distance between his car and the crime writer's. Rain splattered against the windshield as he drove through the opened gate.

As he drove toward Albertson's, John tapped his fingers against the steering wheel, coming up with a plan to get Holly Sparks away from his dad for good.

CHAPTER THIRTY-THREE

HOLLY

HOLLY DID A double take when she spotted the car parked in Clint's garage. He'd always kept his second car parked inside, so she hadn't seen it before. She slowed her car, staring at the blue Ford Fairmont, braking to almost a full stop. But then she spotted movement in the corner of the garage and pressed her foot on the gas, not wanting Clint to catch her gawking at his vehicle.

Sally Hickman had been seen getting into a blue Ford Fairmont with a boy in the backseat. Thinking of John, she turned out of the cul-de-sac and stepped harder on the accelerator. Her mind raced. John was fifteen. That would've made him around nine in late 1984.

Driving a blue Ford and having a son didn't make Clint a killer, she thought after she pulled out of the neighborhood gate. Still, she couldn't purge the image of the car from her mind as she drove to the Major Crimes Unit. Statistically, Clint was one of thousands of people who owned a blue Ford Fairmont in the greater Seattle area alone. It was a coincidence. Plus, the prostitute who'd reported seeing Sally get into the car had been high on meth at the time. Besides, what were the odds that she'd move next door to the man she suspected of killing her sister? Holly tried to put the car out of her mind as she drove, but it kept creeping back in.

When she passed the exit on I-5 that led to the road where she'd been forced off the bridge, she shuddered as her thoughts turned to Jared. Andy had never called her last night to say whether they'd confirmed Jared's alibi with the bartender. Hopefully, he'd be at his office when she got there so she could ask him.

Fifteen minutes later, Holly gripped the plastic bag containing Jared's note as she approached the front desk at the Major Crimes Unit. "I need to see Detective Harris."

The young receptionist's eyes brightened. "Hi, Holly. I absolutely loved your new book," she gushed. "My mom's reading it now."

"Thanks. It's urgent," Holly added, leaning forward to get a glimpse inside Andy's office. "Is he here?"

"Oh. Well, he is, but he's had quite a busy morning." She stood. "Let me just check if he can see you now."

Holly shadowed her to Andy's office. When Holly peered over the receptionist's teased hair, she saw Andy standing behind his desk.

"Holly Sparks is here," the receptionist said.

"Hey, Holly." Andy met her gaze. "Come on in." He pulled his suit jacket off the back of his desk chair and slung it over his shoulders, covering the holstered gun on his hip.

The receptionist stepped aside to make room for Holly to step through the doorway. "Nice to see you," she said before retreating to her desk.

"You too," Holly called over her shoulder. She held out the plastic bag. "Here's the note."

"Thanks." Andy took it from her. "I'll drop it by the latent print lab on my way out."

"Did you talk to Detective O'Malley last night about Jared's alibi?"

The detective shook his head. "I'm afraid not. O'Malley was struck in the arm by a stray bullet yesterday while responding to a domestic disturbance. He never spoke with the bartender to confirm Jared stayed at the bar the night you were driven off the bridge. I'm going to see if I can track the bartender down now." His eyes searched hers. "You doing okay?" he asked, as if he could sense something was bothering her.

"What was the name of the Green River Killer suspect you interviewed in 1985 who drove a blue Ford Fairmont? The one Jared found walking around Star Lake with his son?"

A crease formed between Andy's eyebrows. "The one who passed a polygraph?"

She nodded.

Andy shot a sideways glance at the floor as if working to recall the name. "It was Louie. Louie Prescott."

Her shoulders relaxed. *Not Clint.* "You sure?"

"Yeah. Why?"

She shook her head. "It's nothing." Of course, it hadn't been Clint. And even if it had, the guy had passed a polygraph.

As the detective led the way out of his office, Holly's gaze dropped to a handwritten note on Andy's desk. *Mike's Storage Units #41* was scribbled on a yellow legal pad. Beneath it was a Federal Way address. Holly knew where it was; she'd driven by the storage facility before. That must be where Jared was keeping his car.

"I'll let you know what I find out from the bartender after I speak to him," Andy said as he stepped into the hall.

Holly trailed him out of the Major Crimes Unit, glad to see

the receptionist on the phone when she passed the front desk, so she wouldn't get cornered in a long-winded discussion about her books. Which reminded her, she was supposed to be writing one right now. She pulled a stick of gum from her pocket as she speed-walked to her car, zipping her jacket over her sweater to ward off the damp, chilly breeze.

After she climbed behind the wheel, something came together in the back of her mind. She mentally played back the names Meg's roommate had given her of the older guy Meg had been hanging around when she was pregnant. *Bobby, or Lou, or maybe Denny.*

Holly chewed the inside of her cheek. *Could Lou have been Louie Prescott? Except,* she thought with a sigh, *he'd passed a polygraph and alibis for several of the murders.* The Green River Killer Task Force had ruled him out.

Although, they hadn't asked him about Meg, a voice tugged at the back of her mind.

On the drive back to Tacoma, she forced herself to turn her thoughts to Roxy Vega, knowing if she didn't ready her mind to write the chapter detailing the singer's last night on Earth, she would get lost in trying to solve Meg's murder all day.

After exiting off I-5 forty-five minutes later, she stopped at a red light, feeling clearer in the head than she had in days. The sky brightened as the midday sun peeked through a patch of clouds. Andy would prove whether Jared was the one who'd driven her off the bridge. Jared couldn't have been at that bar the whole time.

But what if Jared was telling the truth? The idea of Jared being innocent still unsettled her. Because if it wasn't Jared who'd tried to kill her, then who had? Holly thought of Roxy Vega, bludgeoned to death by a stranger in a Seattle alleyway—a random act of violence. *Had I simply been the victim of a random road rage incident?*

It had to be Jared, Holly decided, thinking of his threating notes and the man who'd stalked her to her car in the Albertson's parking lot. She exhaled, pressing her back into the seat. Andy would make sure Jared didn't get away with it.

Waiting for the light to turn, she glanced out the passenger window at the newly built, two-story library. She chewed her gum as she surveyed the building, her mind returning to Clint's car and the way his demeanor darkened last night after learning Laurie had told her about his wife's suicide.

A honk erupted behind her, making her jump in her seat.

Looking up to find the light green, Holly hit the gas and made a sharp right turn before pulling into the library's parking lot. Holly knew what Laurie would say if she found her here, digging up old newspaper articles. *Not everything is a mystery waiting to be solved.*

Maybe it was curiosity. Maybe she was jealous after seeing the brunette leave Clint's house this morning. She tapped her index finger on the steering wheel as she parked. No, it was more than that. Maybe it was the blue Ford Fairmont in Clint's garage. Whatever it was, something nagged at her. She needed to find out more about Clint's wife's death.

She climbed out of the car, locked the door, and strode toward the building. There had to be an article about Diana's death. She checked her watch as she walked. If she was going to meet her deadline, she didn't have time for this.

I'll do a quick search, she told herself. *Put my mind at ease, then go back and write for the rest of the day.*

CHAPTER THIRTY-FOUR

JOHN

JOHN PEERED OVER the second-story balcony of the library and studied the back of Holly's head as she hunched over a microfilm reader machine. He was too far away to see what articles she was reading, but it had to be either for the book she was writing or her Green River Killer obsession. From the array of names, maps, photos, lists, and handwritten theories that covered her office wall, it was likely the latter.

Holly jotted something down in a notebook. John's fingers fidgeted with the hem of his shirt as he strained to see what filled Holly's screen. Using a knob at the base of the machine, Holly flipped to the next page of the newspaper before John could make out what she'd been looking at.

What if she was looking into the woman who was last seen at the Albertson's down the street? Her photo was pinned to Holly's wall. *Have they found her?* John wondered. *No,* he decided. He'd watched the news this morning, and they hadn't said anything about her body being discovered. And even if it had, that didn't explain why Holly would be looking up old articles.

John tucked his borrowed copies of *The Onion Field* and *Rebecca*, a gothic fiction novel recommended by his English teacher, under his arm and backed away from the banister. He needed to get closer.

He'd been planning to stop here anyway to look for the true crime book Holly had recommended when he'd spotted her station wagon in the parking lot. After buying a premade sandwich at Albertson's, John had driven to a park his mom used to take him to when he was little and eaten in the car while it rained.

The memory of his mother's laughter as she pushed him on the park swings dissolved into the dull creak of the library stairs beneath his feet. His stomach grumbled, and he lifted his gaze to the large clock above the check-out desk on the first floor. He'd been here for nearly three hours. He hadn't planned on staying so long, but seeing Holly so engrossed in an archival search had piqued his curiosity.

The library was unusually quiet, and when he neared the bottom of the stairs, he could hear the click of the microfilm reader's knob beneath Holly's fingers. Holly faced away from him at the shared computer desk and stretched her neck to the side, keeping her attention focused on the screen.

He could go over and say hello, except Holly might ask how he got here. He didn't need her telling his dad that he'd been driving without a license. Plus, she might turn off the screen or wait to continue her archival search until after he'd gone. From the way she flipped through the archival pages with focused intensity, she hadn't yet found what she was looking for. And he needed to see what was driving her search.

Beside John, a young boy holding a stack of books followed his mother toward the check-out desk. The boy tripped over his own rain boots, sending all but one of his books to the floor with a dense, echoing thud.

Holly turned toward the sound. John spun so she wouldn't see his face and pretended to thumb through a shelf of nonfiction. He traced a finger over a row of Martha Stewart cookbooks and paused when he reached Donald Trump's *The Art of the Deal*. John withdrew the hardcover from the shelf and leafed through the pages of deal-making advice from the real estate mogul.

When he dared look over his shoulder, Holly was refocused on her computer. She'd taken her hand off the mouse and leaned toward the screen. Her jaw flexed as she chewed a piece of gum.

John returned the book to the shelf and moved down a row of magazines behind Holly's computer. Halfway down the row, he stared through an empty space in the shelf. The photo that Holly was staring at made his heart leap into his throat.

It was an image of his house.

It had to be an article about his mom's suicide. John's face seared with anger, thinking of the phone call he'd listened in on last night. That bitch Laurie needed to stop yapping to Holly about what happened to his mother, even though she hadn't gotten it right. It had obviously spurred Holly on a mission to learn more.

Plus, his father had no doubt made it worse by making Holly think he was interested in her. He should never have gone over to her house last night. *I need to put a stop to this before she ruins our lives.* His father clearly did not have a handle on the situation.

Maybe his dad was losing his edge. He was getting older. He was forty-six now. His father's killings had slowed during the last several years. He was being more careful, which was good; it had kept him out of prison.

Had his dad turned soft? A terrifying thought imploded in his mind like a grenade. What if he actually *liked* this woman?

He'd heard his dad humming to himself this morning before

he'd left for work. And he hadn't even killed anyone recently. In a couple of years, as far as John knew.

Good thing he has me, John thought as he watched Holly pop a gum bubble with her lips and scribble in her notebook. *One of us has to keep our head on straight.*

Fortunately, John knew exactly what to do.

CHAPTER THIRTY-FIVE

HOLLY

HOLLY SAT FORWARD in her chair, leaning closer to the microfilm reader. Finally. She'd found what she was looking for. *TACOMA MOTHER DEAD AFTER LEAPING FROM BALCONY.*

Holly was only partly conscious of folding a stick of gum into her mouth as she zoomed in on the article. The house pictured at the top was a different color, but there was no mistaking it—same faux rock on the base of the siding, same picture window above the garage, and same emerald hedges lining the driveway that Clint kept immaculately pruned.

She'd just read the article's first line when a clatter cut through the quiet library. Holly whirled toward the noise. Her shoulders relaxed when she spotted a young mother bending down to help her small boy pick up the array of children's books scattered across the tile floor.

Holly returned her attention to the microfilm reader and twisted the knob beneath the screen to enlarge *The Tacoma Times* article. Holly read it as quickly as her eyes allowed, her focus intent on the screen as she absent-mindedly chewed her gum.

The body of a twenty-nine-year-old wife and mother was discovered in the early hours of January 18 by her husband on their concrete patio after she presumably leapt from their third-story balcony above. She was pronounced dead at the scene.

A suicide note was found at the home, and police are treating her death as a suicide. According to her husband, she had never gotten over her 'baby blues'. He'd been encouraging her to seek help for her depression and reported that she'd been drinking heavily in the months leading up to her death.

Her husband told police that he'd heard her opening a bottle of wine before he went to bed and believes she jumped from the third-story balcony at some point during the night.

Behind her, Holly heard the squeak of sneakers on the tile floor. She spun around, envisioning Jared creeping up behind her before wrapping his hands around her throat, squeezing it shut before she could make a sound.

But there was no one there, at least not that she could see through the rows of bookshelves behind where she sat. Holly exhaled. *It's just someone looking at books.*

Holly turned around and finished reading the article. *An investigation into her death is still ongoing.*

Holly blew a bubble with her gum as she stared at the article. There wasn't as much information as she'd hoped. If there had been an investigation into Diana's death, there had to have been an autopsy. Holly ejected the microfilm from the reading machine and returned it to the index aisle before retrieving another stack of microfilm from later issues of *The Tacoma Times* in 1982.

Holly stifled a yawn when she finally found a second article about Diana's death, published five weeks later.

TACOMA WOMAN'S DEATH RULED A SUICIDE AFTER JUMP FROM BALCONY.

A Pierce County medical examiner has confirmed the manner of Diana Carter's death a suicide after conducting an autopsy and toxicology—

The library lights flicked off. Holly looked around as they turned back on, then glanced at her watch, frozen at 9:45 with condensation trapped beneath the crystal. That must've been the time she went into the Green River. She leaned back in her chair, craning her neck to read the large, two-hand clock on the wall above the front desk. *6:55.* She'd been here all day. It was only now that she registered the hunger pang in the pit of her stomach.

"Ma'am."

Holly turned to see a gray-haired woman wearing a no-nonsense expression standing beside her.

"We close in five minutes."

"Okay, thank you. I'll finish up." Holly hit print on the article and retrieved it from the library's printer before returning the microfilm to the index aisle.

It was dark when she walked through the library parking lot, empty aside from Laurie's station wagon and a white Jeep, which must have belonged to the librarian. Holly quickened her pace as she withdrew Laurie's keys from her jeans pocket, thinking about her purse at the bottom of the Green River. Her only consolation was that she didn't have to rummage through it for her keys.

Once safely inside Laurie's car, Holly locked the driver's door and flipped on the dome light to read the rest of the article. A toxicology report confirmed Diana had alcohol in her system and that her broken neck and head injuries were consistent with a three-story fall onto the concrete. That, along with the suicide note found the morning of her death, contributed to the medical examiner's ruling. The article concluded with a statement that Diana was survived by her husband and seven-year-old son.

Holly tossed the article onto the passenger seat before starting the car's engine, berating herself for letting her curiosity get the better of her. She'd wasted the whole day on a wild goose chase over an innocent man who wasn't even interested in her. And she was no closer to meeting her deadline than she had been this morning.

"Shit."

As she drove, she strained to refocus her thoughts on Roxy Vega, trying to imagine what the punk rock singer had gone through after leaving the bar that fatal night. It wasn't until Holly turned onto the two-lane road that led to her neighborhood that she became aware of the headlights tailing her.

She gripped the wheel tighter as she stared into the glare in the rearview mirror. Her chest tightened, sending each frantic beat climbing into her throat as she forced her attention back to the road. *Jared.*

The car trailed her as she turned into the entrance to her neighborhood, coming to a stop behind her when she braked for the gate. Holly felt to make sure her door was locked, keeping her eyes trained on the headlights shining into her mirror as she lowered her window to punch in the gate code with shaking fingers.

Her pulse throbbed in her ears as she willed the gate to open faster. She beat her palm against the steering wheel after rolling up the window. *Come on, come on.* Holly floored the gas as soon as she had enough space to squeeze through, the headlights behind her following close behind.

The car was still tailing her when she turned into her cul-de-sac. Seeing Clint's house, she debated whether to pull into his drive, wondering if she could make it to Clint's front door before Jared jumped out and attacked her—or worse. When she neared Clint's house, she slowed, about to turn up his driveway, when the car behind her pulled alongside her passenger window.

Her jaw fell open. It was a Tacoma police cruiser. She'd been sure it was Jared. The officer rolled down his window.

"Everything okay, ma'am?"

She swallowed. "Yes. Fine."

"You live here?" He pointed to Clint's house.

"No, actually, I'm staying next door." She gestured toward Laurie's in-laws' home.

"Holly Sparks?"

She nodded, confused. *How did he know my name?*

"Detective Andy Harris asked me to check on your place during my shift tonight. I'll be coming through your neighborhood periodically to make sure there's nothing suspicious." He motioned toward her house. "You expecting any visitors tonight?"

She shook her head. "No."

"Okay, well, if everything's all right, I'll get back to my patrol and drive by a little later. If you notice anything suspicious in the meantime, don't hesitate to call 911."

"Thanks."

He propped his elbow through the open window. "You were driving pretty fast back there. Take it easy next time, okay? This is a neighborhood."

He pulled away, and Holly sank against the seat before pulling into her drive. She got out of the car, still shaken. As she walked to the front door, the phone rang from inside the house. It was still ringing when she stepped inside, and she hurried to the kitchen to answer it before it went to the answering machine.

"Hello?"

"It's Andy. I've been trying to get a hold of you for a few hours. I was starting to worry. You okay?"

"I'm fine." *Aside from wasting the entire day when I should've been writing.* "Sorry, I wasn't home." She glanced in the direction of Clint's house. A bluish glow from a TV flickered against his windowpane, shifting shadows like ghosts dancing across the glass. "Did you speak to the bartender?" She leaned against the wall, preparing for Andy to tell her Jared's alibi checked out, thinking Jared likely got the bartender to lie for him.

"That's why I'm calling. The bartender specifically remembers Jared stepping out of the bar after the third inning, and he doesn't recall seeing Jared again until nearly the end of the Mariner's game. I went to the house where Jared is staying, but no one was home. I'm going to request a search warrant for Jared's storage unit in the morning. With luck, I'll find damage to the passenger side of his car."

"Can you arrest him? I mean, since he lied about his alibi?" She knew the answer as soon as she asked.

"Not without proof he was driving the car that forced you over the bridge. In the meantime, I've requested a Tacoma patrol unit to drive by your house periodically through the night."

"An officer already came by."

"Good. Then stay inside and lock your doors. If you feel unsafe at any point, call 911."

Holly twisted her neck trying to see the front door. She couldn't remember locking it after coming inside.

"Jared shouldn't know where you're staying," Andy added. "The patrol is just to be safe."

After hanging up, Holly decided Andy was right. Jared couldn't know where she was staying. If he did, he would've come for her already. She'd already wasted enough time looking into Clint's wife's death; she couldn't waste any more worrying about Jared. That was why she'd come here. To be safe and to work in peace. Jared had already taken enough from her.

She checked the time on the microwave and resolved to write until at least 1:00 a.m. If she started now and stayed focused, she could get in almost a full workday before going to bed. She grabbed an apple off the counter before turning off the kitchen lights.

On her way to lock the front door, she cast a glance over her shoulder through the kitchen window at the glow coming from Clint's outdoor lights. He might not be interested in her, but at least her cute next-door neighbor wasn't a murderer.

CHAPTER THIRTY-SIX

HOLLY

HOLLY TRUDGED DOWN the carpeted stairs the next morning to refill her coffee. She wore the same sweats as yesterday, having been too tired to undress last night when she'd finally gone to bed at two in the morning. After knocking out three more chapters in her manuscript, she'd succumbed to a deep, dreamless sleep, despite Andy's phone call last night about Jared.

When she neared the bottom of the stairs, movement outside the front window caught her eye. She moved closer to the window, holding her empty mug. It was a mail truck parked in front of her house. The mailman slipped a handful of mail into her letter box before walking to Clint's with a small stack of envelopes tucked under his arm.

As the mail truck pulled away from the curb, Holly set the mug on the entryway table and stepped outside. She wasn't getting any mail sent here, so she hadn't checked the mailbox since she'd moved in. But if Laurie's in-laws were still getting mail delivered, it could be stacking up.

Holly looked down at her slippers and her clothes, noticing

the coffee stain on the front of her sweatshirt, then shot a glance at the quiet house next door. Not that it mattered—Clint wasn't interested in her. She thought of the pretty dark-haired woman she'd seen leaving yesterday morning. But she'd be quick anyway, just in case he was home. Clint may be seeing someone else, but she still had her pride.

She withdrew a stack of mail from the mailbox along with an issue of *The Tacoma Times* wrapped in a plastic bag inside the newspaper box. She cast one last cursory glance at Clint's house before swiftly retreating inside her own.

She carried the mail to the kitchen, retrieving her empty mug on the way. She refilled it with steaming coffee before sliding the bag off the newspaper. It was the Sunday edition. She racked her brain to recall what day it was. *Tuesday?* she wondered, realizing she hadn't checked the news in days.

She flipped through the paper, scouring the headlines for news of the woman who'd gone missing from the Albertson's bus stop last week. But there was no mention of her disappearance or her being found. There was, however, a half-page article detailing Holly's car getting run off the Strander Boulevard Bridge into the Green River. The article didn't mention her name, but that didn't make Holly feel any better. If Jared *had* been the one behind the wheel of the other car and he'd seen the news, he would know she survived. She had no doubt he would strike again. After turning to the last page, Holly slid the paper aside to sort through Norm and Maurine's mail.

She tossed a Domino's coupon and a cable TV flyer in the trash before setting aside a JCPenney catalog addressed to Maurine to give to Laurie. She set an envelope for Norm on top of the catalog. When she reached for the next one, she stopped cold. It had been put in the wrong mailbox. It was for the house next door.

But it wasn't the address that made the air around her feel like it had dropped ten degrees. It was who it was addressed to: *Louie Clinton Prescott.* A hollow chill spread through her limbs.

Numb, Holly stared out the window at Clint's house, imagining a nine-year-old John in the backseat while his dad picked up Sally Hickman in 1984. John would've been waiting in the car while his dad butchered Sally in the woods. Goosebumps crawled across her arms like frost.

No, she thought. Detectives had ruled Louie Prescott out. He'd not only passed a polygraph but also had an alibi for some of the Green River Killer murders. Clint being the suspect that Jared interviewed in 1985 didn't make Clint a killer.

Holly thought of the brunette leaving Clint's house the morning after Clint kissed her in the kitchen. *Was Clint such a good liar that he'd gotten away with the unthinkable?*

Holly turned for the stairs to retrieve her address book to find her contact at the Tacoma Homicide Unit. There was only one way to find out.

❧

"Our casefiles are organized by casefile number." Detective Amanda Corrado handed Holly a handwritten nine-digit number on a legal pad. "This is Diana Carter's casefile number. Sorry I can't help you look."

"That's okay. I know you're busy."

"Yeah, sorry it was a bit of a zoo upstairs. I'd like to say it's not normally like that, but these last few months have been crazy around here." Amanda gestured to the paper in Holly's hand. "That happened before I started in homicide. Our department has had a big turnover since then, and a lot of the detectives working at the time have either retired or transferred to other units. But there's still a few around that we can track down if you have questions."

"Thanks, Amanda." Holly surveyed the wall of file cabinets in the small, windowless room in the basement of the Tacoma Police Department. "And for letting me come down on such short notice."

"No problem. I need to go make a few calls—we got a new homicide this morning, which means I'm up for the next one—but I'll come back down once I'm done. The files can't leave the building, but if you want to photocopy anything, you can use the copier upstairs. Just put everything back when you're done."

"I will. Thanks." Holly turned to the detective, who stood several inches taller than her, even in flats.

"You're lucky you called when you did. We're running out of storage space, so all the closed cases prior to 1985 are going to be moved to the city archives later this week." A beeping filled the room, and she glanced at the pager at her hip. "Shit. I gotta go." She made for the door and threw Holly a glance over her shoulder. "Can you find your way out if I don't make it back?"

"Yeah, no problem."

Holly watched Amanda disappear down the corridor before searching for Diana's file. She'd met Amanda when she'd been researching her third true crime novel, and they'd stayed in touch.

Once Holly found the right file cabinet, it took five minutes of sifting through tightly packed casefiles before she found Diana's. She took the thin file to a small folding table against the wall.

When she opened the file, her eyes caught on Diana's last name—Carter, not Prescott. She'd never taken Clint's last name, which was why Holly hadn't made the connection when Andy told her the last name of the suspect who'd taken the polygraph in 1985.

Holly read through the autopsy report first. While her broken neck and head injuries seemed to match what she'd read in the paper, Holly was surprised to see Diana had sustained other injuries that hadn't been mentioned in the article and couldn't be explained by her fall.

Diana had a linear red mark on her stomach as well as a bruise on her forearm. Holly studied the postmortem photo of Diana's arm lying atop the metal autopsy table. The bruise was oval shaped, the size of a large finger or thumb. Holly flipped to the examiner's report of the injuries on the next page.

The bruising on the right forearm appears consistent with an injury sustained approximately 48 hours prior to death, aligning with the husband's statement that he grabbed her arm to prevent her from drunkenly falling over their indoor stairwell railing two days prior to her fatal fall.

Holly popped a stick of gum into her mouth as she contemplated the examiner's words. Next, she turned to the toxicology report. Her jaw fell open, causing her gum to almost fall onto the page before Holly clamped her mouth shut. Diana's blood alcohol level was 0.05 the night of her death. That was hardly the picture Clint had painted of Diana getting drunkenly depressed and jumping off the balcony. She'd been under the legal driving limit and likely had only one drink.

Holly flipped to the detective's summary report, which was less than a page. Some tension eased from her shoulders as she read through the report, relieved to see the detective had, at least, interviewed all the neighbors and consulted a handwriting expert to compare Diana's handwriting to the suicide note found at her home. A paper fell to the floor. Holly picked it up, her pulse spiking when she saw it was a photocopy of Diana's handwritten suicide note.

Clint,

I can't keep going like this. It's too much. I need to be free of it, of you, and of everything. By the time you read this, ~~*We'll*~~ *I'll be gone. Goodbye forever.*

D

The investigator had added a postscript at the bottom of the report that theorized that Diana had likely planned to kill her son, then herself, but had changed her mind and altered the note.

Holly couldn't believe it. It was plain as day. Clint had to have altered the note, not Diana.

Diana hadn't planned on killing herself. She was leaving Clint—and taking their son with her.

Holly rifled through the pages to study the markings on Diana's stomach from her autopsy photos. Seeing the linear red marking, Holly drew in a sharp breath, nearly inhaling her gum.

Diana hadn't jumped from that balcony. She'd been pushed.

CHAPTER THIRTY-SEVEN

JOHN

BEHIND THE WHEEL of his dad's Ford Fairmont, John dug a hand into the nearly empty bag of ruffled potato chips as he sat across the street from the house he'd been watching for the last hour. He'd seen movement more than once inside the front window, so he knew someone was home.

There were no cars in the driveway, which meant one had to be parked in the garage. A few stray puddles on the street reflected the overcast sky, hinting at more rain on the way. John finished what was left in his can of Coke, wishing he'd thought to bring a book. Although, it was probably better that he hadn't. He needed to stay focused.

He popped another chip into his mouth, glancing at the handwritten, anonymous message lying on the passenger seat. He'd written the note before leaving school, then ripped it from his spiral notebook. He tapped his foot, ignoring the growing pang in his bladder from drinking two Cokes since he'd gotten there. If nothing happened in the next hour, he'd have to leave to find the closest public bathroom.

John reached into the bottom of the bag and stuffed a handful of broken chips into his mouth. A few fell onto his sweatpants, and he looked down to pick them off. Movement caught his eye out the passenger window. He lifted his head to see a petite, older woman being dragged down the sidewalk by a large dalmatian on a taut leash. John sighed, getting beyond bored.

He dropped his gaze to his backpack on the floor of the passenger seat. He didn't even have any homework. All his teachers were too distraught over the news that spread around school that afternoon to divvy out any assignments.

John reclined against the headrest. He checked his watch. If they didn't go out soon, he'd have to leave his note on the front doorstep after dark, which would be a few hours from now.

The groan of a garage door opening across the street drew John's gaze. A gray sedan with two men in the front backed out of the driveway. They had to be Tommy Reed and Holly's ex-fiancé.

After overhearing Laurie tell his dad that Holly's ex-fiancé was staying with Tommy Reed, an ex-drug informant living in Federal Way, John had looked him up in the White Pages. Fortunately, there was only one Thomas Reed listed. John twisted the key in the ignition and followed them out of the suburban neighborhood, making sure to stay at a safe distance.

After fifteen minutes, the sedan turned into a DMV. John followed and parked in the rear corner of the parking lot. Craning his neck to watch the two men get out of the car, John instantly recognized ex-detective Jared Peretti. He'd gained some weight during his time in prison and looked even more muscular than when he'd shouted in John's face after locking his dad out of the interview room. The afternoon light caught a speckle of gray in his jet-black hair.

John waited for the two of them to go inside the building before snatching his note and striding across the parking lot. John pulled his hood over his head and folded the notepaper in half as he walked. When he reached Jared's ride, John tucked the note beneath the windshield wiper of the passenger side. He glanced at the patchy sky. There shouldn't be any rain before they came out.

John strode back to his car with a spring in his step. Soon, his problems—and his father's—would be over.

CHAPTER THIRTY-EIGHT

HOLLY

Holly clenched the wheel, her knuckles pale, as she drove away from the Tacoma Police Department, heading for King County Major Crimes. Amanda had already left when Holly had emerged from the basement, but she'd left a note on Amanda's desk asking her to call when she could. In the meantime, Andy needed to know what she'd discovered. He and Jared had suspected Clint enough in '85 to question him about Sally Hickman's murder and the other presumed Green River Killer victims. Andy would have more clout than she would getting Tacoma PD to reopen Diana's case.

She lowered her visor to block the sun gleaming through the windshield. She also needed to know what Andy found at Jared's storage unit. She passed a payphone on her right, its metal frame glinting from the afternoon sun beneath a towering billboard. Patrick Swayze encircled Demi Moore with his bare arms, their figures awash in a soft, ethereal glow. *Ghost—COMING THIS SUMMER.*

Holly stomped on her brakes and turned into the RadioShack

parking lot, coming to a stop in front of the payphone. She stepped inside the booth and inserted a quarter she found in Laurie's center console before dialing Andy's office. She didn't want to make the nearly hour-long drive to the Major Crimes Unit only to learn Andy was out searching Jared's storage unit.

Andy's phone rang four times before going to his answering machine. Holly's pulse spiked as she hung up. *Maybe Andy is arresting Jared right now.* Holly walked back to the station wagon and dug another quarter out of the center console to call the main line for Major Crimes. Tara answered on the second ring.

"King County Major Crimes, how may I direct your call?"

"Hi, Tara. This is Holly Sparks. I tried calling Andy just now, but he didn't answer. Do you by chance know where he is?"

"Oh, hi, Holly." The receptionist's voice lifted. "How are you?"

Holly tapped her fingers on the payphone glass. "I'm good. Do you know where Detective Harris is?"

"Oh, yes. He got called to a crime scene early this morning. He hasn't come back to the unit yet."

Holly's shoulders sagged. That would mean Andy probably hadn't gone to Jared's storage unit yet.

"How's your new book coming?"

"What?"

"The new book you're writing, aren't you working on—"

"Oh. Right." *The book I'm supposed to send out in less than a week.* "It's great," she lied. "Could you ask him to call me when he gets back?"

"Sure. I just started reading *The Last Broadcast* yesterday. It's so good! It kept me up until nearly two in the morning."

"Thanks, Tara. Talk to you later." Holly hung up before Tara could keep her on the line any longer.

She walked back to the car in a daze. She pulled out onto the road, wishing she would've asked Tara for more details on the crime scene Andy had gotten called to. Major Crimes handled a variety of things, including robberies, homicides, and severe assaults. But it could be something to do with the Green River Task Force. Andy could be tied up for several hours or a couple of weeks, depending on what it was.

A few miles up the road, she passed a self-storage facility, its chain-link fence topped with razor wire, the sign out front promising *Safe, Secure Storage—Month-to-Month Rentals*. She recalled Jared's storage unit address she'd seen on Andy's desk: Mike's Storage Units in Federal Way. She'd driven past it before and knew where it was.

Holly thought of Jared's car sitting in that storage unit. Then of Clint getting away with Diana's murder for all these years. What if Jared got his car fixed before Andy got to it?

She made a U-turn. A honk blared as she changed directions in an intersection. She held up a hand in apology as she sped toward Federal Way. She glanced at the dash. If the storage facility was where she remembered it being, she'd be there in twenty minutes.

❧

Holly drove past unit #41 before parking by the front office of Mike's Storage Units. There were no police vehicles in sight. Holly strode toward the office, making up a story in her head as she took in the building's faded exterior. A bell chimed when she opened the door.

She assessed the older man behind the desk, who looked up from his book when she stepped inside. A mist of musty carpet and stale coffee lingered in the air.

"Can I help you?" The man lowered his book.

When Holly got closer, she saw it was her second true crime novel, *Behind Closed Doors*. She prayed he wouldn't recognize her from her photo on the back and that he hadn't yet read her author's note, telling of her abusive ex-fiancé. If he had, he might not believe the story she was about to give him.

"Um. Hi. Yes. My boyfriend and I have been sharing unit #41, but it's just in his name. Anyway." She blinked as if she were fighting back tears. "We broke up, and he um." She cleared her throat. "He took my key and said I couldn't have it back."

Holly's gaze traveled to a framed photo on the desk of the man and a much younger woman, probably his daughter. They stood in front of a waterfall, both wearing hiking gear. Holly bit her lip and met the man's gaze. "My dad's ashes are inside that storage unit. When I asked my ex to let me have them, he told me *tough shit*." Holly blew a breath out of her mouth and looked up at the stained ceiling.

When she lowered her gaze, the man's eyes widened with concern. He closed his book on the counter without saving his place.

"We were really close, my dad and I," she continued. "And I promised him I would spread his ashes on Mount Rainier—on our favorite hiking trail." She pinched the bridge of her nose. "But now…I'm afraid my ex will just dump him in the trash or something." She met the man's concerned gaze. "I know it's probably no use, but is there any way you could, you know, open it for me?"

He hesitated, seeming to think it over. Holly bit her lip. Maybe she hadn't acted as well as she'd thought.

He opened a binder. "You said it was unit #41?"

"Yes." Her pulse spiked. "That's right."

"Can you confirm your boyfriend, sorry, ex-boyfriend's name that the unit is under?"

"Jared. Jared Peretti."

"My Julie dated an asshole like that once." The man shook his head. "But you're right. It looks like the storage unit is solely in his name. Unfortunately, I can't give you access to the unit without his permission."

The air deflated from her lungs.

"Sorry," he added, seeming to read the disappointment on her face. "I wish I could be more helpful, but I can't violate our security policy. If you can convince your ex to come in and give me permission, I'd be happy to let you in another time."

"That will never happen." She sighed in a final attempt to invoke his sympathy enough to break the rules.

"Again, I'm sorry I couldn't be more helpful."

Holly made no effort to hide her frustration. "Thanks anyway," she said as an idea formed in her mind.

Twenty minutes later, Holly snipped the padlock to unit #41 with a pair of bolt cutters she'd purchased at a nearby Ace Hardware. She'd driven quickly past the storage facility's front office when she returned from the hardware store, hoping the manager didn't recognize her car.

Snapping the lock had been easier than she'd expected. She glanced over her shoulder before lifting the handle of the roll-up door, holding the bolt cutters in one hand. She'd parked behind a different row of units in case the manager came looking for her car.

Seeing Jared's black sedan, she sucked in a breath and moved around to the passenger side.

Spotting the damage to the front bumper, the missing rearview mirror, and the dents and scratches along the passenger side door, she covered her mouth with her hand. Even though she'd expected it, seeing the damage still sent a ripple of shock through her.

Her chest tightened as she stared at the banged-up car door. *He'd tried to kill me. Again.* And he'd almost succeeded.

The rumble of a car's engine pulling into the storage facility's entrance tore her from her thoughts. She cocked her head toward the sound. The engine noise grew louder as if it were about to turn down her row. She swore before pulling the unit's door closed.

Standing still in the dark storage unit, she held her breath and willed the car to keep going as the hum of the engine grew closer. The motor stopped right outside. A deep thud pulsed through her ribs, tension building inside her.

What if it's Andy? she thought. *How am I going to explain my being here?* Outside, a car door opened and shut.

"What's the matter?" asked a male voice that she didn't recognize.

"The lock's been cut. Harris must've found it."

A cold knot formed in Holly's gut. It wasn't Andy. It was Jared. She looked around for a place to hide, but there was less than a foot of room between the car and the walls.

"Shit."

The door lifted. For lack of a better option, Holly dropped to the concrete floor and slid beneath the car. Daylight flooded the small space, and she spotted what must have been Jared's Reeboks stepping toward the car. Dust rose off the floor, giving her the urge to sneeze. Holly covered her mouth and nose with her hand.

"Sonofabitch. I should've gotten it fixed," Jared said. "If anyone asks, my car was damaged already. I'll say it happened before I went to prison. There's no way in hell Harris should've been able to get a search warrant after the alibi we gave them. Harris can't prove my car got this damage the night she went over the bridge, especially if she's not around to testify."

Holly's heart thudded against the floor as Jared's shoes passed by her head. He must know from the news that she survived going over the bridge. Was he plotting to finish what he started?

"Let's get out of here," the other man said. "The cops could be watching this place."

Holly stared at the other man's faded Nikes. He had to be Tommy Reed, the ex-informant Jared was staying with.

"Hang on." Jared's feet moved to the back of the storage unit. "I still need my gun."

He's planning to shoot me, she thought as her sneeze threatened to erupt. She pinched her nose. Behind the car, she heard Jared rifle through a box. The tension in her upper body relaxed slightly as the urge to sneeze dissipated.

"Found it," Jared said.

Holly remembered Jared had a personal revolver, aside from his duty weapon, when they were engaged. His parents had given it to him after he graduated from the police academy.

Holly's gaze followed Jared's feet as he moved toward the front of the car. "I'm going to need some ammo."

Holly's breath caught in her throat as she imagined Jared standing over her bed in the middle of the night, emptying every round from his revolver into her chest.

"Let's go back to the office and buy another lock before we get ripped off," he said before closing the storage unit door.

Holly lay still beneath the car, engulfed in darkness. After hearing the car pull away, she waited a few minutes before crawling out from beneath Jared's sedan. She lifted the door slowly, making sure Jared wasn't already on his way back from the front office with a new lock. The row was empty.

She ducked out of the unit, closing the door behind her before jogging toward her car in the row of units behind this one. Andy might already be on his way. But if he wasn't, he needed to know what she'd found, even though he'd be furious to find out she'd come to Jared's storage unit.

She had to get Andy to arrest Jared before Jared figured out where she was staying—before he could strike for the third time.

CHAPTER THIRTY-NINE

HOLLY

Holly's mind spun the entire drive back from Mike's Storage Units, the suspicion that Clint had murdered his wife pushed aside by the lingering terror of nearly being caught by Jared snooping inside his unit. If Jared *had* been the one stalking her that night at Albertson's, had he then picked up that woman and killed her? *And how many others?* She closed her eyes, envisioning the countless names that covered her upstairs wall. Is *he the Bus Stop Killer?*

When she got home, Holly's answering machine light flashed. She'd deleted the two messages Andy had left her yesterday while she'd been at the library, so this had to be new. Holly pressed play, and a computerized female voice came through the speaker.

"You have one new message from today at 4:16 p.m."

That was less than an hour ago. Hopefully, it was Andy saying he was on his way to the storage unit with a search warrant.

"Hey, Hol. It's Laurie. Just wanted to check in and make sure you're doing okay. You're probably upstairs writing, ignoring my call. Anyway, call me back when you can and let me know you're all right."

Holly lifted the phone off the hook and dialed Andy. Once again, it went to his answering machine. Holly hung up and dialed the main number for Major Crimes.

"King County Major Crimes. How may I direct your call?"

"Hey, Tara. It's Holly again. Has Andy come back from that crime scene yet? I really need to speak with him."

"He did, but I'm afraid he just left. He was in a hurry to go conduct a search of some storage unit in Federal Way."

Holly's grip on the receiver loosened. *Thank God.* Andy will have a warrant out for Jared's arrest as soon as he discovers the damage to Jared's car.

"Did you want me to tell him anything when he gets back?" Tara asked.

"No, that's okay. Thanks." Holly was about to hang up but stopped short. Ever since leaving the storage unit, she couldn't get the image of Jared as the Bus Stop Killer out of her mind. "Tara? Do you know what the crime scene was that Andy got called to this morning?"

"Well…" Tara's breath blew into the line as if she'd pushed the mouthpiece closer to her lips. "I'm not sure if I'm supposed to say this, but I'm sure Detective Harris wouldn't mind me telling you. Female remains were discovered last night along Highway 410. They haven't identified her, but it might be another Green River Killer victim."

Holly stiffened, picturing Jared picking up the woman who'd gone missing from Albertson's after he'd stalked Holly to her car. "Do you know about how long ago she was killed?"

"I'm sorry, I don't."

After hanging up, questions whirled in Holly's head like a tornado. She marched to the living room and flicked on the wood-grained TV. A rabbit ear antenna sat on top. She hoped it got enough of a signal for the local news stations. She flipped through the channels until she found one. An auburn-haired reporter sat behind a news desk wearing a somber expression.

BREAKING NEWS ran across the bottom of the screen in bold red letters.

"We come to you with breaking news this six o'clock hour."

Holly folded her arms. *Jared, what have you done?*

"Family and friends of Rebecca Lopez, reported missing last week after disappearing after leaving a Tacoma Albertson's, are celebrating her safe return home this afternoon." A smiling photo of the young woman appeared in the corner of the screen. "The hairdresser apologized for skipping town without telling friends or relatives where she was going. Ms. Lopez stated she accepted a ride from a stranger, then took a ferry to stay with a friend on Whidbey Island. Ms. Lopez's parents released a statement that they are relieved and happy to know their daughter is safe and sound."

Holly sank onto the couch, staring at Rebecca Lopez's photo on the TV. Jared *hadn't* picked her up. Hadn't killed her. She'd been jumping to conclusions. She rubbed her temples. Maybe Jared's most recent attempt on her life was messing with her head. Making her see patterns that weren't really there.

She thought about her visit to the Tacoma Police Department earlier today. Was she also wrong about Clint killing his wife? Seeing a murder when there wasn't one? Laurie's words came back to her again.

Not everything is a mystery to be solved.

"While that news brings a sigh of relief, we now turn to a far more somber development. We've just learned that a young English teacher at a Tacoma high school has been found strangled to death in her home. Police believe Bethany Valdez was killed in the late hours of last night." The reporter tilted her head toward the camera as a pretty brunette's headshot appeared beside the newscaster on the screen.

Holly's heart dropped into her stomach. It was the woman she'd seen leaving Clint's house. She could hardly believe her eyes. Clint had been seeing John's English teacher, and now she was dead.

"The Tacoma police department has not shared any details related to a suspect in her killing, however, we are told there were no apparent signs of a break in at the teacher's home, which may suggest she knew her killer, who is still at large. Detectives are asking that anyone with information related to her death to please contact the Tacoma Homicide Unit."

The newscaster's words rang in Holly's ears. *Which may suggest she knew her killer.*

She should call Amanda at Tacoma Homicide, tell her about seeing the teacher leaving Clint's house the other morning. She recalled Amanda's pager going off earlier. It could even be Amanda's case.

But from what she'd learned today, Clint had likely already gotten away with one murder. Hell, he'd even passed a polygraph after Jared had brought him in as a Green River Killer suspect. Her mouth went dry. Could he be the notoriously prolific serial killer who'd evaded police all these years?

Once the police knocked on his door, Clint's guard would go up. Dating his son's teacher wasn't a crime, but maybe Holly could get him to admit something before Clint knew anyone suspected him—especially if he had a couple of drinks in his system. Holly stood from the couch.

Andy was handling Jared, at least for now. But she wasn't going to just sit around in the meantime. Holly lifted her fingers to her neck, remembering the ironclad grip of Jared's hands around her throat as if it were yesterday. How helpless she'd felt. How damn tired she was of men like this frightening her. She reached the base of the stairs and looked toward Clint's house.

After changing into jeans and a sweater, Holly quickly applied some makeup. She fluffed her bob with a comb while bending over to let her hair get some volume. When she stood, she hair-sprayed it into place.

When Holly returned downstairs, she gazed out the window at Clint's house again. Daylight was starting to fade. She grabbed the opened bottle of wine that Clint had brought over the other night and headed for the door.

She might not be able to prove anything by going over to Clint's, but she owed it to Diana, to Meg, and to all the others to at least try.

CHAPTER FORTY

HOLLY

"Holly, hi." Clint ran a hand through his thick brown hair.

If her neighbor was unhappy at her presence on his doorstep, he didn't show it.

"I got a piece of your mail yesterday by mistake." Holly extended the envelope toward him.

"Thanks." He glanced at it before letting it drop to his side.

"Also…" Holly smiled, lifting the bottle of red wine by the neck. "I didn't feel like finishing this alone. Want to join me?"

His expression relaxed. "Sure. Come on in." He stepped aside, opening the door wide. "I'll get us some glasses."

As she followed Clint through the main level to the kitchen, Holly took in the spotless house. Not what she had expected for a single father and teenage son. The kitchen was just as immaculate as the rest of the home.

Clint dropped the envelope on the otherwise empty kitchen island. Holly set the wine bottle beside it as Clint retrieved two stemmed glasses from a cupboard.

"Is John home?" Holly glanced at the ceiling.

"He's at baseball practice." Clint emptied what was left in the bottle between the two glasses.

Good, she thought. She needed Clint to feel free to talk, relax, and to have his full attention. Holly lifted her glass and found herself staring at the concrete patio beyond the sliding door. She resisted the shiver that ran through her as she pictured Diana's body lying there after Clint pushed her off the balcony.

"You want to sit on the couch?" He gestured to the room behind her.

She tore her gaze from the slider. "That sounds great."

Clint wore a plaid button-down shirt, similar to what he'd worn every time she'd seen him. His hazel eyes softened as they locked with hers. "Look, I'm sorry for walking out on you the other night."

Holly shook her head. "Don't be. It's my fault. I shouldn't have been discussing your wife's death with Laurie. It's none of my business."

Clint took a drink from his wine. "I overreacted. I guess it's still a touchy subject for me even all these years later."

Holly studied him as he took another drink. *He's a good actor.* She took a small sip from her own. While they were on the subject, she needed to keep him talking.

"Is it hard for you to live here after what happened?"

She half-expected him to bristle at the question, but instead, he seemed to ponder it.

"Surprisingly, no. Most of the time, the house reminds me of the good times with Diana. Makes me feel close to her. I don't think I'll ever leave. It's comforting, the memories I have with her here."

"It must've been such a shock when she died," Holly said, hoping to keep him on the subject.

He nodded. "She wasn't herself that night." He lowered his

gaze to his wine. "I hate myself for going to sleep, knowing she was down here drinking, and how alcohol affected her." He ran a finger along the rim. "It was January, and she always got a little glum in the winter. After she had John, the blues turned into something worse. I should've gotten her help."

Holly placed a hand on his knee. "It's not your fault," she lied.

"John doesn't know this—" Clint lifted his eyes toward a framed photograph above the fireplace mantel.

Holly followed his gaze to a photo of him and John, both dressed in camo, posing on either side of a large deer, each holding up its head by the antlers. Beside it, she realized, was a photo of Clint, Diana, and John when John looked to be about four.

"But in Diana's suicide note," Clint continued, "she mentioned taking John with her. I think she'd gone a little crazy and was contemplating killing him so they wouldn't be apart." He sighed, nearly finishing what was left in his glass. "It still shakes me up just thinking about it."

No, she wasn't. Diana was planning to leave you and take John with her, away from his murderous father. "Wow, that's awful." Holly feigned shock, putting a hand on her heart. This man was an expert at covering his tracks.

Clint slung his arm around the back of Holly's shoulders. Her heart thumped against her chest, imagining him strangling John's teacher the night before.

"Is this okay?"

He must've noticed her body tense.

Holly forced a smile. "It's more than okay."

"I'm out of practice being with a woman."

Liar. Holly took another sip. She searched Clint's eyes, debating how she could bring up the teacher without giving away her suspicion. She wondered if he knew her death was all over the news. She tried to relax against his arm, deciding to wait until he'd had more to drink.

Clint tilted his empty glass toward hers, still half full of what he'd poured her. "You want more wine?"

"That would be great." Holly took another drink.

"I'll open another bottle."

Clint stood and retreated to the kitchen, leaving Holly alone in the living room. She glanced over her shoulder before getting up to take a closer look at the photo on the mantel.

The photo looked to have been taken in front of their house. At the sight of Clint's late wife, her breath stuck in her lungs. She stood beside Clint, her mouth half open in laughter looking at her young son held in Clint's arms. She was beautiful, her blue eyes bright with happiness.

She doesn't look depressed.

Holly stared at the photo a moment longer, when two things suddenly made her blood run cold.

CHAPTER FORTY-ONE

HOLLY

HOLLY PLUCKED THE photo off the mantel.

"I hope you like Merlot. It was all I could find."

She whipped around at the sound of Clint's voice, sloshing what was left of her wine onto her white sweater.

"You okay?" His eyes darkened, seeing the framed photograph in her hand.

"Fine, sorry." She replaced the photo on the mantel, praying he didn't see her hand tremble. "You startled me. I didn't hear you come back from the kitchen."

Holly wanted to scream from what she'd seen in the photograph but tried not to let it show on her face. She cleared her throat, fighting to keep her composure.

"What year was that photo taken?" she managed to ask.

Clint glanced at the photo on the mantel. "About ten years ago."

That was around the same time Meg died.

His expression hardened when her eyes met his. She worked

to calm herself, knowing she had to regain her composure if she wanted to make it home to call Andy.

"You look like you've seen a ghost," he said, appearing to study her.

Time seemed to stand still as she stared into Clint's eyes. In 1980, Clint had brown hair, a young son, and wore a wedding band. He also had a mustache and drove a white pickup. *Lou.* He was the older guy Meg was seeing. He had to have been.

She smoothed a smile over the fear clawing at her chest. "A ghost? No, it's my sweater. It's brand new and it's um…cashmere." She dropped her head toward the large wine stain on the front. "Shit, it's probably ruined." She lifted her gaze. "Could I use your bathroom? I'll try to rinse it out before it sets in."

"Of course." Clint's voice was calm, but his eyes were cold.

Holly set the empty glass on the end table beside the couch, avoiding Clint's chilly stare.

He gestured toward a hallway with his hand. "It's down this hall, second door on your left."

"Thanks." Holly held her breath as she snaked past him, relieved he didn't reach out and grab her as she moved by. She exhaled and kept walking, a thousand thoughts accosting her mind all at once.

Had Clint killed Meg? Just like he killed Diana? And John's teacher?

John. She stopped in her tracks, praying Clint wasn't watching her. If what Meg's roommate had told Holly was true, that meant Clint was the father of Meg's child. Did that make John Meg's son? *No,* she thought. *John is fifteen. Meg's son is eleven.*

She looked at the two matching doors on her left, unable to remember which one Clint said was the bathroom. She darted her gaze toward the front door. *Maybe I should go home. Run out of here before Clint tries to kill me too.* But she had no evidence he killed Meg. What if Andy didn't believe her? Clint was clearly a master at getting away with murder.

No, she needed to stay. Keep him talking. This was her chance to see if she could get him to admit knowing her sister.

Holly opened the first door and felt inside for the light switch. She flicked it on. Instead of a bathroom, a plywood staircase lay before her, leading to what looked like an unfinished basement. She turned around, making sure Clint wasn't watching her, and crept down the steps.

CHAPTER FORTY-TWO

HOLLY

Holly closed the door behind her, hoping Clint would mistake it for the bathroom, and crept down the stairs. There was no railing, so she pressed a hand against a bare stud in the wall when she neared the bottom. Clint not only matched Callie's description of Meg's older boyfriend in 1979, but he also owned a blue Ford car, exactly what Meg and Sally Hickman were seen climbing inside before they died. Holly pictured the car she'd seen in Clint's garage the other day. It looked to be nearly ten years old. And John would've been the right age for the boy the prostitute reported seeing in the backseat. It had been why Jared had brought Clint in for questioning. And been so angry when they'd let him go.

And then there was Clint's wife, Diana. It was too much of a coincidence for Clint not to have killed them all.

Holly looked around the unfinished basement. There was just enough light streaming through the small windows that faced the backyard for her to make out a large open space. There was no dry wall on the walls, only exposed studs and insulation.

Footsteps sounded on the floor above, and she lifted her head toward the sound. *I should go back upstairs before Clint catches me down here, snooping around.*

She stood still. What if he'd already discovered she wasn't in the bathroom? She turned for the stairs. *I should never have come down here. What am I going to say to Clint if he discovers I'm not in the bathroom?*

She'd have to tell him she thought he'd said the bathroom was downstairs—and pray he'd buy it.

She cursed herself for being so stupid. She should've gone straight home and called Andy. *What was I expecting to find down here anyway? A body?*

She passed a doorway on her right. It was the first room she'd seen off of the large open area. She paused and listened for a moment. The footsteps upstairs had stopped.

She peered through the doorway, seeing the studs on the far wall were covered with paper. She stepped inside to get a closer look. When she reached the middle of the room, a yarn hanging from above slapped her cheek. She yanked on it, illuminating a bare lightbulb in the ceiling. Looking at the far wall, she gasped.

Two newspaper articles stood out. The first was from the *Fairbanks Examiner* printed in May 1985. *HORROR ON THE HIGHWAY: Body of Young Fairbanks Woman Found Near Lonely Stretch of Road.* Beneath the headline was a faded photograph of a squad car beside a snow-covered ditch.

When Holly saw the article beside it, her breath caught in her throat. It was an article about Diana's suicide.

Her gaze dropped to the page stuck to the wall beneath the article. It looked to have been ripped from a high school yearbook with rows of teachers' headshots filling the page. One had an X in red marker over her face. Holly swallowed. *John's English teacher.*

Just as she'd thought, Clint had killed her too. Acid burned the back of her throat as the wine threatened to come back up. She forced it back down and glanced at the ceiling. Her pulse pounded in her temples so loudly that it nearly drowned out the thoughts that swarmed and buzzed like a disturbed hive.

Holly turned to the wall beside it. There were more newspaper clippings, just like the wall in her home office. In fact, she'd hung up some of these at home. She scanned the familiar articles covering the murders of Sally Hickman, Jennifer Duran, and Brooke Holtman. All three believed to be Green River Killer Victims.

Holly inched closer, feeling as though she were moving outside of her own body. She froze, seeing the same headline she'd been staring at for the last ten years beneath the three articles. *STRIPPER FOUND DEAD.* She covered her mouth with her hand. Just as she'd thought—*Clint killed Meg.* He was the Bus Stop Killer, not Jared. The one she'd been hunting for all these years. Her lungs locked. The room twisted. The world tilted beneath her feet.

She placed her hands on her knees. *Just breathe.* She stepped back to take in both walls at once, wishing she had a camera. She had to stay calm. Go upstairs. Tell Clint she wasn't feeling well and get the hell out of here so she could tell Andy what she'd found.

She spun around and reached for the string to turn off the light. Before her hand could grasp the yarn, she registered a figure standing in the doorway.

CHAPTER FORTY-THREE

HOLLY

"Hey. Sorry, I didn't mean to scare you."

Her pulse slowed, the fear loosening its grip. He held a baseball bat, which meant he must've just gotten home from practice.

"John." She kept her voice low. "We need to get out of here, you and me."

"What?" He stepped into the room. "Why?"

Holly pointed to the wall behind her, debating how much she should tell him. She moved closer to him as he took in the wall. She studied John's face as it struck her that if Clint was the father of Meg's baby, then John was the half-brother of Meg's son. But there was no time to think about that now. She lowered her voice to a whisper. "I think your dad may have killed these women."

John tore his gaze from the wall covered with an article about his mom's suicide and his English teacher's X'd-out photo. He scoffed. "My dad didn't kill them."

Footsteps creaked atop the ceiling above their heads.

Frustrated, Holly grabbed John by the shoulders, tilting her head to lock eyes with him. She was about to tell him that yes, his father did kill them, but she could see in his eyes that he would never believe her. It was a mistake to think she could convince John of who his father really was. Now, she needed to get out of this house while she still had the chance.

John pointed to the wall beside them. "But he did kill *those* women."

Holly followed the direction of his finger to the wall containing Meg's article and the three presumed Green River Killer victims, then looked to the other wall.

"What?"

John *knew*? Then she remembered the boy in the backseat of the car that picked up Sally Hickman.

Clint had to be lying to John about the others, not wanting him to know he'd killed John's mother. *But how could John be okay with his father killing* any *of them?* She turned to face the tall teenager, her rage at his father fueled not only by discovering he'd killed Meg, but how he'd manipulated his son into keeping this dark secret. The poor kid.

"You don't need to protect your father, John. He should've been the one protecting *you.*"

The door to the basement opened with a *creak.* "John? Is that you down there?" Clint's voice called out.

Holly grabbed John's arm. "Is there a door to outside from down here?"

"Yeah." John pivoted and pointed out the room and to the left. "It's through there."

"John, your father killed all those women. Even your mother." Holly glanced toward the stairwell. "We need to leave. Right now. Come on."

John shook his head. "No. I'm not going anywhere."

"But—" She registered something in the teenage boy's eyes she hadn't seen before. Something dark and sinister. She released his arm and took a step back, recalling John's expression when he saw her office wall covered with details from unsolved murder victims—including Meg. *He'd known that his father had killed Meg when he came to my house.*

Clint's footsteps sounded down the stairs. Her gaze fell to the bat in John's hand. She'd already said far too much. *How far would he go to protect his father?*

Holly turned and rushed toward the doorway, not bothering to try to drag John with her. If she hurried, she could make it to the door leading outside before Clint could catch her. Then, if she could escape and call the police, they'd make sure John was placed in a safe home—away from his father.

Holly reached the doorway when from the corner of her eye she spotted the end of a baseball bat swinging toward her head at full force. A split second later, the impact turned the edges of her world into a black void as she fell to the floor.

A weightlessness came over her, like she was floating. Her vision cleared, and she spotted a woman lying on the basement floor, blood pooling around her head near the doorway. Holly reached out to help her, but her hand wouldn't respond to her command. She studied the woman's face. The woman on the floor was *her.* John squatted beside her unmoving body and pressed two fingers against her neck. Seemingly satisfied, he stood, keeping hold of the bloody bat.

Holly drifted higher, farther away, as the world below began to blur. Clint, John, and her lifeless form faded to nothing before being replaced by a blinding light. Meg emerged from the glow, still looking eighteen, wearing a white dress as she strode toward Holly. A brightness gleamed behind her as Meg outstretched her hand.

"Welcome home, sister."

Meg. Too overcome with emotion to speak, Holly felt herself smile as tears sprung to her eyes. Holly placed her hand in Meg's, wanting to ask her sister so many things, but still too overwhelmed to find her voice. Peace surged through Holly as her sister's arms wrapped around her. There was endless time ahead to ask Meg everything she wanted to know.

Finally, they were together again. Forever. Where no one could ever hurt them or tear them apart.

CHAPTER FORTY-FOUR

JOHN

John lowered the bat, assessing Holly's chest for movement as she lay limp at his feet. Blood pooled from the back of her head onto the concrete floor. He crouched over her, placing two fingers against her neck as his father's footsteps tromped down the stairs.

No pulse. He stood, relieved. He didn't want to have to strike her again with the bat. After Laurie had told him and his father about the crime writer who'd be moving in next door to hide from her abusive ex, John had hoped creeping up on her in the Alberton's parking lot would be enough to scare her away. Unfortunately, it had to come to this.

"What the hell did you do?" he heard his father shout from less than a few feet away.

John spun around.

His dad gaped at Holly's body.

"I didn't have a choice," John said.

His dad put both hands on his head as he shifted his wide-eyed gaze from Holly's body to John to the wall behind him. His jaw fell open. "And what the hell is this?"

John pivoted toward the walls. "Oh. I just like to come down and look at these sometimes. I had them in a box under my bed, but after seeing Holly's wall next door, I wanted a place where I could have them all displayed." *And with Holly moving in next door, I thought it might be safer to get them out of my room. That way, if Holly or the police ever found them, they would blame you, not me.* But John kept that part to himself.

John smiled, looking between the two walls: one with articles from his father's kills and the other from his own. "I'm catching up to you."

"Do you realize what you've done?" He grabbed John by his T-shirt, baring his gritted teeth, and shoved John against the wall. "Have I taught you nothing? How do you expect to get away with this? *Her murder will lead the cops right to our door!*"

John winced, feeling a nail head poke against his spine. "You've never fully let me in. Ever since we came back from that trip to Alaska, you've been distant. Hell, I don't even know if you've killed anyone since then!" John threw up the arm not holding the bat.

"Watch your language," his dad said.

"It feels like you don't think you can trust me. And I'm your *son.*" John let his arm fall to his side. "You haven't even taken me hunting in the last few years."

His father shook his head. "I've failed you as a father. I shouldn't have let you become like me. I wanted more for you."

John gripped the bat in his hand. "But I *am* like you. I'm your son. This is who I am. Who *we* are."

Clint stared down at Holly's body. "And look at what you've done now!" He looked up to meet his son's gaze, his expression more helpless than John had ever seen it. "How did you kill that woman in Fairbanks? You were only a child."

John grinned. "I've been waiting five years for you to ask me that."

CHAPTER FORTY-FIVE

JOHN

Fairbanks, Alaska
May 1985

"What's the matter?"

The woman spun, her hand over her heart atop her wool coat. "Oh," she said, seeing John. A puff of white breath escaped her mouth beneath the dim lights from the bar. "You scared me." She scanned the empty bar parking lot that surrounded them. "What are you doing out here all alone? Are you lost?"

John shook his head. "I'm staying at the motel across the street." He'd been lying awake, unable to go back to sleep after his father had crept into their room. "I heard a car door slam outside and looked out the window. I saw you lifting the hood of your car. You looked like you might need help."

"Well, I do." She dropped her arm to her side and glanced at the engine. "My battery is dead. I got a jump before coming to work, but I should've known it wouldn't start again in this freezing weather."

"Can you call someone?" John motioned toward the bar.

She chewed her lip, seeming to think it over before shaking her head. "My boyfriend's at work." She sighed, looking at her car. "I didn't even bring any jumper cables with me." She turned to John, and her eyes lit up. "Do your parents by chance have any with them at the motel?"

"It's just my dad." John studied the woman, trying to repress the crazy impulse that jumped into his head. "He left me alone. Said he was going to the bar, but he never came back," he lied. John looked around the parking area, adding, "I think he went home with someone."

Her eyes widened as she flicked her gaze to the motel across the road. "You don't look old enough to be left alone all night." She turned to John. "What does he look like?"

"Brown hair. Tall. He was wearing a red plaid shirt and a brown leather jacket."

"Oh, yeah." She nodded. "I saw him leave with Vikki. She's known for turning tri—" Her voice faltered as she held his gaze, seeming to remember she was talking to a ten-year-old boy. "I mean…"

"Turning what?" John cocked his head.

"Nothing." She shrugged. "She just hangs out at the bar sometimes."

"Do you know where she lives?" John stuck his freezing hands into his coat pockets.

"Yeah." She pointed behind John. "Her place is on the other end of that long stretch of highway. But it's too far to walk. Especially in this weather."

John fixed his gaze on her chunky knitted scarf as she tightened it around her neck. "We can take my dad's car." John motioned over his shoulder. "You can drive. After we get to Vikki's house, my dad can take you home."

She blew out another white breath, seeming to debate the idea. John held his breath as his chest felt like it might burst with the surge of nervous excitement fluttering inside him.

"Okay," she said, closing her hood before following him across the road. "My name's Pamela, by the way. What's yours?"

"It's John."

Less than five minutes later, John climbed into the rental car behind Pamela at the motel. He'd nearly chickened out when he crept back inside their room to get the car keys, afraid his dad would wake up and ask him what he was doing. But his father was out cold, snoring even louder than when John had left.

When she started the engine, John's heart thumped in his chest. Would the noise wake his father? John looked back at their motel room as Pamela pulled onto the street, relieved to see the lights were still off.

A minute later, Pamela pulled onto the two-lane highway. John stared at the scarf around her neck, wondering what it would be like to grab the knitted fabric by both ends and pull so tight it squeezed Pamela's throat shut.

John's mind drifted to the bear falling to the snowy forest floor, dead from his father's bullet. John eyed the woman in front of him, bobbing her head to the Prince song playing on the radio, imagining he was the hunter and she was the prey. He leaned over toward the middle seat to peer out the windshield. They were driving down a long, straight stretch of highway with no other cars in sight.

As they sped along, a whirlwind of emotions surged through him at what he was about to do—thrill, anticipation, a strange sense of power. In this moment, he felt more alive than he ever had before. But beneath it all, coiled deep in his chest as Pamela sang along to "Raspberry Beret," was fear.

What if this went horribly wrong? John wasn't sure why, but when his dad shot that bear in the woods, something had changed in him. The power his dad possessed to take the life of such a beast. John needed to know what it felt like to put his prey in his sights, know exactly what he was doing, and pull the trigger. Like his dad did.

John fingered the end of Pamela's soft scarf that hung over the back of her seat as a spike of excitement flowed through him, as if he were about to ride his bike off a big jump.

"I think I'm going to puke," he blurted.

"Oh my gosh." Pamela turned down the radio. "Right now?" She glanced over her shoulder.

"Yeah." John covered his mouth with his hand and made himself gag.

"Let me pull over."

"Hurry," John said.

The car slowed as Pamela braked to a stop beside the short, dirty mound of snow that lined the highway. As soon as the car stopped moving, John grabbed the end of her scarf. The hard part would be grabbing hold of the other end, which was draped in front of her chest. He would have to be quick.

His heart pounded in his ears as she turned around. *Am I really going to do this?*

"Are you okay?" she asked. "Do you need to—"

John wrapped the scarf around his hand and tugged hard. At the same, he reached in front of her and slid his arm down her chest until he grasped the other end. He brought both hands behind the headrest and pulled.

"What are—" She choked out a cough.

John clenched his jaw and tugged harder. If she could still talk, the scarf wasn't tight enough. He pressed the soles of his shoes against her seat and pulled with all his might. Pamela's permed hair swayed wildly around her head as she thrashed in her seat. But she'd stopped talking, which was a sign it was working.

She gasped and wheezed for air before exuding a groan from deep in her chest. John held his breath, straining to keep a tight grip on the scarf as she clawed at the fabric. She leaned forward, but her attempt to pull away from him only helped to tighten his noose. Finally, her flailing slowed. John exhaled.

She twisted her head toward him and swatted her arm aimlessly behind her. She managed to grip the leg of his jeans for a moment before her hand went slack. John heard himself grunt as her head fell to the side. Thankfully, she'd stopped moving. He wasn't sure how much longer he could have maintained his grip.

He kept his feet on her seat and his hold on the scarf for another minute after she went still. When he let go, a bead of sweat dripped into his eye. He wiped the sweat away and studied the corpse in the driver's seat. He'd done it. Just like his dad.

CHAPTER FORTY-SIX

JOHN

JOHN LIFTED HIS gaze to the faded article on the wall from the *Fairbanks Examiner*. "The hardest part was dragging her body out of the car and into that snowy ditch. I couldn't get her as far from the road as I wanted, which was probably why they found her body so quickly."

"Why did you do it?" his dad asked.

"I wanted to know what it felt like to kill. I needed to understand why you did it. After I strangled that bartender with her scarf beside that ditch, I knew. Power. Control. Excitement. A rush. An unexplainable feeling of pure ecstasy. Like the world finally makes sense in that moment. And relax, I'm not going to get caught. I'm good at covering my tracks. Even better than you."

His dad sneered, releasing his hold on John.

"Better than me?" he yelled, his face red with fury. "You killed your fucking teacher! You can't do that. Not if you don't want to go to prison. This is exactly what I was afraid of. Have I taught you nothing?"

John reflected on the smooth feel of his teacher's neck beneath his hold late last night. He closed his eyes, reliving the moment. When his hands first clamped around her throat, she'd clawed at him, but not for long.

As the life drained from his teacher's body—that slut who preyed on underage boys—it was like her energy was being transferred to him. The weaker she became under his grip, the more he crushed her delicate neck, the stronger—and more powerful—he felt.

Feeling his teacher's neck collapse beneath his bare hands had given him a much bigger rush than when he'd strangled that bartender in Fairbanks with her own scarf.

"There's a link to you," his father continued. "I've been waiting all day for you to get home so that we can come up with a story together to make sure you aren't implicated, and now you do *this?*" He extended a hand behind him toward Holly's body.

The pool of blood around her head was growing, John noted. He met his father's eyes. "There was a link to Mom."

His dad's eyes narrowed. "That was different."

"How?" John asked.

"I told you never to talk about that." His dad's voice morphed into a growl.

"Why not?" John shouted. "Don't you think it's time?"

"No." His dad took a step back, nearly bumping into Holly's body with the back of his foot.

"Be careful," John said. "You almost got blood on your shoe."

His father jabbed a long finger into his own chest. "You really have the balls to tell me to be careful right now?" His dad pointed at the two walls. "When you keep this kind of shit?" He pointed to Holly. "And you killed our famous neighbor while she was *in our house?*"

His dad's chest heaved, spittle flying out of his mouth with an audible exhale. For a moment, John worried he might have a heart attack.

"We'll deal with the walls later." His dad lowered his gaze to the dead writer. "Right now, we need to figure out what to do with her body." His father turned and paced the small space, pinching the bridge of his nose.

John really hoped he would make sure not to step in Holly's blood.

"Shh." John moved toward the window and looked out.

"What are you doing?"

"Listen. Do you hear that?"

"Hear what?" His father stepped over Holly and came toward the window. "Stop screwing around, John. We need to get her body out of our house before anyone realizes something has happened—"

"Shh." John put a finger to his lips.

His dad grabbed the back of John's hair. "Don't *shh* me."

John cupped a hand over his dad's mouth. *"Listen."*

His father swatted his hand away, but a man's shout from next door carried through the window before his dad could protest again.

"Holly!" *Bang, bang, bang.*

John smiled. Jared Peretti must've gotten his note. He knew the ex-cop wouldn't be far behind him.

"I know you're in there, Holly!" *Bang, bang, bang.* "Let me in. I just want to talk." *Rap, rap, Rap.* "Holly. Come on."

"Holly!"

John turned to his dad. "I skipped practice and went to the place where Holly's abusive ex-fiancé is staying. Then I followed him and left a note on his car windshield with Holly's address."

The anger in his father's hard-set eyes faded to wide-eyed awe. Outside, an engine revved and tires squealed before a car sped out of their cul-de-sac.

"Holly keeps a baseball bat in her entryway," John said. "We'll take her body over there and make it look like that was the murder weapon. We'll say we saw him pulling on gloves and going around to the backside of her house. Then we heard a scream coming from inside her home before we saw her ex run out of her front door and peel out of the neighborhood. That's when I called the police, and you ran over to see what had happened. If we're lucky," John added, "that prick left his fingerprints on Holly's front doorknob."

His dad shook his head. "There could be other witnesses. We can't lie. What if the Wilsons saw him pound on her door for a few minutes and then leave?"

"The Wilsons are on vacation. So are the Aguilars. It's spring break, remember?"

His father stared out the window, appearing to mull over John's plan.

"We'll make it look like her ex-fiancé broke in from her back door. Then, that sonofabitch who tried to arrest you for Sally's murder will rot in prison for the rest of his life."

His father turned from the window and locked eyes with John. "Go upstairs to the garage. Get the blue tarp. Make sure it's not the gray one. We need it to be big."

John headed out of the room when his dad grabbed his arm. "Before we call 911, you have to get rid of all this souvenir shit on the walls. Burn it in the fireplace, understand?"

John nodded, glad his father had come to agree with his plan. "Blue tarp. Got it."

Then, for the first time since coming downstairs, his father smiled.

CHAPTER FORTY-SEVEN

JOHN

Flashing red and blue lights sliced through the dark cul-de-sac, flooding the quiet street with an eerie, rhythmic glare. From his front porch, John watched his father speak to a tall female detective in Holly's driveway. The first responders had arrived less than ten minutes after John's 911 call. Now, an array of emergency response vehicles was parked in front of Holly's house.

A uniformed officer secured the perimeter of Holly's driveway with yellow crime scene tape as a pair of medics emerged from her house and strode toward the ambulance parked on the street. Clearly, there was nothing they could do. John suppressed a grin, the wake of pride growing inside him. His plan had worked.

John studied his father, gesturing to their house and then Holly's as he spoke to the detective who'd arrived in an unmarked car about fifteen minutes after the first patrol car. She jotted something down in a small notebook before flipping it closed, then said something to his dad before turning for Holly's house.

His dad came back to their yard, looking calm but solemn

when he stepped beneath the glow of the front porch lights beside John. Together they looked on at the scene unfolding next door.

"The detective I spoke with wants to get your statement too before the night is over," his dad said. Lowering his voice, he asked, "Did you burn those articles?"

"Yes." It had pained him to do it, but John knew his father had been right. It was too risky to keep them. It had been childish of him to think he could openly display articles of their kills in their house.

Someday, he'd take his own photographs of his kills and hide them somewhere the police would never find them.

"Why'd you kill your teacher?" His father kept his voice barely above a whisper.

John shrugged. Did his dad really have to ask? "Because I'm just like you. You made me like this. Killing gives me a rush. A thrill. Makes me feel powerful, just like it does for you. And I'm good at it." He withheld the fact they were sleeping together, although he guessed his father already knew.

"Don't get cocky," his dad warned, keeping his gaze trained on the crime scene responders next door. "That's how you get caught."

The tall detective emerged from Holly's house and said something to the officer standing out front. He pointed at John and his dad on their porch. As the detective made her way toward their property line, John's dad put his arm around John.

"Remember to act the part. This was traumatic for you, son. Remember what you're going to say?"

"Of course. I came up with it." His dad should be thanking him, not coaching him. He hadn't seen Holly's wall like John had. At least not as closely. Having Holly next door was a ticking time bomb. It wouldn't have taken Holly long to start suspecting his dad. She'd already looked up his mother's death at the library.

John suppressed a shudder. His dad had no idea how close he'd come to getting caught.

As the detective crossed their front yard and started up the porch steps, John brought tears to his eyes, thinking about the part in *The Call of the Wild* when Buck stands by Thornton's grave, howling into the wilderness, forever loyal even in death. It got to him every time.

The auburn-haired detective extended a hand to John. "I'm Detective Amanda Corrado with Tacoma Homicide. I spoke with your father already."

John assessed her, noting that her eyes were red. Almost as if she'd been crying.

"Homicide?" John croaked, leaning against his father. "You mean she's—" His voice broke so convincingly that he wondered if he should enroll in drama. His father pulled his arm tighter around John's shoulders.

"I'm afraid so." Her mouth turned down into a grim frown. "Can you tell me what happened before you made the 911 call tonight?" She pulled out a small notebook from the inside pocket of her suit jacket.

His dad placed a palm on John's upper back. "You're doing great, son. I know this is hard."

John blew out a breath and let his gaze fall to the ground before meeting the detective's sharp green eyes. With a trembling voice, John told her how he and his dad had heard a man shouting before they looked out the window to see a muscular, dark-haired man in the glow of Holly's porch lights. He shouted Holly's name, saying "It's Jared," and banged on her door relentlessly, demanding she let him in so they could talk.

"When we came outside," John continued, "he was moving around the side of Holly's house. From the exterior lights, it looked like he was pulling on gloves as he walked. Then we heard glass breaking and Holly's scream a minute later. The man who called himself Jared came bolting out her front door and peeled out onto the street, not seeming to notice me and my dad standing outside."

The detective looked up from her notebook. "Did you see what kind of car he was driving?"

"It looked to be a dark sedan, but it was too dark for me to tell more than that."

"Could you see any damage to the passenger side of the vehicle?"

John shook his head. He couldn't say yes, because he hadn't seen what car Jared had been driving. But he knew from what Laurie had told his dad that Holly had been run off the bridge by a dark sedan, which was fortunately also what Jared's roommate drove. "It sped away in such a blur. And I was worried about what had happened to Holly…she seemed like such a nice lady. I mostly remember the taillights speeding away from our street."

The detective snapped her notebook shut. "Thank you. That's very helpful. I knew Holly, and you're right, she was a nice lady." She pulled a business card out of her pocket and handed it to his dad. "If either of you think of anything else, give me a call."

As she crossed their lawn to return to Holly's, his father led John toward the door of their house. "Come on, son. You don't need to see this," he said in a voice loud enough for the detective to hear.

A loud crackle emitted from the radio of the officer standing in Holly's driveway. "This is Officer Garza, and I have Jared Peretti in custody—he's got an active APB on him. I'm en route to book the suspect into Pierce County Jail."

"Hang on," John told his dad as another vehicle pulled to a stop in front of Holly's house.

A white-haired man in a suit jumped out of the unmarked

sedan and climbed over the crime scene tape before rushing up Holly's drive. John recognized him immediately. *Detective Harris.* He'd hardly changed in the last five years since John had sat across from him in that small interview room at the downtown courthouse.

The uniformed officer held up a hand and stepped in front of the detective. "This is an active crime scene. You can't—"

"Holly!" the detective yelled, pushing past the officer.

Detective Corrado met him on Holly's front porch and placed her hands on his shoulders. "I'm sorry, Andy." John heard her say.

"No, no, no!" Andy cried. He sank to his knees.

The two of them must've been close, seeing how distraught he was over her death.

It was a shame Holly had to die, John agreed, but it was a wonderful feeling knowing that asshole detective who'd tried to arrest his dad was going to spend the rest of his life behind bars paying for John's crime.

Served him right.

2013

Tanner folded a piece of gum into his mouth and lifted the small box with the AncestryDNA logo, debating whether or not he wanted to go through with it. He opened the box and pulled out the slim tube for his saliva sample and prepaid mailer to send it back for analysis. If he mailed it tomorrow, he could have a list of his biological relatives, maybe even his parents or a sibling, in six to eight weeks.

Having been adopted through a closed adoption in 1979, this was his best bet for tracking down his birth parents. He set down the box, wondering if they'd ever tried to find him. He doubted it. And if they hadn't wanted to know him, why should he bother?

There had to be a reason for the closed adoption. He liked to imagine his mother got pregnant young, a teenager even. And while she'd wanted to keep him, she'd been forced by her circumstances to give him up. Or maybe that wasn't the case at all. Maybe she'd wanted nothing to do with him.

The detective in him needed to know. But the part of him

that had been rejected by his birth parents wasn't sure that he wanted to. He left the opened box on the kitchen counter and went to change into running gear. He needed to clear his head. He'd make the decision when he got back from his run.

Moving through his sparsely furnished Seattle home, he passed a large window with a view of the Sound at the bottom of the hillside. Before he got to his room, his phone rang in his suit jacket pocket.

It was his homicide sergeant. He was next up for a homicide. He knew before taking the call there would be no run tonight. "Detective Mullholland."

"Mulholland, it's McKinnon. I just got a call from the chief dispatcher. There's been a homicide in Queen Anne. A twenty-eight-year-old female was found dead in her home. It appears to be a strangulation. I'll text you the address."

"Thanks." Tanner turned around. "I'm leaving now."

He ended the call and grabbed the DNA testing kit off the counter, tossing it into the trash on his way out the door. He needed to focus on this new case, not the past.

Some things were better left alone.

❧

"Good morning," John's receptionist greeted him from behind her desk outside his office.

He rested his briefcase on the corner of her desk. "Good morning, Bryn."

"Your coffee and this morning's paper are on your desk," she added, flipping her long, dark hair behind her shoulder.

"Thank you." John's gaze fell to Bryn's neck. He imagined his hands closing around it, then his late father's words echoed in his mind. *There's a link to you.* It had been over ten years since his dad had died of a heart attack, but John often reflected on all he'd taught him.

With age, John had grown to learn his father was right. He couldn't kill people he knew—not if he wanted to continue killing and stay out of prison for the rest of his life.

Inside his office, he spun in his chair to gaze at the twenty-story view of the Seattle waterfront beyond the large window behind his desk. His dad would've been proud of the life he'd built for himself. He didn't have to be a shrink to know that his reason for becoming a criminal defense attorney stemmed from his fear as a kid of his father going to prison. As it turned out, John not only loved his job, but he was also damn good at it.

Since his father's death, John often reflected on the sacrifices his dad had made to protect him, making sure they could continue living their life together—in freedom. He even sacrificed his killing. John had no plans to have children. Instead, he'd committed to carrying out his father's legacy, killing in a way his father couldn't.

He allowed himself to kill once a year. Every summer. He was surprised he'd felt the urge to strangle Bryn since he'd killed only two nights ago.

His thoughts turned to the paper lying on his desk. He couldn't wait to see what it said.

He'd made the front page, just as he'd hoped. He pulled his chair into his desk and unfolded the paper.

SECOND SEATTLE TEACHER STRANGLED IN HOME IN TWELVE MONTHS

A wave of satisfaction rolled through him as he read through the article.

Detectives fear there could be a serial murderer, The Teacher Killer, at large in Seattle.

John read on, wishing his father could see him now. He'd

be so proud. John sighed. He was the only person he could've shared this with.

A knock on his office door made John look up. The door swung open. Simon, his partner, poked his head through the doorway.

"We still on for our hunting trip this October?"

"I'm planning on it."

"Great. I'll book the lodge." Simon gestured to the paper on John's desk. "You read that article? Could be a serial killer. From the sounds of it, he's a smart one too." He cracked a grin. "If he gets caught, maybe we'll get to defend him. Could be great for the firm."

John sat back in the leather chair. He'd known Simon had a cunning, greedy side to him before they'd formed the law firm, which was exactly what John needed in a law partner. Simon was hungry for money, notoriety, and power—a weakness John could leverage if he ever needed to.

"Anyway," Simon added. "You all set for our court hearing at nine?"

John checked his Rolex. "Yep, I'll be ready."

"Great."

John waited for Simon to shut the door before returning his attention to the article. He enjoyed it—until he got to the end. It stated that Detective Tanner Mulholland was the lead investigator. John's leg jiggled beneath the desk. That was a worry. As a defense attorney, John had seen Mulholland in action both in the courtroom and out. He was the most relentless, dedicated, and sharp investigator John had ever encountered.

There was something about Mulholland's tenacity, and him always chewing gum, that reminded John of Holly Sparks. And he didn't like it.

The article concluded with a speculation about the profile

of the killer. *Criminal profilers believe the Teacher Killer is likely a single, professional male, aged thirty to fifty. There is a strong probability he has killed before.*

Surprisingly accurate, John thought. *Although that's not a lot to go on.*

John reflected on his first kill, although it was so wild and unplanned that he usually thought of the young woman in Fairbanks as the one who started it all. But if he were honest with himself, she wasn't.

When he'd gotten out of bed after hearing his parents arguing, he'd come into their bedroom and heard his mother shout from their balcony that she was leaving his dad and taking John with her. His father told her there was no way he would let that happen and stormed inside. John hid behind a door as his father left the room. When John emerged from his hiding spot, his mom was outside, crying while leaning over the balcony.

He couldn't let her take him away from his dad. *How could she do that?* he'd wondered. He went outside to convince her to stay. When she heard the balcony door open, she told him to stay the hell away from her. Taken aback by the nastiness in her tone, he realized that she thought he was his father. *How could she speak to him like that?* John's belly burned like a firecracker about to pop. It rushed up his chest, squeezing his throat, making his face hot. His fists clenched as if he were a volcano ready to explode.

What happened next was unplanned, and a blur in his memory. He'd rushed toward his mother and lifted her legs in a moment of fury. When he'd let go, she'd toppled over the side. He wasn't sure how long he'd stood frozen, staring at her crumpled body on the concrete, but then his dad appeared at his side. If he'd been horrified—or angry—his father hadn't shown it. Instead, he'd placed a hand on John's back.

Go back to bed, son. I'll handle this.

John forced the memory from his mind and turned the page of the *Tribune.* Still, he found himself unable to concentrate on the rest of the news knowing that Mulholland would be spending every waking moment trying to hunt him down. Again, his father's words popped into his mind.

Cops will be less apt to suspect you if you have a wife. A family man.

John skimmed the articles, including one about the Green River Killer, Gary Ridgway, who was being returned to Washington state prison from Colorado, and turned the page. A headline at the top caught his eye.

STARTING FRESH: Sequim dentist opens new Seattle practice after husband's suicide.

Beneath it was a headshot of a smiling, beautiful blond woman wearing a white lab coat.

Intrigued, John took a drink from his coffee and began to read.

⸎

Cameron's office manager, Daniela, leaned her head inside Cameron's partially open office door. "Molly wanted me to let you know that her patient in Room 3 is ready for his exam." Daniela stepped inside Cameron's office, lowering her voice. "He's that hot lawyer I was telling you about. I checked his paperwork, and it says he's single."

Cameron gaped at her. "Daniela!"

Daniela had started working for her two months ago when she'd started her practice, and the two of them had become fast friends. But normally Daniela was more professional.

She smiled. "I'm just saying. He's single, you're single."

"Not interested." She'd given up on love. After Miles, all she wanted was to be safe. Having to cover up the murder of one husband was enough for a lifetime. "Plus, it's against the American Dental Association code of ethics to date your patients."

"So we'll find him another dentist."

Cameron shot Daniela a look. "I'm serious." She stood from her desk and slipped on her lab coat. "Not to mention I'm perfectly happy being single."

Daniela shrugged. "Okay, but you might change your mind after you see him. Unless you're not into that tall, dark, and so-handsome-you-can't-even-think-straight type." She flashed Cameron a wink before disappearing into the hall.

"So unprofessional," Cameron muttered before she stepped out of her office. She walked down the hallway, allowing her mind to wonder what it would be like to have love *and* be safe. To be truly happy with someone.

Cameron's heart fluttered when she spotted the lawyer's profile as he reclined in the dental chair in Room 3. Daniela had understated his looks.

Get a hold of yourself.

She took a deep breath as she entered the room and extended her hand. "Good morning. I'm Dr. Henson."

He sat up, meeting her gaze with his earth-tone brown eyes and a row of perfect teeth that you didn't even have to be a dentist to appreciate. He pressed his smooth, strong hand against hers.

"Hi," he said, his voice warm, his smile easy. "I'm John."

NOTE FROM THE AUTHOR

Gary Ridgway, known as the Green River Killer, was convicted of murdering 49 women. Investigators believe the true number of victims is likely higher. Active in Washington state from the early 1980s, he evaded capture for nearly two decades before his arrest in 2001. He is currently serving life without parole at Washington State Penitentiary in Walla Walla. While Ridgway's crimes gained widespread media attention, the focus should remain on his victims—both those identified and the ones still missing or unsolved. Their stories deserve to be remembered.

ACKNOWLEDGMENTS

I so enjoyed writing this story and am incredibly grateful to everyone who helped along the way. To my editors, Leslie Lutz and Traci Finlay, you are amazing to work with!

Leslie, thank you for working tirelessly with me through many drafts and helping me work through the layers of this story from beginning to end.

Traci, thank you for your feedback at various stages and for polishing the story off by proofreading at the end.

Detective Rolf Norton, thank you for answering my questions about the Green River Killer and my list of procedural questions for this story. As always, any errors are my own.

Special thanks to Spotify for producing a fabulous audiobook. Ferdelle Capistrano and Pete Cross, thank you for bringing this story to life through your talented narration.

To Jack Lawson and Keira Henson, thank you for everything you do for me behind the scenes.

To my friends and family, thank you for your endless encouragement and support.

A heartfelt thank you to all my readers, bookstagrammers, and bloggers who've supported me along this journey. It means the world to me.

Read on for a preview of *The Final Hunt*,
the next book in the Hunt series…

AVAILABLE NOW

PREVIEW
THE FINAL HUNT

PROLOGUE

Simon bent over, placing his hands on his knees when he reached the top of the peak. He tried to find his breath as he looked beyond the tree line and scanned the valley below for the small airstrip and John's plane. The wind had picked up during Simon's frantic trek through the wilderness from where he'd last seen John, and the snow flurries whipped against his face.

You're almost there. Just a little farther. The airstrip was several miles closer to their hunting spot than the lodge where they were staying, but the hike had still taken him nearly two hours.

Sweat dripped into his eyes despite the freezing temperature. He stood up tall and forced his exhausted leg muscles to move down the slope. He took only a few steps before his legs propelled him faster than he could control, sending him face-down into the snow-covered ground between the trees.

"Ahh!"

Pain burned through his abdomen where his body skid atop a rock. He summoned what was left of his adrenaline to pull himself to his feet. Simon gripped the shoulder strap of his hunting rifle and took it slower the rest of the way down, ignoring the burn in his legs. When he reached the clearing, his heart beat rapidly against his ribs. A few inches of snow covered John's yellow Cessna, which remained the only plane parked at the secluded airstrip.

He covered the final few hundred yards as fast as his body allowed. He knew the plane was locked but tried the door handle anyway. Turning his face away from the side window, he hurled the butt of his rifle against the Plexiglass. The window fractured with a resounding *crack* amidst the quiet forest.

Simon threw his rifle into the window again, this time breaking through the acrylic. He reached through the broken shards and lifted the lock before swinging the door open and climbing inside. Somehow, it seemed colder in the plane than outside, but he tore off his hat and gloves, eyeing the radio.

He flipped the red master switch on the instrument panel. Lights illuminated across the controls. Static came through the headset when he pulled it on. With a trembling hand, he pulled the mouthpiece to his lips. Blood trickled down his wrist from where he'd scraped his arm when he reached through the broken window.

Simon pushed the small button on the yoke, readying himself.

"I have an emergency! Can anyone hear me?"

His breath filled the fuselage with puffs of white as he waited for a response.

A crackle came through his headset. "This is Super Cub five-six-Charlie. I read you. What's your emergency?"

Simon lowered his head and exhaled into the mouthpiece. "Oh, thank God."

"Repeat. What's your emergency?"

"I'm in the Frank Church Wilderness. My friend—" his voice broke. Simon swallowed hard and continued. "We were out deer hunting. The guy I'm with was attacked by a bear. A couple of them. About six miles from here."

"Okay, I follow you. I need your location."

"I already told you! We're in the Frank Church Wilderness."

"I understand. But *where* in the Frank Church Wilderness? Are you in the air, or on the ground?"

"I'm not a pilot—I'm in my friend's plane." Simon looked beyond the shattered side window to his right. He squinted to read the sign beside the windsock. "We're parked at the Big Creek airstrip."

"Roger that. Are you with your friend now?"

"No! I told you, he's six miles away!"

"I need you to keep calm, sir. Is he wounded? What's his condition?"

"Um…." Simon thought of the blood that covered John's hunting pack. There were signs of a fight in the snow surrounding it, and John's gun abandoned on the ground. "It's bad, I know that. We were working a ridge, driving deer, walking a couple hundred feet apart. I heard him yell out, like he was in trouble. When I got closer, I saw two bears. I fired at the big one, and I think I hit her, but it didn't slow her down. They took off down a ravine. I shouted for John and heard him scream again—farther away. I headed down the hill and followed the bear tracks to a creek. There was even more blood than where they first got him. I went up and down that creek, calling out his name, looking for blood, or if they dragged him up the other bank. But there was nothing." His voice wobbled before a sob escaped his throat.

"Okay, hang in there. I'll relay that information to the authorities. Help should be there in an hour or so."

"An hour!"

"Well, I'm guessing the rescue will come out of Boise from the Air National Guard."

"All right then, just call them! And hey…thank you."

"To save your battery, you'll want to turn your master switch off for the next forty-five minutes. Then get back on this frequency, and the rescue team will contact you when they're getting close. Got that?"

"I got it."

"One last thing. What's your name? What kind of plane you in?"

"Simon Castelli. I'm in a yellow Cessna. It's the only plane here!"

"You're pretty far out there. Hold tight, stay out of the wind, and hydrate. The rescue team's going to want you with them when they head out to look for your friend."

"But there's not a lot of light left."

"Yeah, I know. But if you can point out where you last saw your friend, it's going to help. You going to be up for that? Are you injured at all?"

Simon rubbed his aching ribs. Tucked inside his coat, he felt the flask John had given him just yesterday to celebrate the trip. Full of Macallan 25-year single malt Scotch.

"I'll be fine. But tell them to hurry—no one's going to last long out there."

CHAPTER ONE

Cameron watched the light snow fall outside her cabin and wondered if any of her husband's remains were still out there. She twisted the stem of her glass between her fingers and turned from the window. The photos from their honeymoon remained on the screen of her laptop. She moved across the cozy room and stopped at the knotty pine bookshelf, buying time before she returned to her ritual of poring over old photographs while consuming too much wine.

She ran her hand across the spines of John's books. There was some fiction, but the shelf was mainly filled with big-game hunting and outdoor guides. Although John had been a prominent criminal defense attorney—arguably the best in the Pacific Northwest—there wasn't a single law book in sight.

John kept long hours and would often work around the clock when preparing for a trial. This cabin, however, was his retreat from it all. When John was alive, the cabin was always more of *his* place. She joined him on occasional weekend trips, but she preferred life in the city.

Since he died, she'd been coming to the cabin, nestled in the North Cascades, every weekend. And sometimes it felt like he was still here.

Cameron's hand stopped on an elk hunting guide. She pulled

the well-worn book from the shelf when something clattered lightly atop the hardwood floor beside her bare feet. She laid the book on the shelf and reached down to pick up the small plastic case, surprised to see it contained an SD card.

The SD cards that she'd brought from their home were from a drawer in John's office. Like everything of John's, they'd been meticulously organized, sorted by the dates the photos were taken. She'd been looking through those same photos over and over for these last three months.

She smiled, thinking of him toting his fancy camera around his neck on all their vacations. She clutched the card in her palm and wondered what old memories were captured in these pictures, waiting to be revisited now. She crossed the room and sat on the worn-out couch beside the dwindling fire in the wood stove.

After taking a large drink of her Merlot, she set the glass on the coffee table among the array of SD cards she'd brought with her for the weekend. Before removing the memory card from her laptop, she paused on a photo of her and John holding up a blue marlin on a chartered fishing boat in Mexico, and laughed.

John had convinced her to go with him on the fishing trip, even though she'd wanted to stay back and lie by the pool. Fishing was never her thing, but she agreed to go along and spend the day with him. She'd reeled in the marlin after only having her line in the water for a few minutes. It was so big John had to help her hold it for the photo. John fished the entire rest of the day without catching a thing. They'd joked about her out-fishing him for years afterward. At least he was smart enough to never ask her to go fishing with him again.

Cameron pulled out the little card and replaced it with the one in her hand.

Her therapist warned her about spending all her weekends up

here. Alone. She told Cameron it was unhealthy for her to keep digging up old memories with a bottle of wine instead of going out with friends and making new ones. That it was keeping her from moving on. Living.

But not yet. That would come.

She opened the contents of the memory card, glad to see there were hundreds of photos. Cameron hardly ever took pictures. It was always John. She clicked on the tiny thumbnail of the first image, which was nothing but a blur of darkness.

She plucked her wineglass from the coffee table and went to the next. The photo was of a woman Cameron didn't recognize leaving a coffee shop; she looked away from the camera, as if unaware of her photo being taken.

Cameron's stomach sank. These were all photos John had stored from some case, taken by his private investigator. There were no new photos of them.

The next photo showed the dark-haired woman getting out of a white SUV. Again, her eyes were diverted from the camera. The photos reminded Cameron of paparazzi stalking a celebrity. She felt an uneasiness creep over her and took a full sip from her wine.

She clicked through several more photos of the same woman. Jogging. Shopping. In all of them, she appeared oblivious of the photographer.

The next photo sent goosebumps down Cameron's limbs and to the top of her scalp. Despite the fire crackling next to her, the cabin suddenly felt cold. The same woman was now obviously deceased.

She lay on her back. Naked. Her skin mottled and a marbled gray. Her lips were a bluish purple, and her eyes were closed. Severe bruising lined her neck. Cameron put a hand over her mouth and clicked to the next photo. It was of the same woman, only zoomed out.

The woman was lying on a bed. Her skin looked even more ashen next to the red bedspread. Cameron looked away and racked her brain for why John would have had these photos. Maybe he'd gotten them from a client he defended. Though it was unlike him to keep evidence like this lying loosely inside his bookshelf.

Cameron clicked to the next photo. She gasped as her glass slipped from her fingers and shattered on the wood floor between her feet.

She stared at the hand-carved cedar bedframe the dead woman was lying on. It was the same bed Cameron had slept in last night. A shirtless man stood at the end of the bed, his reflection captured in the photo by a large mirror above the headboard. He was looking down at the dead woman, and he aimed his black Nikon toward her for the photo.

Cameron recognized the man immediately. She'd know that face anywhere. It was the face she'd been missing and grieving over for the last three months. It was John.

ABOUT THE AUTHOR

Audrey J. Cole is a *USA TODAY* bestselling author, and her work has been translated into multiple languages.

She resides in the Pacific Northwest with her two children. Before writing full time, she worked as a neonatal intensive care nurse for eleven years.

Want to hear about Audrey's next release and get free bonus content to her books? Visit *www.audreyjcole.com*